I0891511

THE PUGILIST AND THE SAILOR

Nadia Ragbar

INVISIBLE PUBLISHING
Halifax | Fredericton | Picton

Library and Archives Canada Cataloguing in Publication

Title: The pugilist and the sailor / Nadia Ragbar.
Names: Ragbar, Nadia, author.
Identifiers: Canadiana (print) 20250206129 | Canadiana (ebook) 20250206137 | ISBN 9781778430718 (softcover) | ISBN 9781778430725 (EPUB)
Subjects: LCGFT: Novels.
Classification: LCC PS8635.A4153 P84 2025 | DDC C813/.6—dc23

Edited by Aeman Ansari
Cover design by Megan Fildes
Typeset in Laurentian with thanks to type designer Rod McDonald

Invisible Publishing is committed to protecting our natural environment. As part of our efforts, both the cover and interior of this book are printed on acid-free 100% post-consumer recycled fibres.

Printed and bound in Canada.

Invisible Publishing | Halifax, Fredericton, and Picton

www.invisiblepublishing.com

Published with the generous assistance of the Canada Council for the Arts, the Ontario Arts Council, and the Government of Canada.

for Mamãe and Papai

PART ONE

JUNE 2012

BRUCE COULDN'T DECIDE where he'd be more comfortable. He held a book in his right hand, his smaller left arm was hitched around his brother Dougie's neck, and Dougie's smaller right arm was around his neck. They were standing in the Everest Grocery parking lot, and he knew he couldn't perch up on the ledge of the concrete planter by the automatic doors because his brother, his conjoined twin, was working. Maybe bracing against the wall, in the shade, by the shopping carts would be a better spot to read? But Dougie had them out on the small strip of grass between the lot's entrance and the sidewalk while he practised his left hook over and over. Bruce and Dougie Reuben were twins joined at the waist. Their separate torsos branched from three legs: the outer legs and the shared middle leg. Bruce commanded the right, Dougie the left, and Bruce desperately wanted to read while his brother worked his shift. Dougie worked security at the parking lot of a twenty-four-hour grocery store downtown. He had to ensure that people weren't parking for free if they weren't buying groceries, seeing as there was a theatre down the street that didn't have its own parking.

It was twelve o'clock and sweltering. They had six hours before their next boxing match. After his shift, Dougie would have some Greek yogurt with nuts and berries and make sure Bruce didn't eat anything too heavy. He had to remember to buy some bananas before he left Everest.

There was a damp spot spreading hopelessly underneath Bruce's right armpit.

"Hey, Dougie—do me a favour? Take off my cap and wipe my forehead." Bruce held his book up in his outer hand in explanation.

Dougie did and readjusted Bruce's cap. He took his shades off and wiped his own face.

"Thanks, Dougie. You must be dying in your uniform." Bruce gave his brother a light pat on the shoulder with his smaller left hand.

They were wearing black cargo pants, as per regulation; their mother, Jane, had taken two pairs, splitting and re-assembling seams to accommodate their larger middle leg. Dougie wore the regulation light blue, short-sleeved shirt, but Bruce refused it and wore a white tee—though the manager would have loved the optics if they both just wore the regulation gear. Jane had cut slits on one side of their shirts to try to accommodate the asymmetry of the hems.

"Christ, this humidity." Dougie bent to grab the water bottle at his feet and took a long slug of water.

"And it's only June."

Bruce hated when Dougie had to work the day shift; Dougie loved when he had to work on Friday nights. He felt like the only sheriff in town. Dougie usually made Bruce yell with him in stereo for effect: "Hey! If you ain't buying groceries, get the hell offa my lot!" Bruce, on the other hand, burned with embarrassment whenever they had to run after someone who was sneaking down the alley. Bruce and Dougie could run at a good clip—they had the rhythm down, and their training as boxers was only a bonus. They planted the shared middle leg and worked their outside legs in tandem, their smaller arms draped around one another's shoulders as they gave chase. It was a bit stilted but terrifyingly fast. Dougie had an extremely high success rate at getting freeloaders off Everest Grocery's property. Their physicality gave the impression that they were pals chumming around, their arms always hanging around the other's neck as though they were children at an eternal Sunday picnic, eating potato salad and racing down to the creek to catch tadpoles. Most of Dougie's co-workers were completely unaware that Bruce was in fact deeply mortified to be approaching thirty-four years old and stuck out on display on the lot. The manager often ("too often," chided Bruce) brought both their names up in praise at staff meetings with the dual intention of showcasing that he was a hip, open-minded, accepting kind of guy rather than some stuffy suit while also trying to shame his fifteen-year-old nephew, the other security guard on staff, into taking the job seriously. The manager failed miserably at both attempts. Bruce wished the manager would just leave his name out of it and focus his merit points solely on Dougie, who was the only Reuben with an Everest employee number.

Bruce dog-eared the page where he had left off his reading and tilted his face up to the blueness above. Lately he had become obsessed with an old sailor named M who had sailed around the world alone—around once and almost around again without stopping. He had all of the responsibilities of staying afloat, staying on course, staying alive, with no one else to lean on. Bruce tried to breathe in the heft of that much open space. It was a sickly kind of seduction that pulled him. He was queasy with attraction to the ocean's writhing and unceasing end. Squinting up at the familiar sky, Bruce struggled to see something deeper in it—some revelation, some winking recognition of his own valour—but his stomach just dropped again. The blue was a flatness that shut him out. Bruce read M as a man who forged a life of his own design, following no compass but his own inner knowing. Bruce could feel himself striving for something just beyond, reaching out, only to twist up inside himself, a kite's tail entangled on itself in the wind. He was standing in a parking lot he'd stood in more often than he cared to admit, with nothing exceptional on the horizon: crisp, brown patches of grass at the edge of the asphalt and a chain-link fence keeping school kids on their side of the back field.

Dougie looked up into the sky for shapes of familiar things shifting in the clouds. He pointed up at a specific cloud that looked just like Irena, their most senior cashier with a big shellacked do, but it had transformed into a regular blob before he could say anything to his brother. Bruce rolled a crick out of his right shoulder and went back to his book. It wasn't a biography but rather an exploration of M's philosophy; the author felt himself to be a student, M his guide. Bruce wore an orange rubber thimble on his thumb so that he could hold his book open and turn the page without his brother's help.

> Of his childhood in Vietnam, M remembers making sling shots, hating school, hating the colonialism of his father's rule, trees, fruits, his mother, his brothers—a kaleidoscope of a vibrant tropical life all around him before the war. He remembers fishing junks on the water moving out with the tide in the morning. The coastline. For some that raw space could act as a magnetic force field pushing you back—deeper back—forcing you to stand down. But for the fishermen who went out into it and for little M, the child, the ocean was not a metaphor. It was simply the earth's most singular manifestation of its own freedom.

Dougie counted the number of minivans in the lot again: five. He had been trying to test his memory by guessing which car belonged to each customer leaving the store; his success rate at guessing the cyclists was one hundred percent. A woman wearing shorts and an army jacket ("in this heat wave?" scoffed Dougie) left carrying only a bunch of bananas, which reminded Dougie not to forget to buy bananas.

"Hey, Bruce. It's pretty dead out here; let's do some extra squats."

"I don't think so." Bruce thumbed another page over.

"Yeah, you're right. We shouldn't wear ourselves out too much. I'm feeling good about tonight."

Dougie was saying this more for his own benefit than anyone else's; he was generally restless in the hours leading up to a bout, keen to distract himself with conversation or errands or action right until the moment their trainer wrapped their hands—all four—and slipped the gloves onto the two strong outer fists. And with the winding of the fabric, everything else would finally begin to recede. But for Bruce it was the opposite: he savoured the long, quiet hours of the morning and then the afternoon before a match. But as the late afternoon closed into evening, his anxiety ratcheted to a distemper that peaked when the announcer called out their names. And once they climbed through the ropes, Bruce resigned himself every time with the silent prayer: *This too shall pass, this too shall pass, this too shall... We're not going to die. I've done this before. Fuck me. Shit.* Bruce was certain he could live in contentment without amateur boxing, but he knew his brother absolutely could not.

Bruce thought back to how long they'd been getting into the ring. Dougie's now long obsession with boxing had begun the summer after Grade Four, so coming on twenty-four years? This realization shocked Bruce, that nearly a quarter of a century later he was still half-heartedly agreeing to go along with it. He always felt he had one foot out, as it were, and yet this was the single thing that had carried forward with unyielding consistency from his childhood: sparring, drills, running, training, weigh-ins, matches. An endless and exhausting number of matches. He never thought of himself as a boxer, but boxing was what he spent most of his time doing.

It was that summer after Grade Four when the Reubens took their first family vacation. Their mother had closed her eyes and swirled lazy eights over the *National Geographic* map, which was folded in a square so as to only consider North America. She touched down and opened her eyes: Fort Lauderdale it was.

"Walter! We'll need the suitcases out of the basement. We're going on vacation next month," she announced to her husband, who had just come in from the field and was washing his hands in the laundry sink.

The twins were elated. They could name tons of kids they knew who were already bored with the idea of travelling by airplane. Now they too would be able to add their expertise to the conversation of 'What I did on my Summer Holiday.' Bruce began research on Fort Lauderdale's flora and fauna.

When the time came, Walter's father, known to all as Père, drove the family to the airport. After he helped Walter unload the luggage, he stooped to hug his grandsons. He held his arms strong and wide to gather them both up, Bruce to his left and Dougie to his right. Both boys with a mop of dark hair like Walter's, eyes bright and sharp from Jane's side. He squeezed them tight and felt them trying to squirm out from his embrace.

"Here's a fiver for each of you to spend on your trip, boys. Enjoy your time."

Dougie spent his before the airplane lifted off the ground. Jane had stopped to buy gum at a kiosk before getting to their gate, and the boys poured over every crisp magazine cover, looking for something remotely interesting and cartoon-like. Dougie gasped and reached out for a picture of two men in shorts locked in a fight; the man facing the camera had his arm wound back, and Dougie could sense that things in his life were about to become exciting, volatile, and fast. He slapped *The Ring: The Bible of Boxing* and his crumpled five-dollar bill up on the counter alongside his mother's Juicy Fruit.

On his very first airplane ride, he didn't care to look out the window or play with his barf bag. He was completely transfixed by the pictures, the ads, the scores—this new world inside this new magazine. Bruce had never seen him so focused. Dougie was educated in Fort Lauderdale. He spent his vacation boxing imaginary opponents at the beach, in the restaurant, at the bowling alley, in the wetlands. At the end of the two weeks, when they got back home, Dougie begged for boxing lessons and offered up Bruce's saved five dollars as an installment on a pair of gloves they could share between them. Walter and Jane agreed to the new extracurricular activity as long as Bruce was a hundred percent on board. That's when Dougie began his campaign: he gave Bruce his serving of dessert, he let Bruce pick the shows they would watch, and he helped Bruce make a diorama of the Everglades.

"So how 'bout it, Brucie?"

"I dunno, Dougie. I don't even know how to fight."

"That's the whole point! That's what they teach you! C'mon—it'll be fun. And then we'll always be able to stick up for ourselves. It'll be so cool."

Bruce was moulding plasticine into a palm tree. "Well, okay. I guess we can try it out. But you gotta let me quit if I feel like it."

"Don't worry. You're gonna love it, Brucie. Trust me."

Dougie's shift on the lot had ended, bananas not forgotten, the black satin, jerry-rigged shorts donned. At the beginning of the match, the ref paraded the twins in front of the judges' table and around the ring. This was mostly a theatrical flourish on the ref's part; he could sense a rowdiness simmering in the crowded room, which he welcomed, and he wanted to crank the heat up after the very poorly attended snooze-fest that had been the afternoon's bout. Bruce closed his eyes for just a bit longer than a blink, letting himself be dragged by the arm and subtly pushed forward by Dougie, who was now more in command of their shared middle leg. The crowd was chanting: "Bull…shit! Bull…shit! Bull…shit!" For those who had been following Boxing Ontario closely over the years, there was a deep and bitter divide about whether the twins should be allowed to compete as a single athlete. The ref—who came down on the *yes* side of the debate ("Because, shit, what a stroke of luck to be alive to witness such a phenomenon up close," he defended)—deposited the twins at their corner. And in the red corner, from Windsor-Essex County, Tony Marlowe was similarly foisted in front of the crowd. Closing his eyes once more, Bruce could hear the cheers swell like a velvet wave, rolling, the lushness folding in on itself. When he looked at the judges, he saw a child—presumably a judge's son—sitting at the table as well: a perfect bowl cut, eyes wide in wonder at seeing the Reuben Beast. Bruce raised his gloved hand and waved; he smiled, but his mouth guard shaped it into more of a grimace. The boy's eyes grew wider.

Their trainer, Dom, was tightening Dougie's helmet as Dougie coached his brother: "Keep yourself protected, Brucie. I gotta good feeling about this one. And shit, remember to stay light on your outside foot, man."

Bruce rolled his eyes, squeezing them tight one last time before they'd have to get wailed on by Marlowe, who weighed in at ninety-one kilograms and had a reputation for never getting knocked off his feet.

The bell rang, and all three met in the centre of the ring to sort out their differences for the next three minutes. Marlowe winked at Bruce in the seconds before Dougie connected his glove to the side of Marlowe's rubber helmet.

That night, though they both did what they could, Dougie and Bruce lost to Marlowe. The crowd had been satisfyingly rowdy, but the ref was disappointed by the outcome. By eleven o'clock they were at the bar, where Dougie performed a thorough postmortem. The twins sat on one side of a booth, each with an arm around the other. The bar was loud and busy and dimly lit. The walls were a mash up of black-and-white portraits, bright abstracts, concert fliers, and the beginnings of a mural of Sisyphus, everything scribbled over with thick layers of graffiti. Setting his glass down, Bruce felt tipsy already as Dougie pounded back his pint. Alongside the zing of blood, Bruce had the synthetic cedar smell of Dougie's pomade filling his nose, and his top lip was swollen and pink like a newborn mouse.

"Seriously, you gotta be less flat footed—lighter on the ball of your outside foot—so I can move in faster with my left." Dougie lightened up his scolding: "At any rate, Marlowe just got lucky."

Bruce didn't respond. During the match he had caught Marlowe's eye before Marlowe plowed a fist through his shoulder. Bruce had flailed backward, the force swinging Dougie to the fore, his outstretched fist connecting with the side of Marlowe's jaw. But in that moment Marlowe didn't look "just lucky" to Bruce. Marlowe looked like a bear lumbering out of hibernation, hungry for something other than berries. Bruce wiped the condensation from his cold pint, swiped his hand over his face, then scratched deep in the nook where his left side met Dougie's right. There was a rash starting to form where he and Dougie were joined. A dry, scaly itch that started in the crevice where their torso split above their navels and crept only towards Bruce's ribs. Dougie was always the twin with better skin.

"When we get home, I'll show you a trick to stay lighter. It's all in our balance."

Dougie lifted the empty pitcher to the waitress, who was already on her way to the table. She took it without smiling but gave a nod. Bruce noticed that the waitress never looked directly at him, preferring only to zero in on Dougie; Dougie hadn't noticed this.

"Maybe we should start jogging to your job at Ogilvie's? Sneak in extra workouts wherever we can?"

"That's not going to work, Dougie. We run enough."

Bruce was really scratching his side now, trying as best as he could to be discreet but unable to satiate the terrible gnawing opening up under his nails. He decided against chiding his brother for drinking. They both knew they needed to cut out the booze if Dougie really wanted them to make a breakthrough, but Bruce didn't want to push this agenda. He was definitely not vying for a spot on the national team.

By the time their pints were empty, Dougie was telling Bruce a story they both already knew: "...and then I told him—"

The twins spoke in unison: "No jury alive would believe that horseshit."

"I know. I remember." Bruce laughed at Dougie, remembering that the person his brother was getting so riled up over was barely a teenager. Lippy, but hardly able to grow a mustache.

"Another?"

"No, I'm done. Let's go. My face still hurts."

Dougie held the empty pitcher up to the waitress again, turning to his brother. "A quick one." Dougie started singing, then paused. "I've had the theme song to *Three's Company* stuck in my head all day. Ever since we saw that San Diego plate in the lot. That was weird, right? Why would anyone from San Diego ever need to come to Toronto?"

Bruce was using all of his mental faculties to ignore the itch. Before he could block it out, the first lines of the song were on repeat in his head. "Great. Thanks, Dougie."

"You know we're set to fight Wesley Patrice in a couple months?" Dougie was drumming the table with one hand in time to the song playing in the bar.

"Unghhhhhh. Do we really have to fight that guy?"

"Uh, of course we do."

"That guy fights dirty. You saw how he sabotaged Olivier before their match."

"Patrice is a snake."

Dougie gripped his neck to shrug out some tension and started talking about Bruce's delayed blocks. He used his weak arm to thump on Bruce's shoulder, indicating the vulnerable spot that opened up when Bruce was slow to react. Bruce was getting drunk and not getting the gist of his brother's demonstration; instead he noticed the crow's feet gathering when Dougie smiled. Bruce realized he must be getting them too, there on his own face. He was fighting not to feel drunk, putting his glass back down too deliberately, looking at his brother, the ridges of that ear he'd spent his whole life examining, so much so that it had become an alien object. A thing chewed up and spit out and left to harden on the right side of Dougie's head. He had to take it on faith that the left ear was of similar ilk. He fingered the ridge of his own outside ear as Dougie's arm continued to thump on his shoulder. Bruce let his small arm dangle, so familiar and fraternal, around his brother's neck. He noticed, really for the first time, that Dougie's face had become broader, harder, tougher since those days when they were twenty; he thought about how his own face must've been so soft and optimistic back then. They were identical, but Dougie's face was a bit longer, his eyes more deeply set, his cheekbones sharper. There was something wolfish about him. About them both.

Ignoring what Dougie was saying about his technique, Bruce continued on about the Patrice and Olivier bout: "It's not a coincidence that Olivier got jumped the night before their match. Broke his nose and three ribs."

"But Olivier still got in the ring with him eventually," Dougie offered.

"I overheard some guys at the gym saying Olivier got ambushed by a bunch of Patrice's friends."

"Which guys at the gym? Why didn't I hear this?" Dougie was baffled that he had misssed this piece of intel.

"You were busy talking to Dom about protein shakes. Whatever, it happened outside some 7-Eleven near his house. His face was totally mangled. Dude, he still kind of walks with a limp."

"He's hands down a better boxer than Patrice. Mangled or not. He's just got real shit luck."

Bruce observed that his brother chalked an awful lot of things up to luck: Marlowe's win, Olivier's loss. He drank from his newly refilled pint.

"Run Run Run" came over the speakers and instantly took him back to when they had first moved to the city and he was really into The Velvet Underground. He remembered that first night after they had moved. They had unloaded boxes, hugged their parents goodbye, and then decided to grab a late-night slice of pizza. Standing in line, Bruce had reached into his back pocket for his wallet and grazed the bare arm of a drunk girl behind him. She was repulsed by that accidental intimacy, wiping her arm off on her boyfriend's jacket sleeve. Her boyfriend pretended to be busy, reading the menu above the counter. When Bruce tried to apologize, the girl had flinched, terrified he'd make contact again. Later, as the twins made their way out of the narrow restaurant, Dougie purposely jammed into them while they squirted hot sauce onto their slices. He called the girl facile, and she cleverly responded with a bleary-eyed middle finger. Bruce had been humiliated by every second of the whole encounter and couldn't muster the appetite to eat his slice. He handed it over to Dougie. As they got back to their apartment, he remembered his brother saying, "Don't let assholes make you feel like an asshole."

After he'd eaten about a quarter of it, Dougie gave him back his slice. Bruce was grateful for it.

Leaving the bar, they staggered towards their basement apartment, the same one they had unpacked their boxes into fourteen years ago. Dougie was whistling. He was feeling great. His entire body was sore, his head felt pleasantly light, he wasn't on the Everest schedule for tomorrow, and he took deep, deep breaths. He had his arm around his brother, his best friend. Dougie had a slightly quicker pace and was pulling Bruce up into step.

Dougie and Bruce grew up in the country on their parents' farm. When they were kids, Dougie used to love acting out scenes from *Butch Cassidy and the Sundance Kid.* They'd play in an old barn at the edge of their property, and he'd get them up into the loft and pretend they were going to jump off a cliff into a river. Sometimes he was Butch with the plan; sometimes he was the Kid, saying he didn't know how to swim. Sometimes he would play both simultaneously: "They're sneaking up on us on all sides... I've got a plan, Kid, but it's dangerous... What plan's that? I ain't jumping off no more cliffs for you, Butch."

"Wait, you can't be both. I'm Kid. I'm definitely not jumping down from here." Bruce planted a hand on his seven-year-old hip.

"No, you don't have to jump—you can be a rancher who lets Butch and Kid hide in your barn and distracts the enemy. Here. Move this hay to hide me, then pretend that they're cornering me and trick them into leaving."

Bruce picked up a long stick to use as his rifle. "Are you men here to work? Go milk them cows. I didn't think so. Now get outta my barn if you ain't gonna work, or I'll shoot. No, I ain't seen Butch Cassidy or the Sundance Kid. Pew pew pew."

"Great. Thanks, Rancher Bob. Me and Kid, we owe you one. The coast is clear—we gotta run. Hey, Bob, you should come with us. We're on our way to find gold, and we need a lookout. We need someone we can trust, someone who's tough and smart. We'll split the money with you three ways."

Bruce was tired from the match and the drinks and didn't want to march along at Dougie's brisk pace. Bruce leaned back to the right, creating resistance as he turned his head to examine the houses and porches lined with bikes, if for no other reason than to weigh down the lurching of Dougie's forward momentum. This was a silent negotiation being played out through their muscles and tendons and shared leg while they each sifted through their own thoughts. Then Dougie turned, pretending to shoot at his brother: "Pew, pew, pew." Bruce rolled his eyes, and Dougie laughed, using his limp hand to pat Bruce's shoulder, slowing his pace down incrementally.

"Fuck that Patrice match, Dougie. I'll fight anyone else but him. You want to run more? I'll run more. I just don't trust him."

"Let his guys try to come for us. You forget that we're the goddamned, most feared, most revered Reuben-fuckin'-Beast."

"Why don't we report Patrice to the league and get him booted? For everyone's sake."

"I'm not afraid of Patrice or his guys. They can't do shit to us."

All of Dougie's *S*s had turned to mush; Bruce knew that once his brother was drunk, he was even more stubborn and his bravado tilted toward the obnoxious. Bruce unconsciously balled up both fists; he wanted to scream but didn't. A fire was sparking in his belly, and he tamped it down quickly, quietly. He felt helpless, not about Patrice, but about Dougie's unwillingness to hear him out yet again. He scratched where his rash continued to take over new ground on his side.

The next morning was overcast, the pressing humidity threatening a rain that would be a welcome balm, if only it would ever arrive. The twins strode into Bruce's work at Ogilvie and Associates, each feeling the heft of the other, each body aching from separate exertions, a slight pounding shared across both of their temples.

"Morning, Bruce. Hiya, Dougie. I just made some fresh coffee, and there's donuts. Bruce, the credit card statements for the appliance repair account are on your desk."

Lana was Bruce's boss three days a week in the one room that housed her bookkeeping firm. Bruce was her only employee. She had bought a deacon's bench specifically to accommodate the twins at Bruce's desk, which was situated directly behind her own. They were all lined up facing the front of the room as though sitting in a classroom; Lana never liked sitting with her back to the door, and all sides of the room were currently occupied by the photocopier, coffee station, filing cabinets, storage cupboards, bankers boxes, and coat rack. Though she was constantly talking over her shoulder to the twins, she very much enjoyed having an extra person around for the conversation, particularly because she wasn't required to have Dougie on salary.

"Thanks, Lana. I'll finish off their expense report first thing."

"So, Lana, cut the crap... I know you're dying to spill the beans. Did you propose to Gary this weekend?" Dougie wanted all the gossip.

"He said yes! I sent him out this morning to buy my ring. The proposal was really beautiful, if I do say so myself. I told him, look, we aren't getting any younger, and Gary, I'd rather live with your bad habits than get to know the good side of anyone else on this earth."

Lana was aglow, as any new fiancée would be. Her hair was a freshly dyed crimson. She wore a navy pant suit and fiddled with the baubles on one earlobe. Bruce and Dougie were grinning like drunk teenagers at the news. The brothers had always been genuinely taken aback by the small kindnesses that Lana mindlessly dropped like breadcrumbs around her. She fashioned ice packs on the mornings when they came in with black eyes, and she always kept painkillers stocked in the stationery cabinet. She let Bruce do what he had to do without ever looking over his shoulder, and in return his effort at work was always sincere; he never let himself get bored or distracted by his brother.

"Our congratulations, Lana. That's wonderful! You really deserve the best." Bruce was happy for his boss. They stood, and Dougie reeled Lana in for a hug over the desk.

"The wedding's going to be at the end of the year—we might just do a small New Year's thing at some restaurant. What do you guys think? You'll be there, of course?"

Bruce and Dougie both nodded. Generally they avoided formal situations, but they'd be there, no question.

Bruce had gotten the job after seeing the words *HELP WANTED* sharpied in uneven capital letters on a piece of paper taped to Lana's window. Dougie had made it physically difficult for Bruce to walk toward the door, dreading the utter tedium that surely lay in wait. But Bruce knew what he wanted; he was sure of his competencies. He lunged them both forward, offered to work the rest of that day for free in lieu of an interview, and was hired on the spot.

"I don't know if Gary will finally tell his dad about us. He's senile as a goat, so it's neither here nor there—I just figure at this point we have to make a choice, and then we can spend the rest of our time making it be the right one."

Lana sank into her captain's chair and swivelled to check her voice mail. She punched the number pad of her phone with the eraser end of a new pencil. She swiped a light layer of dust off a framed photograph of herself and Gary on vacation and readjusted its angle.

When Bruce had landed his new job at Ogilvie, Dougie took him out for dinner to celebrate. Dougie was impressed that Bruce had listened to his guts, undeterred even by him, but he was mostly relieved because he and Lana had hit it off right from the start. While Bruce had been getting caught up on an unwieldy account, Dougie had had time to strategize, his head lolled back and his free arm draped over his eyes to block out the fluorescent bulb. All the while visualizing foot sequences. His was the back foot; he imagined sitting most of their weight there and then shifting it into the middle foot, pushing off the back, giving momentum to Bruce's front foot stepping in first, landing with a hook. Get in fast, stay low, keep the drive in the back legs for power. Left cross. Reset. Again.

"I have a good feeling about this, Bruce."

"Me too, actually. I'm happy to be working again. I mean, Everest's great and all, but I'm happy to do something that I'm good at."

"I can't believe you find joy in accounting."

"Well it's not as exciting as boxing, but I like when things get squared up. When the numbers appear jumbled but then emerge ordered."

Dougie raised his glass. "To doing well, the things few can do."

Bruce met Dougie's glass with his and then took a sip. "There are a lot of bookkeepers in the world. I'm just one out of millions."

"That's right—one in a million, and Lana's lucky to have you."

"Thanks, Dougie." Bruce was unable to stop himself from grinning.

There was something about being at work at Ogilvie's that made Bruce feel useful and competent. He respected his new boss, who was not judgmental; he could see that already in the way she was with Dougie. In the last place he worked, his boss had treated him sourly and ignored Dougie outright. He had found fault with everything that Bruce did. He needled and manipulated things in the hopes that Bruce would quit and let the company off the hook for any wrongful dismissal and discrimination charges.

"This is going to be a great year for us; I can feel it in our bones. I see special things in our future." Dougie put his soup spoon down.

"Like what?"

"Big things. Huge. Me and you."

Dougie and his brother had a standing agreement that if Bruce took their shadow boxing training seriously, he could spend as long as he wanted at the library doing his research. Dougie wasn't particularly interested in Bruce's obsession with sailing around the world ("circumnavigation," Bruce corrected). It had started when they watched a documentary about sailors in a race around the world, and from that moment on, Dougie could feel Bruce growing wistful and nostalgic for the sea. Dougie and Bruce had never been strong swimmers, though Dougie knew that with a bit of intensive training they could definitely master a tandem butterfly crawl. He could picture it: merman legs, all three kicking like a single fin, their outer arms strong and in sync. Smooth and fast, undulating through the water. Dougie encouraged his brother's fascination with single-handed sailing because it generally seemed to lift his spirits, but it was obvious to him that the people who wanted to get in a boat and sail clear around the earth by themselves were all completely mentally and emotionally unstable.

Bruce had been re-reading his copy of *The Life and Art of Being M* and was in search of something that would immerse him more deeply into a seafaring state of mind. He was charmed by an illustrated guide to sailing knots that he had spread open on a table. They were standing as he bent over the book, and he could feel Dougie restlessly swaying forward and back, ever so slightly.

"We can look for something for you too, Dougie."

"Nah, I'm good." Dougie was bored but kept his lips zipped, fighting hard to keep up his end of their agreement.

Bruce happened across the differences between the square knot, which was a simple way to join two similar ropes, and the sheet bend, which was a more secure way to join two lines of different materials or thickness.

"Cool," offered Dougie tightly when his brother pointed it out, amused.

"So? Which knot would you say we're joined by?" Bruce didn't expect Dougie to respond, but he suspected they'd have different answers.

Before Bruce returned to the knots, he caught sight of a woman sitting on the nearby staircase leading up to the third floor. Long black hair, jeans, sneakers, black t-shirt. A jacket was bunched on her lap, obscuring the title of her book. She looked up and made eye contact with Bruce.

What Dougie saw was his brother comically frozen, seemingly rapt and staring. Dougie followed his gaze: a girl. He looked back at Bruce and then back at her, but he couldn't see what the hold-up was about.

"Brucie, you good? Let's get what you need and then get outta here. I'm scheduled on the lot tonight. I need some air."

What Dougie had missed was that look that had forced Bruce to do a slight double take so his mind could catch up with his heart. He didn't dare breathe. She was lovely. She was looking right at him, and he couldn't move a muscle. And then she went back to reading.

But as she sat on the steps, leaning into the banister to let someone pass, Bruce felt a shimmer of something he recognized: she seemed to Bruce to be a part of the world but somehow not of it, a shark stalking a beach. And Bruce realized that all his life he had been doing the same, although less gracefully. Less poised and beautiful and unrestrained. His hands were sweaty, and his throat was dry. Hair fell out from behind her ear, and she left it there covering her face as she read.

Eventually she got up from the spiral staircase, and Bruce had them surreptitiously trail her through the building. They had to pass sideways through narrow lanes of cookbooks, art history, psychology, dream analysis, playwriting, manga, horror, mystery, and a wall of DVDs. They surprised a few library patrons, who either jumped up from crouching at a bottom shelf or got themselves jumbled while trying to move around to let the twins squeeze past. Most were taken aback but were too polite to mention their inconvenience or shock. Bruce got Dougie to help him grab books and pile them into the crook of his right arm to make it look like he had a reason to be searching through the aisles. Anything to increase the chance that he might catch sight of her again. Dougie did this grudgingly at first and then continued out of sheer disbelief at his brother's uncharacteristic behaviour.

As they emerged from the hushed stacks, light flooded through the large second-storey windows. A silver-haired woman in a brown knitted vest over a pink-and-teal short-sleeved blouse was sitting in one of the few comfy, padded chairs facing the stacks, reading the *Sing Tao Daily*. When she spied the twins, she dropped her newspaper and began gesturing urgently and telling them something that they assumed was meant to be helpful. Then she covered her shy smile with her hand.

"Good afternoon." Bruce smiled at her over his growing pile of books.

Dougie gave her a thumbs up and whispered, "Cool shoes."

She raised both legs up to show off her gleaming Jordans, giving two thumbs up in return, "My grandson!" she laughed.

What the twins didn't understand was that she spoke Teochew and that she was telling them about Chang and Eng Bunker from Thailand—Siam—who were first to be labelled as Siamese twins. Their biography was over on the other side by the computers; she had read some of it last year to practise her English, but it was too long, a little boring, and she had given up after a few pages. Interesting pictures though. They had lots and lots of kids.

Bruce had lost sight of the woman from the stairs and hated to admit that it was time to leave. He found an empty study carrel where he abandoned his books and stretched out his arm. Dougie patted his shoulder with his smaller hand and silently pointed across the room with the other.

The woman was heading for the stairs. Bruce quickly scooped up as many of the discarded books as he could but then hesitated, leaving some space between himself and the woman as they went downstairs. When she lined up to check out her materials, Bruce and Dougie got in line behind her. The librarian asked the woman to verify her address in order to renew her card, and Dougie could feel his brother straining against his tether, straining against hope to hear her response, to learn anything about her that he absolutely could.

As she turned to leave, she saw the twins again. She took them in without flinching or registering surprise. Dougie had to drag his brother up to the librarian's desk, and then she was gone. Bruce blinked rapidly. Should he have said something? Did she see him? Of course she saw him. Did she notice only three legs? Maybe not? He should've asked about her book. Maybe she didn't actually see him? Bruce's heart had been pitched out of the briny sea and now lay heaving on a parched and chalky shore.

For the rest of the day, Bruce wondered about this woman. He made a tally of assumptions about her: she used the library, so she must like to read and probably hated technology or something; she was there during the day, so she didn't work a regular job. He kept recalling the sight of her sitting and reading, wholly absorbed. But then what was the exact look on her face when she made eye contact with him? It wasn't surprise, nor was it a blank stare. Not curiosity. Bruce gave himself permission to feel that she had seen him and accepted him. For the most part, he felt that he—as a person—passed by unseen by others; he honestly couldn't remember ever being regarded like that by a stranger, by a woman, by someone who wasn't his mother or Lana. It was as though she felt that it was okay for Bruce and okay for Dougie, that it was completely natural for them to be there in the library, in line behind her, like anyone else. And so, dipping into that surf, Bruce knew he wanted the chance to get to know her, to hear what her voice sounded like, what she thought about the things she read, how she, herself, came to be. He didn't know how this would ever be possible. Maybe he was asking for too much. But maybe not. He couldn't be sure that he was really feeling the way he was feeling. He was being crazy. He was punch drunk. He shouldn't seriously be thinking these things. Would he see her again? He had unknowingly been clawing at the rash on his side, and Dougie slapped his wrist away. "Quit it, ya fleabag." Dougie wasn't suffering from the same affliction that was terrorizing his brother's body now.

Bruce dropped his hand and smiled sheepishly at no one in particular.

Over the next few days, Dougie was dragged back to the library more times than ever before. Bruce never fessed up, but Dougie knew the exact reason why; he saw how distracted his brother was, how many times they left without taking any books home. Bruce had them take a detour there on their way to the gym so that he could ask about any volunteer positions—there were none at the moment, unless the twins wanted to help elementary school kids with their homework one night a week for at least a year, which they did not.

Bruce had a small gym bag slung on his shoulder, and Dougie held his bag at his side by the shorter handles. The streetcar would be too crammed at rush hour, and so they both instinctively knew—without having to say a word to each other—that they would walk the hour it would take to get to the gym from the library.

Dougie just wanted to keep his brother focused on their next match. He wanted to double down on their practice time. He felt sharp and clear and more determined than ever. But he needed Bruce to be as sharp and as clear, although he conceded that Bruce would never really be as determined. Dougie had to erase any distance that might be yawning between them because time and again he had seen what a talent Bruce could be in the ring when he was in the right headspace. They had to detour around roadwork in one half of the intersection: the smell of hot tar and exhaust, the rumble of heavy machines, the poor guy sweating in his safety vest and steel-toed boots holding the stop sign. Dougie was grateful for the gifts that boxing had bestowed on him his whole life: physical strength, mental clarity, purpose, and joy. And all he wanted was for Bruce to open himself up to feeling these things too. What else was there in life, really? These were the things that everyone was on a relentless hunt for, and here they were with it all right in their laps. Dougie's success as a boxer was directly tied to Bruce's concentration and endurance, so they needed to be one muscle reacting, one synapse firing, one behemoth with a single goal once the bell rang. One swimmer with a blistering, ferocious butterfly crawl. Luckily he had enough drive for the both of them.

When they were finally at the gym, Dougie moved them in front of the mirror as often as he could. He held Bruce's gaze in the glass, reinforcing with a look that where one was, so was the other. Always.

Bruce looked at himself turning one half of a long skipping rope with his one strong arm. Their tank tops were now sweat-stained, each bunching up a little higher on their joined side. Dougie started speeding up his end of the rope, catching Bruce's eye in the mirror. Bruce sped up too. As Bruce turned, he tried to see himself in that mirror with fresh eyes, to see what a stranger might see, having never seen anyone like him before. He stared at all three legs pumping without missing a beat. There was that beefy middle leg, which he had spent his whole life thinking was the single feature others defined them by, that translated the singular *him* into a plural *them*, that made him who he was: an aberration of human form, the femur gone wrong. He looked at how strong and massive it was, the shoe on it a size larger than the shoes on their outside feet. But then he tried to look at only his half of their reflection. Naturally it was difficult to hone in on just himself; none of his movements were happening in isolation, and his brother's small right arm was there, fleshy and dangling around his neck. He turned his end of the rope, and it whirred past his ear faster and faster still. Almost automatically his focus pulled back out. He looked at the two of them again, the "Reuben Beast," as Dom had branded them. His idea had been to encourage them to reclaim that idea of monstrosity for themselves.

"Okay. That's time," Dougie called. "Shadow boxing now. Let's go through those new drills Dom gave us."

In each of the twins' secret hearts, separate impulses were percolating as they punched combinations at their reflections. Dougie wanted to keep the two of them firmly rooted; Bruce wanted to find his wings.

They had to get the timing down of their step out: their ability to roll out of an opponent's range smoothly, quickly, so both of them would be clear of an incoming hook. They had to be twice as fast because they were twice as wide.

Bruce forced himself to stop thinking about the girl from the library and concentrate on the drills. He felt strong today. They were better at the drills than they had been last week. Dougie eventually called time, smiling, also feeling strong and confident.

A few days later, they were back in the gym, this time with Dom. They had been working with him for a decade or so, the longest they had been with one trainer. He was thick-necked and stocky, and kept his balding head shaved. Dom was from a family of storied boxers in the city, but the legacy would end with him; his son was a dentist, and both his daughters were teachers. This made his wife laugh because those were the two authority figures Dom had hated the most as a kid.

"Dougie, that's great. Bruce, you've got to follow through with your jab. Hit your opponent and then keep punching right goddamned through him. You're acting like you're scared. The punching bag's not going to bite you. Hit the fucker like you actually want to win the fight."

Dom knew what he was talking about. A ring of pictures crowned the perimeter of the gym, each with a different man caught in some variation of the same pose: sweating and spent, the ref hoisting one bulbous fist in the air. In every picture Dom was in the background behind the ropes, his own meaty fist thrown up also, a wild frenzy in his eyes, an eyetooth missing in his smile.

"Boys, don't waste the singular, most precious advantage that you have. What some would see as your God-given curse is actually His most unique gift bestowed upon you. But only you can turn it from plight to promise."

"Cut him some slack, Dom. He's trying—aren't you, Brucie?" Dougie picked up his water bottle and sprayed his hair and face down before taking aim at his mouth.

"Okay. I got it—punch through the bag. Okay. My fist will more or less come out on the other side, somehow."

"Attaboy, Brucie." Dougie threw a few uppercuts and worked to bring his arm back in quickly while Bruce craned his face away from the onslaught.

Bruce knew Dom wasn't going to let him off easy, and so he mustered up what might he could. As he let Dom carry on with his instructions, his mind flashed to all of the time he'd spent in gyms with his brother, for his brother. He remembered their creepy high school gym teacher who was desperately trying to get them to join the wrestling team. Bruce couldn't imagine the logistics of how wrestling would work. He couldn't see any dignity for them on the mat; they'd be a joke, scrambling all over themselves. Dougie had had no time for it. He'd had a suspicion that if he and his brother were alive a hundred and fifty years ago their gym teacher was the type who would've tried to sell them to a carnival freak show.

"C'mon. Focus, Bruce. This bag is every person who's ever turned you down for a job or a date or whatever. This bag avoids making eye contact with you when you ask for the time. This bag thinks that you don't belong here. This bag feels like it's better than you. This bag thinks you're weak and is going to whoop your ass unless you do something about it. So do something."

Bruce and Dougie planted their middle leg, and Bruce squirrelled his outside leg around a bit. He felt awkward and still unwilling. He hit the bag while Dom screamed at him for something better. He hit the bag again. He remembered he had to start the payroll for that florist shop. He swung again and missed the bag. Dom told him not to waste everyone's time. *Get into your body, Bruce* was a mantra that Dom had been trying to hammer into Bruce since day one.

"You're overthinking it, Brucie," Dougie offered helpfully.

He tried to loosen the reins in his mind. Dom telling him to keep his rhythm. Dom still insisting that he stop wasting everyone's time. He felt some space opening inside him that was welling up with a musty sadness and defiance and a general disappointment, and he focused his attention there. He felt his loneliness, despite the fact that he had never been alone his entire life. He nudged around a sense that he was invisible but that he was also under a glaring spotlight the minute they stepped out in public. He got into his body through that widening, weeping hole. And then his next punch connected. And the next. Dougie yelling affirmations into his ear. He pretended that the bag was Dom. Dom telling him he was small and insignificant and incompetent. Bruce felt his own weight and Dougie's too. He felt his arm and his shoulder and his thighs and his back—and Dougie's too. He wasn't invisible. He took up space. They took up space. He started to feel more deeply that Dougie's weight was also his own, that the mass and strength of Dougie's body was also his to use. He hit as hard as he could. He wasn't small. Bruce's shoulder was strained, aching up into his neck. He kept jerking back and popping forth. Waiting for the bag to be in the right spot. That initial sadness in his gut amounting to something that wasn't exactly words now but felt something like *here...here...here* stuck on repeat. He drove his right fist into and—he was pleased to finally note—through the bag.

Bruce plowed his fist through three more times.

"Well, hell, Bruce, you're still alive in there. Do you feel it now?"

Bruce had to admit, reluctantly, that Dom was a minor genius. For a moment he understood exactly why Dougie needed to keep doing all of this. He concentrated on catching his breath, the smell of sweat, the force of his own heart beating: *here, here, here*. Dougie used his outside fist to bump Bruce's left arm up with his glove, trying to mimic as best he could the pictures around them. That weak arm a bird's wing unfurling.

"Okay, boys. I'll see you in a couple days."

"Dom, can we talk about the Patrice match?" Bruce was out on a limb, solo.

"What is it?"

"Well, basically"—Bruce had been rehearsing this next part all morning so he could get the gist out before he lost Dom's attention—"he flouts all the rules of decent sportsmanship."

Dougie had that playground sense that his fun was about to get curtailed. "Bruce, he's a boxer! Dom, don't listen to him. He just got freaked out by Olivier."

"Dom, Olivier got jumped by Patrice's guys. In the street."

"Look, I don't really know. They never found the guys. Olivier's okay, though. He still fought Patrice and lived to tell the tale."

"See, Bruce, you're overthinking again." Dougie basked in the shimmer of being right.

Bruce wanted to react with the force and speed of an undeniable comeback, but he couldn't generate it fast enough. A loathsome helplessness smothered his right to get angry.

"Run some more. And goddammit, get yourselves in sync," said Dom over his shoulder.

Later that evening Dougie was on the lot, still amped up from practice. He loved the atmosphere of being in the boxing club: the other boxers sparring, the sounds of all the bags, the skipping ropes, the pads being hit. He loved being there first thing in the morning when everything about a new day felt promising. But equally he loved being there for a fight night, regardless of whether the Reuben Beast was fighting or watching other fighters. When the lights were dimmed, except over the ring, the atmosphere pressed with urgency and adrenaline. He soaked all of it up while he was there and took it with him everywhere he went.

"Check it out—the snappy couple getting out of the Beamer—there's no way they've come to the Everest on a Friday night to do their groceries. C'mon, Bruce. Let's do this."

Dougie and Bruce were on the couple without even breaking into a sweat.

"Evening. Now I know you're not thinking of parking here without patronizing our establishment tonight."

The man instinctively put an arm around his wife, who instinctively tightened her grip on her purse.

Dougie pushed a bit harder. "We'll have to ask you to park elsewhere, sir. This is not a public lot."

"Oh. But we were just going inside," the woman improvised, unsure of where exactly to let her gaze land on the twins.

Dougie made a sort of grand gesture with his arm. "Well in you get—the door's thatta way."

"There's a special on at the deli counter," Bruce offered. He didn't think Dougie should have to do all the work alone while he just stood there. "We'll be out here keeping an eye on your car the whole time you're inside shopping tonight."

The couple were flustered as they hustled back to the parking spot, embarrassed and indignant.

"Genius, Brucie! You're a real cowboy, you know that?"

Earlier that morning at the gym, before their session with Dom, Dougie and Bruce had been working on the speed bag ("the uvula," Bruce had dubbed it), a teardrop hanging from a wooden platform. They had started slowly alternating Dougie's left jab and Bruce's right cross, building speed punch by punch to get the bag spinning, timing the rhythm to hit it in the right spot at the right time, aiming right down the middle. Dougie loved working the speed bag; he loved the moment when they both clicked into place, locked in together, their one-two jab-cross getting faster and more accurate.

Dom had called them into his office. It was a cluttered room. A fan on the top of a filing cabinet was oscillating; pages under an eight-pound free weight on the desk ruffled, then were still, and then ruffled again. The wall was thick with layers of paint; it was chipped all along one side of the window, the rust and putty colours of the original bricks muscling their way back into the dingy white office. Dougie and Dom were sharing pleasantries as Bruce nodded along, and then Dom made his proposal.

Since then Dougie had been waiting for the right time to continue the conversation with his brother. Bruce seemed pretty loose now, so he dove right in.

"Um. So what do you think about going up for the Golden Gloves tournament? It'll be hard work, you know—I can't lie to you. But like Dom said, we're ready now, and we've got enough bouts under our belts to qualify. Not to mention we could win the whole damn thing. Do you know what that could mean for us? To hold the title of Golden Gloves Provincial Champions? That's huge. It puts us in a whole new class. Even if we'll be too old to compete on the national team, at least we'll go out having accomplished something."

Bruce didn't have a good feeling in his gut about this; he had dreaded everything about the tournament from the second Dom had called them back into his office, sitting at his desk working a hand gripper in his left hand without pause. The registration deadline was looming, and they needed to give him their answer sooner rather than later. Boxing turned Bruce's innards to cottage cheese.

"The tournament is at the end of the year. That gives us a couple of months to step up our training. And you heard Dom say he'll make us his top priority. You know he meant it. Bruce, he believes in us. You may not see it or feel it the way I do, but we're gifted in the ring. We're good at this. Plus, c'mon, there is no one else like us. Show me another set of conjoined boxers anywhere in the world. We've got a natural advantage that no one sees coming. Most of our opponents—you know what they think when they know they're gonna fight us? They think we're weak, that between the two of us we still don't muster up to half a man. Hell, the reason Boxing Ontario lets the two of us fight a single opponent in the first place is because they think we share a brain between us. But Bruce, we're strong, we're fit, we're fast. We're good. You might not believe it, but I'll believe it for both of us until you're ready. We gotta at least try for the tournament heavyweight title. You won't regret this. Trust me."

Dougie finally stopped for air. Bruce twisted his torso out to the right and held some of the night air inside him for a few long seconds. Everest Grocery was lit up like a squat lighthouse. The twins had to move out of the way for a beat-up old car awkwardly trying to navigate out of the lot: a teenager with her dad, learning how to drive. She laboured through a protracted three-point turn to painfully wrench the red Toyota Tercel around. It stopped at the curb, the right signal blinking, waiting, waiting, waiting, though no other car was in sight. The girl was laughing, her hands gripping the wheel at ten and two, her father in hysterics, barely able to catch his breath. Bruce tried to remember the last time he was swept away in that kind of joyful undertow. He felt the weight of Dougie's arm slung around his neck, his own arm in mirror image around his brother.

Bruce was still trying to figure out how to ease up on the boxing if not ditch it altogether. He didn't think it was possible to devote any more time to it. Already, their whole lives had revolved around the sport. But then he looked at his brother, who was grinning like an idiot.

"So? Just think about it. Sleep on it. Don't rush to a decision." Dougie was sure he could work Bruce over by the end of the weekend. His inside hand gave Bruce's shoulder a pat and a little rub. "Only thing is the deadline to register is Monday, so we do have to let Dom know right away."

Dougie had been coasting on a thermal of exhilaration since that morning's chat with Dom. They had spent their lives training for this moment, this tournament. Everything that made Dougie the man he was, all of it made sense in relief against a championship title: being conjoined, spending so much time as a kid in boxing classes and at the gym, going through different trainers, driving to matches, running, sparring, staying focused all through their young adult lives. Becoming the Reuben Beast. Taking what others found abnormal or scary about him and his brother and shaping that into a form that was agile, beautiful, powerful, frightening, and undeniable. That was their purpose; this was their calling.

Dougie was sailing around the world, and he wasn't going to stop now, at the halfway mark. He just couldn't.

The Tercel honked from behind. The girl rolled down her window, and her dad leaned over her, apologizing as the car crawled back into the lot and then lurched to a halt. And then lurched to a start. The twins could hear the dad killing himself with laughter.

Dougie was whistling and re-imagining the end of the Marlowe match, imagining punching the smug look right off his face. Imagining his own arm now drained of all tension and might, being raised up high by its wrist.

The next day Bruce and Dougie were back at Everest doing their grocery shopping when Bruce was hit with a startling discovery, nearly ramming his side of the cart into a pyramid of watermelons. *Holy shit. Her books will be due back three weeks since that day.*

"What's up? Grab a melon while you're there."

"That girl. She'll have to go back to return her books. We were there on a Wednesday before your shift...so we just have to go back in a couple days. That'll be three weeks."

"What if she renews them?"

"Hmmmmm."

"You can't be serious about going back to the library. Bruce, you're killing me with the goddamned library."

"We can just stop by in the afternoon for a little while. Why don't you get some boxing biographies?"

"No."

"Dougie, please. Just let me do this one thing."

Dougie was comparing prices on cheese. "You're stalking that poor girl. Get it together, Bruce."

Bruce felt desperately ashamed that his brother was right.

"What if we go to the library again on Wednesday and by some remote chance she's actually there this time? You're telling me you'll actually walk up to her and start talking? What's the rest of your brilliant plan?"

Bruce had no plan. His ears were burning with shame.

"Listen, I get it. You think she's cute. But then what?"

Dougie's manager was wheeling a mop bucket toward them and nodded at the twins as a cleanup request interrupted the overhead music.

"Get real, Brucie. Let it go."

Bruce swallowed hard on the lump in his throat. What had he been doing? This was a woman he had laid his eyes on for a couple of minutes, weeks ago. Maybe his brother was right. He had no game.

The truth was, if Bruce had pushed back, Dougie would've gone to the library every day. He loved his brother and wanted him to feel happy, but it was also true that Dougie wanted to box. Dougie wanted to beat every single opponent they had lined up into the winter. But in order to win, he needed Bruce. He needed Bruce more than Bruce needed that girl, a total stranger to both of them. Bruce would be able to forget her once they were champions of their weight class. In time Bruce could find another girl to have a crush on.

Bruce and Dougie both hated the song that was playing as Dougie's co-worker, Nikki, scanned their groceries at the checkout, and Dougie said as much to her. Dougie had made sure they got into Nikki's line; she made Everest awesome because she was awesome. Nikki gestured with her eyes and a tilt of her chin behind Dougie; the three of them watched the manager hopelessly attacking a giant olive oil spill in aisle five. Nikki told Dougie to grab a pack of gum from the display, and she tossed it in their bag. "Today's employee discount." She winked and blew a small bubble.

Bruce's feelings were still bruised as they carried their bags home, but he didn't bother to say anything. He knew that Dougie's cavalier attitude was ultimately sparing him from a potentially greater humiliation. But to be perfectly honest, he wasn't ready to let it go yet; he just needed to figure out what he would do if he saw her again, and then he'd find a way to get his brother's co-operation by Wednesday.

They arrived home to their half of a semi-detached Edwardian. A short flight of narrow cement stairs led down to their basement suite, and a set of wide, well-worn wooden steps led up to a deep square porch at the front door. The entire lot was comfortably wide, and the residents of their half often forgot that they were attached to a whole other house. Bruce and Dougie were friendly enough with the rotating cast of roommates that circulated above them on their side at 44 Hudd Street, but none of them ever got to know the terse couple who owned the half at 42. Forty-four was sliding into the shabby side of "lived-in." The paint was peeling from the window frames, the ragged lawn was only ever mowed sporadically, and very long grass clustered around the young but sturdy tree out front. The walkway to the porch was cracked and warned of eventual upheaval. Forty-two, on the other hand, had never been a rental, and so their paint was always fresh, the windows double-paned. Their very bright security lights were always at the ready, and the front yard was designed in the style of a Japanese Zen garden. Both Bruce and Dougie agreed the overall vibe was less Zen and more uptight. Just next to 42 was a one-storey white stucco-and-brick church, with an arched doorway flanked on either side by three tall, arched windows and three more miniature arched windows in the gable above. The twins didn't know what happened inside, but the agreed-upon vibe from the outside was that a giant had uprooted this quaint little morsel, which had been nestled deep in the forest of a European fable, and transplanted it down in this city on a whim.

The twins could more or less shuffle down their cement stairs easily, needing only to adjust themselves to a forty-five-degree angle. At some early age, they had unconsciously agreed that the direction they were coming from would determine who took the lead when going up or down a flight of stairs. Today they were walking south, and because the house was on Bruce's side, he took the first step down. They always each carried a set of keys to eliminate the possibility of fumbling or dropping them when they were at the door since there wasn't room enough to really bend or stoop, especially with bags in hand.

They trundled in and through the hallway into the galley kitchen and dropped their bags. They pulled out a bench tucked by their table and sat to untie their shoes. As they stood emptying the bags on the counter, Bruce noticed Dougie pressing hard into his left temple with his outside hand. Dougie did this intermittently as he put things in the fridge. Bruce put a jar of salsa down and reached for a glass, stretching over as far as he could to flick the tap on. He offered Dougie the water.

Dougie opened his eyes and took the glass, observing his brother's worry. "Must be the heat. Hopefully we're not coming down with anything."

"Do you need to lie down?"

"Maybe just a quick nap." Dougie's stomach was churning.

They manoeuvred gently onto the bed and lay on top of the covers until Dougie finally fell asleep. Bruce lay down, glancing over at Dougie every few minutes to see that he was resting okay, and let his thoughts turn back to the girl. He remembered her long black hair.

Bruce also dozed off, waking as the sun was going down. He woke up hungry, but Dougie was sleeping soundly. He propped himself up to lean across his brother's torso and opened the drawer of Dougie's bedside table where Dougie kept an emergency stash of protein bars. Bruce used his teeth to tear the wrapper open. He relented that it wasn't fair to drag his brother back to the library like he'd been doing. It was true that he had no idea how he would approach the girl to introduce himself, assuming he even saw her again. He couldn't imagine a scenario where he would be able to charm her into a friendship by just randomly approaching her out of the blue. He crumpled the foil wrapper and tossed it into the trash, and something in that very simple movement, a soft underhand toss of the crinkled ball into the garbage, led Bruce to an equally simple idea: a letter.

JUNE 1996

From early on the twins had been able to naturally work out how to afford one another a little space. They couldn't ignore what was going on with the other, but they knew when something would not be spoken of.

Dougie had lost his virginity at the end of high school with Corrine Dumont. She read science fiction with an insatiable appetite and wanted to become a veterinarian. She only listened to oldies music on AM radio and still held firmly to the self-assuredness that she'd had as a three-year-old. She was blessed in that the only approval she sought after came from her ancient pet turtle, Chelonii, and together she and Chelonii had decided to carve their own paths. She had spent the year sitting in front of Dougie and Bruce in English class. Dougie was impressed by the fact that Corrine answered questions with a lot of sass but without being a smart aleck. She was sent to the office for calling their teacher an imperialist when he spent a week forcing the class to relearn how to use commas properly. Dougie asked her if she was going to the "Instead-of-Bullshit-Prom" bonfire at the Lloyds' farm. She hadn't been planning on it but reconsidered when Dougie asked her to.

After school on the day of the bonfire, Dougie and Bruce took a long walk around their family's field with Dougie playing out a few likely scenarios between him and Corrine. He had wanted Bruce to also ask someone so they could double date. He suggested asking Corrine's friend—the one with the headgear—but they'd never had any classes with her and neither could remember her name. Bruce was worried about having something else to do while Dougie was otherwise occupied. He settled on making sure he was never without his Walkman at all times from then on. He reassured Dougie that he was completely fine with anything that Dougie wanted to do; he was perfectly happy not doing it yet. They both agreed that it would be best if they did it for the first time one after the other, rather than at the same time. This was for the girls, who they wanted to make sure didn't feel too weird about it, and for themselves, since they weren't exactly sure how the logistics were going to work out yet. Dougie felt pretty good about their talk, and they went back into the house to look for fresh batteries for Bruce's Walkman.

That night Bruce surprised himself with how much fun he had at the party. There were about forty kids who had all decided not to go to the prom. There were all sorts of people Bruce didn't expect to see there. Bruce talked for a long time with Ian Kapoor, who had the reputation of being a loner but turned out to be really hilarious. While taking swigs from his flask and then passing it to Bruce, Ian explained the plot of a short film he was making. Bruce was warmed by the rye in the flask and wished they had talked at least once at school in the past five years.

"No matter." Ian clapped him on the back and said he would write a part for the twins in his movie. He was deeply influenced by French New Wave cinema, so Bruce would have to smoke in it a lot.

Corrine was also having a better time than she ever imagined she would have, and she was glad that she had accepted Dougie's invitation. Dougie was trying to convince her that boxing wasn't actually barbaric, that there was grace and nobility and skill to it. Bodies didn't lie; there was something very honest about the body. He demonstrated his point by coaxing her into punching him in the arm as hard as she could. She was uncommonly strong, and she blushed the whole time. Corrine was thrilled to be sitting out in the dark with other kids, facing a dangerously large fire. Sparks rose up, disappearing to stars. Dougie reached out for Corrine's hand, and she let him take it.

Dougie and Corrine kissed for a long time after she drove the twins home in her parents' car. She was sitting behind the wheel, and Dougie leaned in through the window. Bruce was pressed flat against the car, drunk and drumming the roof with his right hand, headphones on.

Corrine had enrolled in an aquatic ecology camp in Peterborough and was leaving in two weeks. She and Dougie had sex a week after the bonfire. Corrine picked the twins up, and they drove around, eating candy and pretzels that she had grabbed from her parents' pantry. Dougie had snuck out an almost-empty bottle of scotch, but he let Bruce have most of it. They drove around until her parents were sure to have left for the Maxwells' dinner party, and then they went back to Corrine's. She could have introduced them to her parents and said they were all going to watch a movie, but she was suddenly feeling guarded and preferred to avoid having to talk about the twins with her parents. In the morning they would've interrogated her about the movie, and the boys, and how their grades were, and how long they had been friends, and what their plans were for the future, and how they liked being joined, and all.

Corrine's room was painted a colour she called *mantis* and Dougie called *green*. She felt certain that Chelonii liked the twins and approved of her particular choice; she assured them they would have known for sure if Chelonii didn't like them. The boys had no idea what she meant exactly and just sat on the edge of the bed, staring down at the turtle. Dougie was perfectly giddy; Bruce put his headphones on and closed his eyes. Corrine exhaled a deep breath, took off her t-shirt, and let Dougie touch her tiny breasts with his left hand.

AUGUST 2012

On their way to Ogilvie's on Monday morning, the sun got itself trapped in the streetcar's dirty back window. Bruce and Dougie each paid their fare and sardined themselves midway through the car. Dougie was playing googly eyes with a baby, trying for a smile. Bruce hung himself from a hand grip, feeling every jolt and sway from the track move through his body. They had gotten up just before five a.m. to go running, and Dom would've been elated to know that for the whole run Bruce kept telling himself to get into his body, trying to come to terms with the sad reality that he wasn't going to be able to get back into his bed. He had to give his brother an answer about the tournament by the time they returned home from their run. He was of two minds about it. It was a four-day tournament, and that was an awful lot of days in a row to punch people and get beat up in exchange. But it was basically just one weekend, and Dougie would be elated even if they didn't win the title. So ultimately he had told his brother to tell Dom yes, but with the caveat that they needed to take a long break after the tournament. Bruce had expected Dougie to give him the usual rousing pep talk about how much Bruce would love it and wouldn't regret this decision. But he didn't. Bruce had been surprised by the softness in Dougie's reaction. Dougie had turned to face him, as much as was possible for the two of them to do so, craning around to look Bruce in the eyes, and said, "Thank you."

Bruce focused his attention on his legs—he could feel the blood coursing through them, and with his eyes closed, he couldn't feel any difference between the right and the middle. He imagined that the dips and bends of the track were the ocean's swell. The hiss of music escaping the earbuds of a girl sitting near them became the wind filling up the sails. He forced his eyes to stay closed almost the whole way. He willed himself to forget about the coffee shops, the bank, the cyclists, the recycling and green bins put out, the taxis, the dentist on the corner, the pho place, the widows on their porches for the day.

He imagined M sailing away from home forever, making a decision to commit only to the sea and becoming entirely engulfed by that choice. In 1969, when he knew he wouldn't return, M had telegraphed his wife back in France saying only *We shall meet again*, though Bruce knew he would've written it in French. Bruce didn't know how it felt to say goodbye to someone you loved and to leave them behind. How would he have chosen to say goodbye to Dougie? How would they each be different without the weight of the other? Had he and Dougie been born simply identical twins, rather than conjoined, their lifetime of dilemmas would have been completely different. Neither twin, nor their parents, ever allowed themselves to think these thoughts because what good would that bring when this was their reality? Jane and Walter were happy in the life and home they had built, and they had strived to instill that contentment in their sons no matter what obstacles arose.

However this morning Bruce's heart was beating fast. With his eyes closed and off in his own world, for only the fourth time in his life, he dared himself to tentatively clear the dense brush that hid a forbidden path in his imagination. Had their cells cleaved as they were intended, or had his parents allowed the doctors to separate them, Bruce might now, at thirty-four years old, be driving to work by himself because he had learned how to drive at sixteen. Maybe he had fallen in love for the first time in high school and then again a number of times since then. He saw himself with a careless, entitled kind of confidence, able to move through the world without mapping out exactly how he was going to do it. It was his right arm now that draped casually, not around Dougie's neck, but around the passenger seat's headrest as he looked out the back windshield to reverse out of a parking space. It was the most commonplace gesture, and he was able to do it without batting an eye because he'd parallel parked a car a thousand times: running errands for his parents, picking up a girlfriend to go away for the weekend, meeting up with friends that Dougie hadn't met yet. And when he dropped Dougie off at the airport, he simply said, "Later," with a quick hug in the car before he had to drive away to let in a waiting minivan. And maybe Dougie was a famous pro boxer. And he lived in a big house in Vegas with his wife, an Olympian triathlete, and their goofy daredevil kids. And Bruce had turned out to be an—

Bruce swallowed wrong and started choking. Dougie looked over and began to soothe his brother's chest with his inside arm.

"I'm okay. It's okay," Bruce sputtered.

"Sorry, Brucie. I didn't bring my water bottle."

Bruce was still coughing and waving off the concerned looks from Dougie and the mother next to him with her baby. The baby was kicking its legs uproariously. The mother dug out an unopened bottle of water from deep inside the baby's diaper bag, and Dougie accepted it, thanking her.

Each of the three times in the past that Bruce had indulged in this type of fantasy, his body almost immediately put a stop to it. This clandestine imagining of himself without Dougie was something he would never utter out loud. In fact the thought of him existing without Dougie right there with him was not something that had ever occurred to him as a child and maybe just once or twice as a teenager. And one time when he was about twenty-three. Every time he had lingered near the edge of these dark woods, it had been because he was faced with the desire for something that only he wanted. When Bruce was fourteen, he had tried to negotiate with Dougie to switch out the boxing for chess club. Dougie didn't see the point; it made no sense to him. He'd have nothing to do while Bruce played chess, and their mother agreed they should compromise on hobbies they could both participate in. At eighteen he was ready to move downtown, but Dougie wanted to stay at home for a few more years to put in some real time with a new trainer nearby who recognized their potential. He did help them improve considerably, but he ended up moving to Whistler a year later. And when they were in their early twenties, Bruce had wanted to apply to university. He had completed a bookkeeping certificate after high school, but for a short period of time he had had a dream of going to university, taking more advanced courses in accounting or maybe even something further afield. He hadn't known exactly what it would have been, but he had felt excited about the prospect of being immersed in something new: architecture or law or astrophysics. Without fail, when he allowed the vista of an independent life to widen in front of him, he started to choke, breaking into an alarming and uncontrollable barking fit that couldn't be calmed or quieted for a very long minute or two—until he could retrain his mind's eye to focus on the present moment, this moment when his body was involuntarily loud and insistent in its inability to breathe. Trapped in this way, he was forced to let go of everything else in his mind as the sole means to equilibrium.

But before Bruce was able to come back to himself, a fragment of one of his earliest memories became dislodged. He and Dougie were three years old, and their mother had taken them to a playground. A lady yelled at them for taking up too much space, for playing too rough—a little monster, she had called them. She claimed they had nearly endangered her baby daughter who was plopped in the sandbox, who was supposed to be there when they probably weren't. Being scolded by a mom who wasn't his mom made Bruce erupt in immediate wide-mouthed wailing. He remembered his mom had turned to him and said, "Christ, Brucie. Come on, stand your ground." She said that he wasn't to let some stranger with her baby tell them what was or was not normal. Jane was seething, but little Bruce, the child, had mistakenly felt that his mother's rage was directed at him and his weakness, that his mother was disgusted by him because he was ashamed, embarrassed for being different from any other person he had ever seen. Over the years he never asked Dougie if he remembered that day because Bruce also remembered that Dougie had told the woman in his three-year-old way: "It's not nice to talk about people's bodies, you know." And Jane had kissed the top of Dougie's sun-warmed head before telling the lady to go to hell and that her crying baby was overdue for a nap and likely had heatstroke. Bruce felt he must've continued to cry for some time after the lady and her baby had left the sandbox.

At the stop people rushed past the twins, pushing off the streetcar, pooling out of all the doors and onto College Street.

Dougie's voice cut through his brother's memories. "There's two seats at the back."

At the back of the streetcar, Bruce pulled out his book about M. He couldn't concentrate and kept reading and re-reading the same line: *The sun that rises over open water does not have time to pander to an audience.* When he finally forced himself to stop glossing over the words and focus on what was directly in front of him, he immediately understood M's philosophy to be an echo of his mother's own unflinching sensibility.

> Whether I am here—the sole, insignificant witness paying homage—or at home—under the dark of my bed covers, shivering with fever, my mind reeling with delirium—is irrelevant. That perfect, eviscerating fire burns and burns out there in the vast dark of space and forces the earth's waves and sky to reinterpret its intensity into reflections and refractions that are safe for us to behold. The sun is ferociously itself with no patience for apology, self-doubt, or self-loathing.

Bruce had turned to M for shelter, for some kind reassurances, but it was just more tough love, as it had been from his mother. The callous irony was not lost on him. The words he read were yet another indictment of Bruce's failure to stand up for himself with his brother, and of the weakness he felt because of his self-doubt. A glowing spotlight exposing his shame.

He forged ahead in his reading so as to push past what he was feeling.

> When M eventually made landfall in Tahiti, those words were found scrawled across the deck of his boat in something the local children said could only

> have been human blood. The ones who had skipped school to snoop around had read the missive with their own eyes, and they later boasted to the others with gleeful terror. They conferred an authority upon themselves that arose from bearing witness to M's madness, reluctantly acknowledging that, yes, the strange words smeared across the hull were written in a French they could understand because they had learned it in school. Against their will.

His eyes scanned the printed words, but the notion that M had been steeped in madness when he had made his declarations about being "ferociously" himself, akin to the sun, was utterly lost on Bruce. In Bruce's head all he heard was a cacophony of M's voice, his mother's voice, and his own: *Why can't you be more like him? Why can't you be more like him? Why can't you be more like him?* Waves lapping the shore. He gave up reading and thumbed through the book, looking at the fine-lined illustrations until Dougie yanked the cord to bring the streetcar to a halt.

Once off the streetcar, there were a few brief moments that their shadows were cast out long ahead of them; then finally they were taken in by the shade of the buildings for the rest of the way to Ogilvie's.

ANKA RAMRATAN
AUGUST 2012

IN A BACHELOR APARTMENT NOT TOO FAR AWAY from where Bruce and Dougie lived, Anka Ramratan was twisted up under her sheets while someone banged on her window and yelled through the open screen.

"Anka, wake up. I know you're in there. The sun is shining, you degenerate." Diane had invited herself over for breakfast. "Anka, I have coffee. I drank mine. I'm gonna drink yours too if I have to stand out here for much longer."

Anka rolled out of bed, her sheet wrapped around her shoulders, and went to the door. As soon as she was faced with her friend, Diane muttered, "Oh, shit," and put the coffee and grocery bag down. She gathered Anka, wrapped in a sheet burrito, into a hug. "It's crap. I'm so sorry."

Diane came armed with breakfast food, tabloid magazines, whisky, nail polish, and a set of jacks. The jacks were a last-minute addition at the Everest checkout—the package had been tucked into the gum display, discarded by a previous customer.

Today marked a year since Anka's parents had died.

Anka unwrapped herself. "Jesus, it's so hot already. I'm okay."

She bent to pick up her coffee and then checked the mailbox. She wanted to deflect some of this well-meaning attention; Anka didn't want to be forced to face all of her grief in front of someone else, even if it was her best friend. "Come inside. I got the craziest thing the other day," she said, her fist still clutching the sheet to her heart.

Inside Anka tidied the bed, folding the sheet in half, and in half, and in half again. "I got a letter from a secret admirer."

"What? Like online?" Diane had unpacked the grocery bag and was beginning to assemble breakfast.

"No. In my mailbox outside. Totally old-fashioned."

"Creepy."

"Maybe. Actually, a bit sweet? I dunno. Unusual."

"Who's it from? Do you know them? Please tell me they didn't ask for money or photos?"

"No, nothing like that. Just a regular guy introducing himself. Trying to be neighbourly? Apparently he's seen me around, but I'm not sure who he is. I thought maybe he had come into the laundromat, but a lot of guys come in and they're all kind of anti-social. I dunno. Maybe someone I just haven't paid attention to."

"How do you know he isn't some pervy weirdo?"

Anka turned on the radio. "Should I write him back?"

"Probably not. Lemme see it."

Anka took the two steps to get from her bed to her extremely compact desk and passed over a folded piece of paper that had been ripped from a spiral-bound notebook.

Diane was immediately unimpressed as she unfolded the paper. "Someone has seriously given you a ransom note."

Anka laughed, feeling foolish, and tried to snatch the letter back, but Diane twisted herself out of reach and read it quickly while she had the chance.

August 22, 2012

Dear Anka (I think),

Hi. My name is Bruce Reuben. I'm not trying to bother you, but I've seen you around, and you seem really cool. I live nearby next to that tiny Hungarian church. I'm really sorry if this is a little strange. I'm not trying to be weird. I only wanted to say hi and to be a kind neighbour.

Very Best Regards,
Bruce Reuben, age thirty-four. Bookkeeper

PS. I'm not sure if this your name. Please forgive me for being presumptuous. It was a name I saw on a hydro bill in your mailbox, and I am extremely (like, really, really) sorry for prying. If you are reading this and you are a woman with long black hair, then this letter is for you.

Diane folded the letter back up and handed it over. "Hmmmmm. Mmmhmmm."

"What?" Anka asked, even though she knew what that sound meant.

"It is a little strange."

Anka tossed the letter on her desk and decided to drop the subject. She took the three steps from her office to the corner of the room that was her kitchen to make some fresh coffee. The stovetop espresso maker and the kettle occupied the stove's two burners. She topped off her lukewarm, to-go coffee with a heavy splash of whisky and poured some into Diane's waiting mug. In her previous life, when she took for granted that both of her parents were alive, she might have been dismissive about something out of the ordinary like this letter. The "before" Anka would've shuddered at the thought of a stranger knowing where she lived and would've promptly discarded the letter. But here in the "after," she was alone in her tiny one-room apartment. She didn't care any more about how things were supposed to look or expected to be. It was an odd intimacy to have a stranger's handwriting addressing her. The first time she read the letter, her stomach had dropped but also her cheeks had flushed. It was disorienting to feel something like curiosity threading through her grief. She felt reckless and didn't care about what could happen to her. She felt cracked open. She took a sip and then glugged more whisky into her paper cup.

A letter introducing himself had been Bruce's big move. He figured what he really wanted to write would almost guarantee his arrest. He wanted to tell her that there was a quality that he could vaguely recognize about her that was also the same about him, some sense of being on the outside of things. However he didn't know how to write that in a sentence that made any sense. He decided against writing that he thought she was agonizingly beautiful and he had never thought that about anyone before. While Dougie was asleep, Bruce had struggled through four drafts to land on those seven terse sentences and a whole day's debate with himself about whether he should mention overhearing the librarian recite her address. He also nixed the idea of mentioning that he and Dougie had celebrated their birthday last week. Ultimately he decided to keep the letter as short as possible and deal with questions as they came, if they came. As it was he barely stood a chance of getting this woman's attention or interest. His biggest hope was that he hadn't freaked her out. He decided he'd lie low on going to the library for a while and give her some space.

Once the letter had been folded, he re-purposed the envelope from the birthday card their parents had given them and tried to very casually open up a conversation with Dougie while they were eating dinner.

"So I have a quick errand to run tonight."

"Sure. What is it?"

"Or we could do it tomorrow. Whatever. It's nothing really."

"Cool."

"Um. I have to deliver a letter?"

"There's a mailbox on the corner"—Dougie paused to finish chewing—"near the gym. Just wait till we go train."

"Well. Ungggggh… It's for that girl." Bruce was blushing and could only look down at his plate.

"What? Okay, Casanova. Wow, I did not see that coming."

"I thought I would introduce myself somehow. I dunno. It's kind of random."

"Can I read it? Did you tell her about us? Did you tell her about the Golden Gloves tournament?"

"No." Bruce was regretting his strategy. "Forget it. It's probably a mistake."

"No way. We'll go when we're done eating." Dougie gave his brother's chest a little rub and a pat.

Bruce was feeling nervous now that everything was set. He pushed away his plate and gulped down his glass of water, which did nothing to satiate his thirst.

Dougie filled in the silence: "Do you see it?"

"Huh?"

"Well it's no coincidence to me that the more we're boxing, the braver you're getting."

Bruce had never thought he'd ever want to approach having a relationship; he'd always assumed that a girlfriend was not in the cards for him, though for Dougie it was the opposite. Dougie had always figured why the hell not? The only time Bruce had been kissed was by Stacey Houseman, who had been dared to kiss him and then Dougie, each on the lips, during lunch recess in Grade Six. It seemed as if their entire class had heard and closed in around the three of them to make sure no one could break free. Stacey's friend who had instigated the dare had pushed her toward Bruce, who was stock still, ears perked on full alert. He saw Stacey's freckles up close, a spray of brown across her nose, before he closed his eyes and felt a soft, glancing peck just over the corner of his mouth. His heart was beating like that of a fox narrowly spared by a hound. He turned to find Dougie and Stacey kissing; Dougie had even wrapped an arm around her.

According to Dougie, Stacey had swirled her tongue around his for a glorious number of seconds before she pried herself away from the twins, squealing and screeching ("retching," according to Bruce). Dougie, wide-eyed and with a hand to his head, watched Stacey run away, braids flying behind her, all the girls glimmering around the schoolyard like dandelion seeds on the wind.

Bruce couldn't say what had shifted so suddenly in his mind that allowed for him to carefully tear the paper from a notebook and get the words down ("it's definitely not the boxing," he assured Dougie), let alone convince himself to walk over to the address he had quietly typed into his phone a few weeks ago. Dougie had to take the lead up the front steps when it became clear that Bruce's nerves suddenly might not let him release the letter from his grip. Bruce was forced to follow behind his brother, remembering the brief moment of eye contact between him and the woman.

"There's some mail in here, Bruce. I wonder if any of it is hers."

"Quit it—let's just get out of here."

Dougie flipped through the couple of items. "These are for dudes. But here—try this one." Dougie held up a hydro bill.

"What am I supposed to do with that?"

"Just address your letter to her. Maybe that's a better approach than 'To Whom It May Concern.'"

"I didn't write that."

"That way she'll at least know it's for her and not for Mr. Vincenzo Bruno." Dougie was now brandishing an envelope from GoodLife Fitness.

"Fine." Bruce huffed as he dug the stub of a pencil out of his pants pocket.

"You carry a pencil around?"

Dougie put all the mail back while Bruce positioned the letter against the front door and managed to scribble something furiously.

"There. Okay. Let's get outta here."

Bruce took the lead down the stairs with his heart wild in amazement, and as they walked away, he grinned at Dougie in wide-eyed, disbelieving wonder that he had taken so blind a leap off a cliff. He didn't know if it would come to anything, but something about taking decisive action had him stepping a little more lightly, and he carried his half of the Reuben Beast a little more upright.

walked over to the [illegible] he had [illegible] from his [illegible] [illegible] [illegible] [illegible] [illegible] [illegible] [illegible] [illegible] [illegible] [illegible] [illegible] [illegible] [illegible] [illegible] [illegible] [illegible] [illegible]

"There's [illegible] [illegible] [illegible] [illegible] [illegible] [illegible] [illegible] [illegible]

[illegible] [illegible]—let's [illegible] [illegible] [illegible]"

Doug [illegible] [illegible] through the [illegible] [illegible] [illegible] [illegible] [illegible] [illegible] [illegible] [illegible] [illegible] [illegible] [illegible] [illegible] [illegible] half up [illegible] [illegible]

"What am I supposed to do with that?"

"[illegible] [illegible] [illegible] [illegible] [illegible] [illegible] [illegible] [illegible] [illegible] [illegible] [illegible] [illegible] [illegible] [illegible] [illegible]"

"[illegible] [illegible] [illegible]"

"[illegible] she'll at least know it's [illegible] and not [illegible] [illegible] [illegible] [illegible] [illegible] was now [illegible] [illegible] [illegible] [illegible] [illegible] [illegible]

"[illegible] [illegible] [illegible] [illegible] [illegible] [illegible] [illegible] [illegible] of a [illegible] [illegible] [illegible] [illegible]"

"[illegible] [illegible] [illegible] [illegible]"

[illegible] [illegible] [illegible] [illegible] [illegible] [illegible] [illegible] [illegible] [illegible] [illegible] [illegible] [illegible] [illegible] [illegible] [illegible] [illegible] [illegible] [illegible]

"[illegible] [illegible] [illegible] [illegible] [illegible]"

[illegible] [illegible]

ANKA RAMRATAN
AUGUST 2011

ANKA WAS A BEAST LEFT TO DIE in the middle of the desert; the sun-baked bones of her skull had been left for someone to eventually discover and muse over. The last few very numb days had been spent talking to the doctors and police officers and figuring out what to do with the house and all their stuff and her stuff and their bills and the food in their fridge. She had refused all of Diane's offers of help because she wasn't ready to receive any of it.

The call had come while Anka was parked in front of her computer about to revamp her résumé. And just like that her life flopped over into the "after." She found that she couldn't get up from her desk for some time. Eventually she tapped her screen back to life in an attempt at a small and mindless gesture. But seeing the cursor blinking non-stop at the edge of the word *excel* made her throw her keyboard toward the kitchen floor. Later, when her Auntie Sab picked her up, she packed Anka a bag, grabbed the keyboard, wrapped the cord around it three times, and left it on the counter. The letter keys that had fallen out were left where they had landed. Auntie Sab gathered Anka and her bag in one fell swoop. She was shorter than her niece by a head but somehow bore her up.

Curled tight into a corner of Uncle Charlie and Auntie Sab's sectional, Anka was holding a mug of steaming tea but not drinking it. "I don't think I can do the eulogies."

"Oh"—Sab had her fists full of damp tissues as she snatched two more; all the garbage bins in the house were overflowing with tear-soaked Kleenex—"don' worry 'bout anyt'ing. You don' have to do anyt'ing. Honestly."

It would be a big funeral with extended family, and out of town family, and overseas family—enough to fill two vast kingdoms.

"I want to stand for them, I do. I mean, it was always us three together. But I don't know if I can. I wish I'd been with them that night."

It took Sab a good while to compose herself. "Don' ever say t'ings like dat. Dat is…*that* is a poison." She dropped the wad of Kleenex and took up her tea. "My dear, wishes are dangerous. Dey are a steep mountain you cyan't climb." Sab forced herself, fighting through tears, to finish her thought: "You are a blessing. Your life is a blessing and their greatest legacy. Say it. Lemme hear you say it, Priyanka."

Anka opened her mouth, but no sound would emerge. She took a small sip of her tea. She could hear Grandpa Ramsay upstairs.

Grandpa Ramsay was in his bedroom, continuing to wither with every moment that passed. Arguing feebly against the cruelty of the gods. Coughing, his innards feeling wrung out. Unable to comprehend why he was still here, at age ninety-one, under his weighted blanket. There had to be a way he could give up his own life in exchange for the return of his great-niece and her husband. What was the point of living so long if it meant outliving everyone?

ANKA RAMRATAN
NOVEMBER 2011

LATE IN THE FALL, Anka had called Diane first thing one morning, her voice thick on the line. "Hey, it's me, I'm at the bus station."

"What's going on?"

"Nothing. I need some time, some space. Just to vanish into thin air, maybe."

"What? Anka, wait. What are you talking about? You sound weird."

"Don't worry. It's nothing crazy. I just need a change of scene. I got a job."

"A job? What? You have a job. You're at the fucking bus station? Like, the Greyhound? You have a job, and you should be there working, doing all your radio-assisting shit right now."

"It's fine. I'm fine."

"This is insane. Anka, you're scaring me."

"Don't be mad. Don't get mad. I got a job at a factory canning tomatoes. It's just for a little while."

"What the fuck? Tomatoes? Where?"

"I can't be in the city anymore. My brain won't turn off. I need to do some kind of work, like something exhausting. So I thought, whatever, why not this?"

Diane didn't say anything. She did not understand what was happening. She could only imagine what her friend was feeling. She could sympathize, but she didn't really know this kind of grief up close; she intended to, and would be able to, call her mom later. She was scared shitless for Anka.

"Anka, are you sure about this? You still haven't told me where you're going."

"They've just called boarding for my bus. Don't worry—I'll send you my address as soon as I get set up."

"A factory job? Dude, this isn't fucking Dickens. Let me come meet you; we'll get something to eat."

"It's already done. I applied online. Don't worry. It's legit. I gotta go. I'll call you tonight."

Diane was out of bed, hurriedly getting her jeans on and trying to keep her friend on the line. "What about your apartment? And your stuff?"

"Subletting to an international student I met at work. She's nice. I really have to go."

Diane didn't get the chance to ask the rest of her questions. She was half-dressed and had her keys and wallet, but Anka was gone.

Anka stood in the sombre, slow-moving bus line. Everyone stone faced. The smell of exhaust and the grime of the cement walls reassured Anka that she was making the right move. The plan was to keep outrunning the intrusive thoughts. She had an image of her parents, whole and shining and lovely, and she was fighting to keep it that way. Not the way they had been found—in a wreck. She boarded the bus, lumbering behind her duffel bag through the narrow aisle to a seat at the back. The bus was not full; no one sat next to her. She stared at the headrest in front of her.

Her parents had gone to a party that night, a retirement party for someone at her dad's work in the suburbs north of the city. When she shifted her gaze to stare into her hands on her lap, she could see Stella and Mukesh clear as day, getting ready for the party. She imagined her mother at her vanity putting on her jhumka earrings, heavy, yellow-gold filigree bells inherited from her own mother. When Anka was a teenager, Stella had told her that when she was growing up she thought these earrings were the most glamorous things in the house. The things of Bollywood romances or official state dinners. Anka wanted to stay here for a while with the earrings, earrings passed down from her grandma that now belonged to her. Stella had worn them for all the special occasions: weddings, New Year's, Anka's graduation. Anka used to secretly try them on in front of the mirror; they had had enough weight to drag on her lobes, and she could almost feel that weight there now.

While her mom was at her vanity, she imagined her dad in the adjoining bathroom clapping aftershave onto his cheeks.

The rumble of the bus was enough to lull Anka further into the daydream, and she imagined her parents' conversation as though it were a movie unfolding before her, their lilting voices so distinct in her ear.

"Mukesh, who t'rows demselves a retirement party at fifty? Is a slap in the face to the rest of the team, nuh?"

Anka knew her mom found the work parties a chore. She used to complain about all the small talk and the cliquey wives.

Then her dad would say, *"Especially since all a we will be clockin' in Monday mornin'. He always showing off he'self. But don' worry—we won' stay long."*

"You always say dat."

Anka could hear Mukesh whistling. *"Priyanka sure she don' wan' come? He invite de whole family."*

"She wouldn't. She still upset wit' me after de blow up we had."

"She missin' out."

Anka remembered the fight that she and her mom had had on the phone the night before the party. Her mom was always harping on about her lack of ambition, lamenting that she had been such a good student, always so bright. But Stella was tearing her hair out because here they were *in dis country for a betta opportunity for she chile, and here was she chile wastin' every betta opportunity.* Stella could not, for the life of her, understand why Priyanka couldn't stick with anything for the long haul. A better job had opened up at Anka's work, and Stella could not contain her impatience when Anka didn't pursue it: *Priyanka cookin' up every excuse in de book as to why she cyan't submit she résumé. I woulda kill for half de brains Priyanka get.* Anka remembered her mom had called her lazy, so she had slammed the phone down while she could still hear her mom stchewing her teeth. Anka had felt like a teenager again.

Anka shifted back to imagining her dad coming out of the bathroom to put on his shirt, ironed and laid out on the bed. She imagined her mom resigned to the tedious night ahead.

"I wish we didn' have to go till to dey house, way out behind God back."

"You over t'inking t'ings. We'll have some drinks, a nice meal, and den leave."

"Don't kid you'self! Tell me one time we haven't been de last people to leave anywhere? You ever lef' a party early?"

"Early in de morning? All the time!"

Stella stchewed her teeth.

Anka imagined that she hadn't hung up on her mom. That they had ended their call laughing about something. That Anka had been able to give both her parents an out for that night. Intrusive thoughts about what happened at the end of the party threatened, so Anka forced herself to look up from her hands in her lap and stare out the window. She forcibly ignored the lanes of traffic alongside the bus and looked further out to the horizon, watching the city spiral out into highways and trees and farmland and small towns.

That Southern Ontario landscape was all quite familiar—the green highway signs, the scrubby green grass, deciduous trees, coniferous trees, the highway cutting through, the quality of this particular light making these shades and hues. This was the only infrastructure and ocean of land that she had ever existed in, but she didn't recognize anything of herself in these contours. She didn't feel connected to what she saw out her window, surfaces that held no depths for her. Not in the way her parents felt about Guyana. For both her mother and father, their selfhood and national pride were inextricably linked to the taste of fruits from their neighbours' trees, the particular vibrancy that radiated from the green and blue and yellow and pink and heat of everything alive in their memories. They were formed from that clay; everything around them in the atmosphere had swirled into the double-helix deep inside them, and they vowed never to bend their Guyanese accents to suit whichever land came next. For Anka, born here but not feeling entirely of this place, there was nothing now but the present obligation to show up for this new job in the morning.

When Anka got off the bus three hours later, she found herself stretching her legs out at the bus station in a charming-enough town. A lump, which was also a gaping wound, was throbbing in her throat. She had one more quick bus to take, but it wouldn't arrive for a couple hours. She asked the ticket collector for directions to the public library, where she could wait in relative comfort. Tears had been silently slipping and routinely, rhythmically wiped away the whole bus ride. She felt inside out—raw and grotesque. The ticket collector drew a map that consisted of four long lines, and without calling attention to it, she pulled three quick tissues from the box next to her computer and passed them through the small hole in the plexiglass window. Anka was grateful for the small amount of dignity this austere and efficient gesture offered her.

It was early evening by the time Anka's trip came to an end. In her pocket she had the address for an apartment she had managed to find online before she left Toronto. It was a boxy, three-storey, light brown building, with dark brown doors and trim. Dusty balconies with room enough for only one plastic patio chair. An outcropping of mediocrity in the middle of a vast parking lot. Anka thought it would do just fine.

In the morning she began her training on the sorting line, picking out subpar tomatoes from a steady current that always, always moved forward. She appreciated the sparseness of the line—everyone wearing the same white coveralls, aprons, protective face masks—and the constant noise of the enormous machines. Her entire field of vision was taken up by slick red rubies.

She made no effort to befriend anyone; she worked her shift and picked up all the extra ones she could. She went home, ate instant ramen noodles, slept, and did her single load of laundry once a week. There were days when she just couldn't keep from constantly tearing up, unable to outrun an oozing regret, the futility of wishing that this terrible, irreversible thing had simply not happened. The sagging defeat of that helplessness. To be here, alive, without her parents. Though she was an adult, she still felt small and scared and not wise enough to be on her own like this. She did not put up any pictures or get any plants. She had a futon, her cell phone, and her laptop.

She sat on the futon after a shift and thought back to that retirement party, to the last people who got to spend time with her parents. They were boring, elitist, yuppie strangers who worked with her dad for decades at the bank and still didn't know a thing about him. She knew from a police report that her parents had left the party at 9:45 p.m., which absolutely floored her because all her life she had never left a family party with her parents before 2 a.m. This was definitive evidence that the host didn't have any of her dad's favourite El Dorado twelve-year-old rum on hand. She could well imagine her mother's surprise when her dad had been ready to leave so early.

She imagined her mother jumping up from some wingback chair when her dad made the move to go. Stella would have been so relieved she could've kissed her husband's soft, clean-shaven cheek. Anka imagined a cake had been cut and paper plates with blue-and-white frosted wedges had been distributed, and a gaggle of gleaming-eyed kids of varying ages were hauling their sugary bounty back to the basement.

Anka thought of family parties where it would take a generous thirty minutes to kiss and bid each person farewell. There was always another last-minute gaff between her mom and her aunt, her dad and her uncle laughing about something only they understood. Little Anka standing by the door roasting with her jacket and shoes on for an extra fifteen or twenty minutes, practically falling asleep on her feet, her cousins already gone home. Her aunt handing Stella a generous chunk of the cake packed in a large margarine container. Eyes brightly shining.

At a work party, though, Anka imagined the goodbyes were swift—one general wave to everyone in the room, a quick exchange with the host at the door, and vamos.

Anka also knew from the report that it had rained that night, and she saw her mother shiver against the seatbelt in the cool night air, the humidity broken after a heavy and quick downpour. When she got to this part in her daydream, she liked to imagine that her mom had felt that being strapped in and ready to drive away from a tedious obligation was its own kind of freedom.

She pictured her dad feeling more defeated. *"Party was a lil' stale. No music."*

Stella laughed, relieved that they felt the same. *"I know. I t'ink Lisa was vex all night. I overheard she and Mike quarrelling in de laundry room."*

"For someone who can retire early, he couldn' serve up anyt'ing besides Peach Schnapps? I nurse one tin of Coke de whole night."

"Serves yuh right."

"Dat man so cheap, ras."

Anka pictured herself in the passenger seat instead of her mom, looking up at a crescent moon that followed alongside her window before they got back to the highway.

And this was where, each time, Anka put the brakes on her imagining. It was difficult to halt the momentum of her daydreams; she would abruptly get up and pace the room, or shake her whole body out, or put on loud music, or jump around, or do push ups, or try to run away from home. Or all of the above at the same time.

But sometimes, by some grace, there was respite. One night, when she got to that last scene of her daydream, she allowed herself to feel it all, to submit without thought to the pain she felt. Her grief ebbed for a moment, and a feeling of spaciousness began to open up around her heart, so much so that she could lay down, fall asleep, and then wake up fractionally calmer. When she focused here, without an intense longing or missing, she could again feel her mom and dad present in that space. And when she did, she could talk directly to them rather than watch a scene play out across her mind's eye. If she could find the spaciousness around her grief, she could keep up a steady current of conversation and intent listening—she could keep the sorrow at bay. When she waded into that space, she could remember how it felt to lounge about on her parents' bed just chatting about whatever. Cool, smooth sheets, warm lamplight, and the feeling of having a harbour, even when she didn't particularly need one. And when she coaxed herself deep into this feeling, so that she was there again on their cosy bed instead of here on a lumpy futon that who knew how many strangers before her had slept on, she would pick up any stray conversation with them, her parents, Stella and Mukesh. At first it was just Anka talking to herself and concentrating on milking the sweetness of their love for as long as she could. But after a few days and nights, she began to sense their responses. Her dad was the first one to chime in: *Why you don' poach an egg wit' toast fuh dinner?*

The worker stationed across from Anka on the line was a fifty-eight-year-old woman. Her husband was postponing his retirement because the two of them were now raising her grandson whose mother was an addict. They loved their daughter terribly, and they held onto a very painful hope for her. Anka could feel this woman's fatigue, and resolve, and anger, and impatience barely contained. She hardly complained about having to stand through the duration of the shift. She was curt when she spoke, except on their lunch break when she sometimes spoke of the desires she had for her grandson: to keep him straight, polite, studious. He was only in the second grade, but once he got over his bedwetting, he'd be bound for university, this line be damned.

At first Anka appreciated the anonymity of being reduced to a tiny cog in a giant machine each time she set foot inside the factory doors. But it didn't take her long to learn the ropes, and then she saw that in actuality the line gave her mind far too much freedom. She was adrift, floating. She talked to her parents for whole shifts sometimes. At first they were understanding of her decision to be there—they agreed that she was doing the right thing by carving out the time and space to be gentle and quiet with herself—but after a time her mom started up the nagging. Her dad kept using the word *potential*, the phrase *not living up*. Sometimes he said it in French, which meant he was really upset, though this puzzled Anka because he didn't know any French when he was alive. Sometimes she could hear her mother's laugh jingling underneath the endless atmospheric drone around her. While her body was chained to the monotony of the line, her mind wandered back to family beach trips every summer, the seat belt digging into her neck as they drove out of the city. She had always loved that moment, in the car, just before she could see the water, when they had come off the highway and driven into and out of a series of small towns, passing the landmark church, and arrived at that one last town. Anka was thrilled at being able to pinpoint the precise moment when the very hard, very long asphalt road was about to fall off into a soft, shimmering horizon. That slight haze—framed by storefronts rising on either side, like a director blocking the idea of a scene with the frame of their fingers—signalled the promise of what could not yet be wholly seen. And then in a blink or two, the main drag of the beach town they were driving through became just the beach. She remembered unbuckling, standing up, and hugging her mom's seat from behind, her arms around her mom's neck and shoulders, her parents laughing and not scolding because they all loved going to the beach so much. Her mom feeding single potato chips to her dad while he found a parking spot. The sun announcing to everyone that, for now, he was humbly at their service and that all wishes would be granted while he was on duty. His ministrations would not discriminate; it was an open bar, an "all you can eat" buffet.

Diane kept sending her emails about breathing properly and being in the Now. One by one, Anka read and then deleted them. It was a hopeful day for Diane when, nearly seven months later, Anka finally relented and agreed that it was unnecessary to punish herself on the line, that she'd come back to the city and try to let herself resume her life there, somehow. She admitted that she missed Diane and that all along it had felt easier to miss someone she knew she would see again, that she didn't need to punish herself in this way either. She also understood more acutely than ever that she couldn't actually know anything with certainty and so it was stupid to be far away from her friend instead of close. Anka began to feel more and more like a tourist peering into the assortments of grief in other people's lives. She thought back to that Greyhound bus with everyone boarding like a zombie, and she now understood that they were all equally awash in the high and low tides of grief that the moon, with her clipboard, had mercilessly assigned them.

She couldn't yet bring herself to spend any of the insurance money that had come to her, so she chose instead to just scrape by. Once she had moved back, she considered all of her communication, marketing, editing, writing, teaching, and researching skills and then got a job at the Fraser Street Laundromat. She imagined her father rolling his eyes, but she ignored him. She figured she could let the money sit for now; one day she'd do something like go back to school, or buy a house, or blow it all. Maybe she'd treat Diane to a trip somewhere or she'd donate it to a charity. She'd send her ex-line mate a cheque for her grandson's university tuition. Or else she'd just go and buy herself a one-way ticket to Mars.

JANE REUBEN
AUGUST 1978

JANE REUBEN WAS TWENTY-THREE and couldn't get comfortable, fielding early and sporadic contractions. Her sandy hair—recently cut into a feathered style that she hated—was pasted to the sides of her face. She was becoming inconsolable in the waiting, but the contractions were too irregular and far apart to warrant going to the hospital. She wrestled herself out from the rumpled, frustratingly warm sheets of her bed, the bedroom windows opening out to afternoon sun, bright farmland, and birds chirping, the whole goddamned idyllic lot of it. She raised her arms up above her head, wrenching the floral drapes shut, and for a moment she could breathe in this new darkness, clutching the heavy, textured cotton in her dry, red fists. She stood like this for a while, still four weeks ahead of her due date, attached to her bedroom curtains as though in vertical ascent of a craggy rock face, her whole body sticky with sweat, and at an utter loss for what to do with herself next.

She heard the pause of her husband's bare feet on the hardwood along with a laugh that he quickly stifled. "Just try to relax, Janie."

Walter had no idea what to tell his enormously pregnant wife. His father had predicted twins, possibly even triplets, but they wouldn't know for sure until they were born. Four months ago, Dr. Halpern had told her that she could try to get in for an ultrasound at a hospital down in Toronto but that they were incredibly busy and probably booked solid now; he suspected she could just be patient and wait it out. That was how it was always done in their modest corner of the world, and all of his other patients had been perfectly satisfied with that.

Jane didn't move or speak, her head turned to the side, staring at the wall. Walter suspected he had said the exact wrong thing and adjusted: "Can I get you anything?" They had been together since they were teenagers and would be good foils for one another throughout their lives—Jane very direct and straightforward, Walter easy and steadfast.

"I need to get out of this house. I'm going for a walk. Put my overnight bag in the truck."

To get out to the main two-lane highway that faced the farmhouse, Jane first trundled as best as she could down their very long, straight gravel drive. She turned left onto the narrow country road that rarely saw any traffic and that came to an end just a stone's throw over at an identical, perpendicular country road lined with young poplars. Here she turned right and walked just a ways down to the highway. It was busy with north- and southbound traffic that was always passing through to somewhere else. She would invariably turn right, heading south into town.

Walter watched her from the door, the gravel scrunching loudly under each footfall, until she was out of sight. He was an uncommonly patient man, and he watched her for almost seven minutes before the trees blocked her from view. He assumed she would walk out to the main road and back, so he sat in a rocking chair waiting for any slight breeze to ease across the porch. He closed his eyes and rocked, every few minutes looking up for the sight of her coming back along the country lane. He waited for what now felt like an uncomfortable amount of time and then went to the truck. Both Walter and Jane had thought their new truck was the most beautiful thing they had ever seen: a two-tone, sky-blue-and-white GMC with an all-blue cloth and vinyl interior. They deliberated for quite a while before deciding on this truck because it was not at all practical for the farm. But it was so beautiful, especially with its lush blue carpeting, that they got the dealership to throw in mud guards and promised one another that they'd keep it as pristine as they could for as long as they could. He slid the overnight bag into the truck's cab, started the ignition, rubbed his hand along the smooth blue dash before taking the wheel, and rolled down the driveway. She needed her space, but he did not want her out there alone suddenly giving birth.

There wasn't far for her to go, just a two-lane stretch of road ahead and behind. Walter drove to the point where he was sure she could've gotten to by now, but Jane was nowhere to be seen. His extremely pregnant wife had vanished into thin air. There was just the enormity of the clear blue sky and the enveloping softness of the blue cab all around him. He put his hazards on and slowed to a crawl, checking his mirrors and scanning the fields. He waited for a car in the opposite lane to pass and then made a U-turn, scanning the opposite horizon for Jane. He sped past the narrow road that led back to their farm. The roads were more sloping and winding going north. Once again he flipped on his hazards and slowed right down. Still no Janie. Walter was getting anxious, regretting having waited so long before he started following her. He pulled onto the shoulder next to a stand selling bushels of fresh corn. A girl, about fourteen, was reading a book while working the stand. Walter complimented the corn and described his wife. "She's pregnant," he said and gestured comically wide out front and around his sides, "and wearing a purple, tent-like kind of dress. On the impatient side today."

"Yeah, she got out of Mrs. Morrison's car and started walking that way." The girl jerked a thumb directly behind her.

"Where was Mrs. Morrison headed?" In one smooth, habitual movement, Walter removed his cap, swiped his forehead, and replaced his cap.

Mrs. Morrison had worked at the post office for twenty-five years. Even if people were complete strangers to one another, like Walter and this girl, it was assumed that everyone knew Mrs. Morrison.

"She bought half a dozen ears of corn and drove away."

"Did my wife say anything to you?"

The girl dog-eared her page and tightened her ponytail. "She asked me to bag a dozen ears and set them aside till she came back."

"Where the hell was she going?"

The girl met Walter's gaze briefly and exhaled all of her breath. "Well there's really nothing down that road except, um, a path that takes you to the lake, and some kids sometimes have parties and make out down there at night."

The girl was blushing furiously and had her eyes set squarely on her book again. Walter gave her money for the corn, tucked the lot in the truck, and tore off down the dirt road. He stopped when the road came to a dead end, and then sure enough, he started along a well-worn path through the trees. A breeze had finally picked up and was shaking all the leaves like so many castanets. He caught a glimpse of cool water through the greenery, and then Walter saw Jane's purple back as she walked into the lake.

"Jane! Janie! What the hell are you doing? Jane!"

He was running, splashing and lifting his knees high through the water until he could reach her and put his hands firmly on her shoulders.

The water was level to where Jane had hiked up her dress, gathered up under her breasts, around the globe of her belly. "Jesus Christ, Walter! I'm pregnant, not deaf. I came out here to stop thinking. Drive me to the hospital. I'm ready to get this kid out of me."

"How far apart are your contractions? Dr. Halpern will just send us home."

As if on cue, Jane had a contraction out there in the lake, and Walter had to agree that it was time.

In the delivery room nine hours later, Dr. Halpern shot up from between Jane's knees and said, "Look. I'm afraid there's something."

Four and a half hours after a touch-and-go Caesarean section, the first wails of her tiny sons finally rang out.

Jane reached her arms out for them over the surgical divide. She kept them outstretched while a nurse took the babies to get cleaned up. She kept holding her arms aloft while Dr. Halpern and two nurses whispered and huddled together around the babies. Jane didn't lower her arms. "Halpern! What's going on? Get Walter in here."

Dr. Halpern nodded to one of the nurses, and she swung the door open to let Walter Reuben in to see his family.

The younger of the two nurses brought the twins over to Jane and awkwardly manoeuvred them to lie on Jane's chest, struggling to wrest her arm free from under them.

Jane, alive with adrenaline, smiled and looked up at Walter. Walter was looking toward Dr. Halpern.

The babies were nuzzled together, not making any sound, eyes shut tight. Their arms tangled around each other, their torsos coming together, entwined and somehow still fused. Walter counted arms, hands, fingers: four, four, twenty. He counted legs: three. Three, three, three. Heads and shoulders: two. Bodies: one. Basically just one.

Jane was cooing and naming them. "That one is definitely a Douglas, and this one is Bruce. He looks like a Bruce, don't you think, Walter?"

Walter looked down at his sons and kissed his wife's chapped lips. If she registered anything out of the ordinary with their babies, she didn't reveal it in that moment. One baby became unsettled and started crying out—Walter couldn't yet be sure if it was Bruce or Douglas—and then the other baby followed suit. If nothing else, their voices were hale and hearty. All the members of the Reuben family wrapped their arms around one another.

Jane woke up in her hospital room at dusk following the birth of her sons, awakened by the sound of quiet conversation on the other side of the curtain divider. She was sharing a room with another woman who had given birth three days ago and whose mother was visiting. Jane couldn't understand the language they were speaking softly, but she could tell that that the visiting mother had brought the new mother a home-cooked meal. The room was filled with the smell of fried onions, and Jane could have cried she was so moved by that tenderness. She had no idea where her own mother was anymore and had gotten very used to taking care of herself. While she was pregnant, she had cooked so many meals that she had filled their chest freezer to the brim. She knew she wasn't going to reach out to notify her dad that he was now a grandfather to twins because they had simply drifted too far apart. Jane had Walter, and they both had Père, and their family was going to work just fine. A smile began to creep across Jane's face, thrilled by the word *twins*. Their boys. She was blinking rapidly to keep the tears at bay, so much had been flooding her mind from the moment she had opened her eyes.

Walter was drinking from a Styrofoam cup, and he jumped from his chair as she propped herself up on her elbows. The twins were in the nursery with every other baby born that week.

Walter didn't quite know where to start. "So."

"Yup." Jane smiled.

He sat a hip down on the bed with her. "Our boys?"

"They're something, aren't they? Twins, Walter. Père was right."

"Dr. Halpern wanted to talk to us when you got up."

"Unghhhhhh. I've had my fill of Halpern."

Walter's dam burst. "Janie. The boys, I figure we'll let them go ahead and operate. I mean, it's the leg. I've been checking up on them, and as far as I can tell, it's just that one leg. They seem okay otherwise, each with their own torsos and all. It shouldn't be so hard. Halpern's a good doctor, right? Or maybe he'll get a specialist from Toronto? They're tough little guys; I can tell already."

Jane scooched herself up against the pillows. She reached out for Walter's cup. "I've never understood how you can drink cold coffee."

"I'll sneak you in a fresh one if you'd like."

"I want to see my boys."

"The nurse will bring them in when it's time to feed them."

Dr. Halpern had slipped into the room unnoticed and now squeezed up to the side of the bed, removing the cup from Jane's hand.

It took a few minutes for Walter and Jane to notice that Dr. Halpern was there crowded at the head of the bed with them. Jane moved to sip the last bit of that cold coffee, only to find her hand empty and Halpern flipping through a chart.

"Halpern, can I see my sons now?" Jane had to look up over her shoulder to where the doctor had sandwiched himself, awkward and uncomfortably close, behind her IV stand.

He took his time looking up from his notes and then finally offered, "Walter and I spoke briefly." He paused for another long moment in order to solidify his authority. A fly at the window buzzed and twitched.

Jane opened her mouth to hurry Halpern along. A crick was forming in her neck, forced as she was to twist her head in order to glance in the doctor's direction. He continued: "It is my medical opinion that your sons' only hope for a normal life is with surgery. However I would be remiss in my duty if I didn't inform you of the inherent risks and almost certain possibility of death for one if not both of your sons."

Walter was quick to clip the doctor short. "But isn't it just that one leg? They don't seem attached anywhere else."

"Yes, that may well be, but a major artery runs through the leg. And it's not so much the leg, but rather the hips, and whatever organs internally. And so."

"What's your recommendation?" Jane surprised Walter with her conciliatory tone.

"It is a potentially life-threatening surgery, and something like this has never been performed at our modest hospital. It would be a first. Especially for someone so early in their career such as myself. However my recommendation is to move forwa—" Halpern interrupted himself with a sneeze before continuing. "Excuse me. The sooner the better."

There was something about that last phrase—"the sooner the better"—that rankled Jane. It was almost as though it were better for Halpern's schedule and not for her sons' lives. And she didn't hesitate to say so: "Halpern, please acknowledge to me that you understand that we're not talking about servicing our truck. We don't need a mechanic."

Jane was no longer contorting herself to look at the doctor but rather staring straight ahead to the foot of her bed, where she felt would have been a more natural and professional place for him to stand.

Jane and her sons were released from the hospital a week after they were born. She sat with them out on the porch, waiting for Walter to come in from mowing the lawn. She had been telling her sons about the farm, about the new truck and all the problems the old one had been giving them, and about how if you turned right onto the road at the end of the drive, Père lived in the next farmstead over. When she heard the lawnmower cut off and the silence spread itself out again—but before Walter came to grab a beer and sit with them—she gave her boys some advice: "Never bend for this place. Force the world to rise up to meet you. Because you, my children, are perfect."

In those very early days when the boys were still just two weeks old, she had tried to breastfeed, but without the help of the nurses at the hospital, Bruce, Dougie, and Jane were often all left frustrated. Jane's nipples were starting to crack, her breasts painfully engorged, and the babies were still always hungry. One morning just before dawn, in the dark of their bedroom, she was struggling to get out of bed fast enough to respond to the crying from the bassinet just out of reach. Still recovering from her unexpected C-section, she rolled onto her side to try to push her body up and get her knees out over the edge of the bed. Walter was snoring through the crying, and she could've murdered him right there in the bed, except that she needed his extra set of hands so badly these days. Finally she was sitting at the edge of the bed, but she still needed a minute to gather her reserves and launch herself to standing. Dougie and Bruce were insistent, calling out for her to come, come right now, we need you, we're hungry, right now. She had had a painful time breastfeeding them a few hours ago, and she couldn't imagine it would be any different now. Jane felt a bottomless despair that she had never experienced before, a deep shame that she was failing to provide her babies with the very basic necessities of survival. She was afraid to admit that she had taken on something that was too big for her to handle and couldn't manage. Sobs racked her body. She didn't know what she was doing; her own mother wasn't around to offer any help or advice, and neither was Walter's. She had a few friends, but she and Walter were the first to become parents. The pain in her chest, in her heart, in her abdomen, in her gut was swallowing her whole, and she couldn't breathe. It took everything in her to stay sitting upright, holding on to the edge of the bed.

Walter moved in to sit close and tilted his wife's head down to rest on his shoulder. He had woken up, alarmed by the sound: Jane hadn't cried in years. The last time he knew of was when they were eighteen, at his mother's funeral. He remembered how stoic Jane had been, so composed, supporting him even at that age, up until the final moments when the casket was taken out by him, his father, and the other the pallbearers. In the aching hush of the church, a primal and ancient anguish erupted from Jane, the sounds of a terribly wounded animal, sobs that she couldn't push down or control any longer. In his eighteen years, Walter had never witnessed that in anyone. And here, five years later, he was no more experienced and still didn't know what to do. He knew enough not to tell Jane what he had mostly been thinking since their sons had come home: *how hard could breastfeeding be? Don't you just pop them on and that's it?* Instead he kissed her greasy hair and went to the bassinet, which the twins were already almost too wide to fit into.

"Walter, I need you to go get Mrs. Morrison. I need her advice."

"Okay. The post office opens at nine." Walter had Bruce and Dougie in his arms and was bouncing the way Jane did. They were still crying.

Jane's tears were still coming, but the sobs were quieting. Walter brought the babies to her. She offered a nipple to one, but that baby couldn't get a good latch, and they were both reaching out for her. She twisted her body to allow him to switch sides, but she was uncomfortable and it still wasn't right. She realized none of them would physically survive if she let herself slide any further into that slick pit of helplessness. She tried with the other baby to get him to latch properly, to no better effect.

"I'm going to make bottles. Can you bring them to the kitchen?" She had laid the babies on the bed and was holding her aching breasts.

Downstairs Jane mixed evaporated milk with water and sugar as one of her nurses had told her to. She filled the bottles, looking out to the field in the reliable, slowly brightening morning, and after three deep breaths, she pressed the heels of her palms to her eyes and locked away that abject despair and shame in a box at the back of her brain.

When she was joined by her family, she was sitting up tall against the back of her chair, her feet planted on the floor. She reached out for her babies and cradled them, holding a bottle to Bruce's mouth while Walter pulled a chair close to feed Dougie. The kitchen was silent, save the ticking of the wall clock and a crow outside. Jane looked into Bruce's chestnut eyes, and he stared back intently, deep into hers. Deep into her being. She calmed down considerably as the sun continued to rise, daybreak rinsing just enough of the uncertainty away that she could think again.

"Walter, it is better that they're together, don't you think?"

"Joined?"

"Yes. They're meant to be there for one another." Jane was watching Dougie now as he stared up at his father. "They'll never feel alone. That terror of really being on your own in the world."

"Don't you think it'll be hard for them like this?"

"No matter who comes and goes, if anything ever happens to us, it will be impossible for them to be lonely."

"Sure, but they'll have each other even if they're, you know, separate."

"Hmm. Mmhmm."

Walter rubbed her knee with his free hand and remembered how close Jane had been to his mother. Every Sunday Jane had had a standing date to come over, not to spend time with him, but rather with his mom, who would teach her how to bake something new each week. His mother was quick to tease and laugh, and she enjoyed

Jane's company. Walter had no idea what they used to talk about all afternoon, but he was happiest when the kitchen smelled of sugar and cinnamon and was filled with Jane's chortling. He wished he could just run over next door and rouse his mom instead of having to wait until the post office opened to drive into town and then figure out when Mrs. Morrison would be on a break to come and steady them on their feet.

"Do you really trust Halpern? He said they might not survive surgery. Can we take that risk?" Jane asked, searching his face for a definitive answer. "How can we gamble with their lives?"

"We could find another doctor in the city. A specialist. See what they say."

"I suppose." Jane passed the empty bottle to Walter to set down on the pine table. "But this is how they came to us. Maybe we're not supposed to make them be anything other than who they are. What if that's the job?"

"We should start by asking Halpern for a referral."

Jane snorted.

"I'm sure we don't have to decide on anything right away. They look pretty happy right now." Walter stroked the bottoms of all three tiny feet. "How can toes be so small?"

Jane propped the boys up on her shoulder, leaning her head to the side to give Dougie some more room. The weight of them felt reassuring against her body. These two boys had come to her, and she silently vowed to them in the kitchen that morning not to get too scared, to always be grateful for what she had been so blessed to receive. She promised to do things differently than her own mother had—she would never abandon them or force them to be something other than they were. She was strong enough to bear it all, and she would teach them to do the same. She just needed Mrs. Morrison, who had five grown children and twice as many grandchildren, to advise her a bit on what to do with the intense pain in her breasts, and then their family could take it from there.

Over the next few weeks, Halpern arranged for an endless number of X-rays and tests and milestone checkups. He arranged for his photo to appear in the papers with the twins, and then he arranged for a referral to a specialist in Toronto. The newborns were generally in good health, alert, and growing quickly.

When they finally saw him, the Toronto specialist agreed with Halpern that they shared an enlarged pancreas, and though they had their own intestinal tracts, he couldn't be sure if part of one's was intertwined with the other's. As well, one twin had only one small kidney and an almost nonexistent spleen. One twin looked to have slightly elevated blood pressure. His prognosis was a thirty percent chance that both boys would survive the fifteen-to-seventeen-hour surgery. But there would also be significant prep work to do before the surgery could take place.

On the way home from the appointment, Walter realized that he agreed with Jane: they had two happy, vibrant, alert sons now. Was it fair to look at Bruce and Dougie and take a gamble that one or both may not survive?

At six weeks, when she went to get them from the bassinet after a nap, they both smiled up at her for the first time, and tough-as-nails Jane Reuben squealed with delight, radiant in a love so pure. And by the time Bruce and Dougie were six months old and had figured out how to crawl, Jane could hardly keep up with them. She noticed as they got bigger, their inside arms remained tiny and they would naturally tuck them around one another to keep them out of the way while they went about their business of finding things to put into their mouths. Halpern had once suggested that rather than separate them, Jane and Walter should consider amputation of the third leg, which would make things simpler—edge them a little closer to "normal"—in his estimation: "You know, two legs instead of three?" Jane had never wanted to punch anyone in her life, and yet she daydreamed about clocking Halpern many times throughout her days. What she and Walter could see, however, was how easily Bruce and Dougie naturally moved about, with no pain and often of one mind, as far as they could surmise.

JANE REUBEN
JANUARY 1985

BY THE TIME 1985 HAD FRESHLY ROLLED IN, the twins were midway through the second grade at E. J. Smythe Public School and Jane noticed a change in their behaviour. They seemed miserable and very easy to set off; any slight change of plans and she would have to watch out for whining, tears, and screams of protest. Don't dare run out of marmalade for toast in the morning. It was like having toddlers all over again. Walter escaped somewhere out on the farm every time the twins got emotional, which was just as well as far as Jane was concerned. But she found it strange; she knew Dougie and she knew Bruce and she knew something was not right. When each outburst had finally subsided, they always just answered Jane's probing in unison with: "Nothing. Nothing's wrong." She had some suspicions and wondered what was going on at school all day, and on the bus rides home, and who exactly the lunchroom monitor was.

One morning Bruce burst into tears as he and Dougie were getting their winter coat on. Jane braced herself for whatever minor infraction might have detonated this bomb.

"It's too hot. I don't want to wear this coat with Dougie!"

Dougie wrangled himself out of the coat and tore off his toque. "Yeah, it's too hot. Get me outta here!"

Bruce was inconsolable, and Dougie wouldn't stop squirming. The bus was due in eight minutes, and it usually took them twelve minutes to walk out to the stop.

Jane yanked the front door open and said with more edge in her voice than she realized, "It's winter. Your ears'll damn well fall off from frostbite."

Truth be told, once the door was open, Jane felt that it was unseasonably mild out. She wasn't budging on this though. She stepped around them as they flailed on the ground, one kicking and crying and the other rolling about blowing raspberries, and she stomped, growling, down the drive. After a few minutes, she noticed she'd been clenching her teeth and fists. They had let her walk for longer than she anticipated, and she saw the school bus drive past their stop. Jane wanted to have a tantrum too; essentially she was having one, though she barely admitted it. Having to drive them in would set her morning back; it wouldn't be by much, but she had been looking forward to some time alone to work in a quiet house. She turned back, and they had their coat on, unzipped, and were putting their boots back on. Bruce was swiping his nose dry, and Dougie was telling him, "It's okay." Jane dropped her shoulders and exhaled.

"What's going on, Bruce? Why were you crying?"

No answer.

"You're both getting too old to be behaving like this."

Silence except for Bruce's shattered breathing.

Jane grabbed her keys. "C'mon, in you get."

The drive to school was quiet, and she could sense Bruce barely keeping himself together.

They managed to get to school just before the bell, so she watched them walk themselves in and gave the teacher at the door a crisp wave. She decided then to volunteer for pizza lunch at the end of that week.

That Friday she poured a plastic cup of Orange Drink for a girl with clearly self-cut, uneven bangs and a sweatshirt too short at the wrists. The girl touched Jane's elbow gently and motioned that she wanted to tell her a secret. "Mrs. Reuben, Kevin is really, really mean to the twins."

Jane bent down to the girl's little desk. "Which one's Kevin?"

The girl looked down at her hands for a while. Jane was starting to lose her patience with all these tight-lipped kids. She squeezed and relaxed her grip on the pitcher a few times. "What's your name?"

Then Jane noticed that from her lap the girl had been quietly but urgently jabbing her tiny index finger to their right, behind Jane. Jane added a little more to the girl's cup. "Thanks," the girl whispered.

Jane swivelled on her heel and approached the boy. "Kevin? Would you like some Orange Drink?"

The boy didn't answer. He just stared back at her and grunted through a too-big bite of pepperoni pizza without breaking eye contact, smacking his greasy lips while he chomped. Jane knew she had her man.

Kevin Shannon was the one real bully that Bruce and Dougie ever had. Every day, before and after school and at every recess, he'd follow them around relentlessly cussing out their whole family. The twins learned words they had never heard before; he'd called Bruce a pussy, and Bruce had been utterly confused. The more they tried to ignore him and tell the outdoor teacher, the more bile Kevin summoned from deep within. He never got physical, but he talked about fantastical, awful, violent things. Both twins were uncomfortable and scared. They saw that Kevin wasn't tormenting anyone else, and they resigned themselves to this fate, such as it was. Bruce had a hard time falling asleep and cried on more than one morning while being dragged to school. Kevin had been describing in detail how he could separate the twins with a chainsaw, and Bruce wanted to barf.

Jane had not known any of this, but she could see cruelty in Kevin's stare. The teacher stepped out of the room, and the kids instantly got louder and more animated in their conversations. Jane took this opportunity to crouch to Kevin's level. She made the effort to soften her approach and told him she was Bruce and Dougie's mom. In a calm and almost apologetic tone, she told him that she had already called the police who would get in touch with his dad, though she didn't know exactly when that would be. She kept her expressions measured, her manner in no way threatening, and in a move that she knew would confuse the boy, she looked at him gently and said, "Good luck." She stood and refilled his cup.

Neither twin knew why, but after pizza lunch in January, Kevin Shannon spent his whole afternoon recess by himself in the bathroom. After school they got on the bus without him threatening to set their hair on fire or tear out their intestines with a rusty meat hook. When they got home, Jane asked them how the rest of their day had been.

"Fine."

"What did you do?"

"Nothing."

"What did you learn today?"

"Nothing."

"Did you have fun?"

"Yep."

Jane noticed, however, that there were no tears that weekend. Walter must have noticed he didn't need to make up any excuses to get out of the house. Jane wasn't sure how long this peace would hold, so she decided to volunteer for pizza lunches for the rest of the school year.

JANE REUBEN
JULY 1988

WHEN THE TWINS WERE ON THE CUSP OF TURNING TEN, they decided they wanted to learn how to box. One evening when Jane was getting dinner ready, the twins were following her around the kitchen, right underfoot.

"Mom, we've agreed. Can you sign us up now?"

"Go bring your laundry basket to the top of the stairs so I can wash your clothes tonight."

"Yeah, yeah, sure." Dougie didn't care about the laundry. "Are you going to let us?"

"Boxing? Are you sure? Bruce?"

Bruce shrugged his shoulder. "I guess."

Jane bumped into the boys as she was turning away from the sink. "If you're going to be right under me while I'm cooking, shell these peas."

Bruce took the bowl from her.

"Well it's all right with your father and me, if you're both interested."

"Yes! This is going to be so awesome!" Dougie was doing a little victory shimmy as they went to the table.

Jane smiled to herself. She had been unsure of how to strike a balance between teaching them to be flexible in how they physically adapted to the world, and encouraging them to feel indomitable, that sometimes the world would have to adapt to them. Walter was of the mind that having them help on the farm would be enough to make them disciplined and physically strong. But she was looking for something more: she wanted to inspire in her sons a sense that they could do something exceptional, not in spite of their bodies but because of them. She wanted them to feel in control. In control of their bodies together and in control of their destinies. Able to trust themselves to face whomever or whatever might oppose them in life. Fighting in a structured environment might be the key for her almost-ten-year-olds to ground themselves in a world they never saw themselves reflected in, to protect themselves, emotionally, more than anything else. And this notion in turn made her feel more in control, that as their mother she had the power to give Dougie and Bruce something concrete that would prove to them, and to anyone who doubted them, that they were tough and had value.

What Jane hadn't consciously understood at this point was her underlying belief that if her sons grew up to feel strong in body and mind, it would be a testament to the fact that she and Walter had made the right choice not to separate them, that she had followed her maternal instincts and they had been proven right.

"Mom, we're done the peas."

"What are we having for dinner?"

She gathered up the empty shells, relieving the boys of their kitchen duty. "Laundry basket."

To be honest she was relieved that they had come up with an after-school activity of their own free will because she had been drawing a blank. She had been watching them for cues about where their innate talents lay and had suggested different activities that neither twin jumped at: hockey, soccer, painting, Boy Scouts, piano. Boxing was much better. She remembered when she had had to scare the kid who used to bully them. She knew that as they got older they'd face bigger foes than that brat, and she wanted to ensure that they would be able to handle that sort of thing on their own, that her sons' sense of self-worth would never be shaken by other people's ignorance or mean-spiritedness. Up to this point, she had thought any activity they dedicated themselves to could've offered this confidence, but she had still been trying to figure out which would be the most accessible to them. Now it dawned on her that boxing specifically would give them tangible proof of the value of their conjoined bodies.

She could hear them horsing around at the top of the stairs.

As a girl at their age, she had wished she had a skill that could've bolstered her when she felt weak, something she could have relied on because she couldn't rely on her parents—one was physically absent and the other emotionally vacant. She'd had no siblings to conspire with or lean on. It was one thing to feel confident, but she also wanted them to feel good and solid in their shared body. Imposing and righteous. This would allow them to know that their place in the world was solid and good. It had never occurred to her that children could learn how to box, but she thought boxing sounded like just the thing.

JANE REUBEN
SEPTEMBER 1992

JANE WAS SITTING WITH ONE OTHER PARENT in the folding chairs set up by the gym door. She would have preferred to be by the window; the was air thick with teenage sweat and hormones, alt rock blaring out of crappy speakers, and the staccato slaps of a jump rope hitting the floor. Eventually she took off her jacket but left her scarf on.

The other parent was eager to chat. "I was expecting Walter. How are your boys liking the new coach?" he asked.

"They're fine. It's all good—they haven't said either way."

"My daughter's the one in the middle. There."

Jane usually wasn't the one who drove the twins to boxing class, but tonight Walter had had to help Père fix his back gate. The man she was sitting two seats away from, Alan, shouted over to her that the other parents didn't stick around; it was usually just him and Walter who stayed to watch.

He hopped one seat closer. "I used to be really against the idea of Alice coming here to learn how to fight. I thought it was a little strange as a hobby, you know. Especially for Alice. She's really into frilly, girly things. My wife won't set foot in here because Alice cold turkeyed ballet thc day before a performance."

"Mmhmmm." Jane nodded but didn't look over at Alan as he went on.

"She just decided she was going to do this instead, and she doesn't take no for an answer—you know what I mean?"

Jane smiled a thin, tightly pursed smile out of obligation as Alan continued.

"Alice is badass."

The kids were paired up, practising the same combination with one throwing punches and ducking a mimed jab from their partner. The kids were slow and cumbersome but sincerely concentrating with all their might, some mouthing out the count. The instructor was paired up with Alan's daughter and was using blue pool noodles at a distance with her instead of sparing with pads. Jane could tell she was good though; her movements were more elegant, smoother and faster than the others, including Dougie and Bruce. Her hair was in a thick ponytail down her back. Jane noticed that her boys were paired up with a guy who was obviously older than the rest of the students, all of whom were around fourteen. She saw a tattoo on his forearm. And she also saw how her sons came together to operate their outside fists as a coherent unit, both ducking that implied jab. She swelled with pride to see them in the gym like this, handling themselves easily against someone who was older, taller, stronger.

"Your sons are pretty badass too."

Jane finally turned to Alan and let herself beam, laughing out: "Damn right."

"The one on the right is a bit slow on the count though."

At the end of the class, Jane waved to Alan as they crossed the parking lot to their cars. "I'll tell Walter you said hi."

Dougie raised his hand as Alice and her dad got in their car. The parking lot was fuller now with parents waiting to pick up their kids, all the headlights on in the falling dark.

"Mom, you didn't need to stay, you know. You could've dropped us off like every other parent."

"Alan stays."

"Unghhhhhhhh. Alan, Mom? You want to be like Alan?" Bruce could often hear Alan from the sidelines giving out encouragement and advice.

"Dad stays. Anyway, how's this new coach?" Jane was buckling in and quickly double checking her mirrors.

Both twins said, "He's fine."

"Alice is really good," Jane offered.

"Yeah."

Jane noticed as she was backing the truck up and out of the strip mall that Dougie and Bruce shared a look, and Dougie had a big grin.

"Brucie, Alan thought you were a little behind the count during that ducking jabbing thing you guys were doing at the beginning."

"Unghhhhhhhh. Mom! Alan is not the coach."

"He's not wrong though," Dougie pointed out.

"Shut up, Doug."

"Well I thought you guys did great. You both looked great today. I was really happy I could come see you practise."

"Really?" Dougie was sitting forward and holding the side of his mother's headrest to keep firmly in place. "Because I've been thinking. Instead of just doing all these, like, classes, me and Bruce should start to train in the amateur league now. Join a registered boxing club."

Bruce's eyebrows were raised to high heaven. "Wait, what? Since when have you been thinking this?"

"All the time, Bruce. Dude. This is something we're good at. Don't you ever consider taking it to the next level?"

Bruce threw his head back and let out an exasperated cry. "No. No way, dude."

"You're going to say no to the Olympics, Bruce? Seriously. The O-lyyymm-piiics?" Dougie drew the word out incredulously.

Jane eyed them through the rearview mirror. "We'll talk about this with your dad when he gets back from fixing the gate." She noticed Bruce was sullen, staring out the window and Dougie was staring straight ahead out the front windshield.

"What's there to talk about?" both boys said in unison.

Dougie held her gaze for a moment in the rearview mirror.

Bruce was massaging his outside thigh up and down from hip to knee. "You said that we'd see how this coach was and that if he was as bad with us as Coach Vanier that we'd be done. That would be it."

"Yeah, but this guy seems cool. You saw how he paired us up with Donovan? Donovan is on his way to going pro. C'mon, and the pool noodles? Classy, right?"

Under his breath Bruce muttered, "I have to finish so much math homework tonight." Both his fists were clenched as he stared holes through the window without paying attention to anything that was passing by. He mouthed the word *fuck* so his mother wouldn't hear him.

Jane turned on the radio, which was playing the same station that had been on in the gym. She automatically switched it to CBC. Jane was still feeling puffed up from seeing how much her boys commanded their space while they boxed. She thought of Alan calling them badass, and she laughed out loud. The boys thought she was laughing at whatever the talk radio was on about. Jane took the exit to the highway heading back home and switched the station back to whatever loud thing it had been on before. For a minute there was nothing in the world she had to worry about. Jane had never realized the intensity of the tension constantly stalking the background of her thoughts, slouching in her shoulders, squeezing at her neck—always some worry about her family and home and livelihood. There was an ever-present feeling of guilt alongside the quiet fear that her sons would feel lost or lonely out in the world. So she worked hard to project the opposite. She deliberately only spoke the words that would affirm the beauty of who they were, as they were. She couldn't remember a time since becoming a mother—truthfully even prior to that—that she had experienced an ease that had nothing looming over it.

JANE MONTGOMERY
MAY 1964

WHEN JANE WAS YOUNG, up until she was nine, her mother always dressed her up too fancy for the neighbourhood they lived in: patent leather Mary Janes and one of her three wide-skirted party dresses with ruffles running down from the shoulders and across the bodice, rather than the standard polyester and corduroy fare for school. Jane had heard the gossip on the street about her mother and their family: *She thinks she's a movie star*; *Like she's better than us*; *Always with that ridiculous coat, no matter the weather*; *Can't even keep her husband at home*.

But Jane saw how her mother studiously ignored the women as they passed, smoothing down her slick blonde bob then pulling the collar of her fur coat tight to her throat. Her mother had long, slender fingers, the nails glossy and painted, in contrast to Jane's blunt and sturdy ones.

In the morning she would coo to her, "my kitten, my little kitten," while tapping out her cigarette ash, holding Jane still between her knees as she forced her hair into braids. This time of day was when Jane tried to be good and keep her dress clean, wanting to bask in her mother's good graces while the mood lasted. But by the time she came home from school, Jane's hair would be a flyaway mess, her socks muddy, and her dress hem unravelling, a ribbon on the edge of the little puffed sleeve torn loose. Her mother would examine her each evening before supper, stern and rougher than in the morning. "You dreadful little cow. You can't manage to keep yourself together, can you?" The grip around her arm would be too tight, the push aside forceful. "Go get changed." A nearly empty glass next to the ashtray most afternoons. Jane would run, sliding in her socked feet to her bedroom with her mother yelling, "Chrissakes! Stop running in the house! You're driving me crazy!" Jane would pull on her play clothes, eager to escape the scrutiny, determined that the next day she'd do better at keeping herself presentable and avoid causing her mother's warmth to sour yet again.

It was difficult though. One day Jane had refused to move during each recess, standing by the door instead of joining her friends, assuring the outdoor teacher that she was fine, that she didn't want to go play. Her dress had come home as close to pristine as she could manage; her shoes had been a bit scuffed though, and she had frantically tried to spit shine them before presenting herself in front of her mother. Jane—so proud of herself, chest puffed, arms ramrod straight at her sides—was ready for her inspection, ready for her mother to gently cup her cheek and tweak her nose, her bright little kitten. *Go out and play—supper's almost ready.* Instead Jane came home to an empty, wordless house. No cigarettes resting in the ashtray, no supper on the stove, no inspection. Only dust sparkling through the sunlight. Jane sat on the sofa watching the front door until it finally opened; her dad was home from the shop where he worked as a mechanic. She had sprung up with relief when she heard the door open, but she held herself back when she realized it wasn't her mother. Jane and her father stared at one another, embalmed in the amber light before sunset, until he told her: "Go get changed."

That soft coral cloud of a dress was the last one she was ever forced to wear, and she stuffed it into a bag and pushed it to the back of her closet. But she hoarded all of her mother's nail polish bottles in a shoebox under her bed and would pull them out at night, the pert candy colours whispering dark things to her, asking her questions that she could not bear to answer: *Where's your mommy? Where are all her pretty clothes? She took her precious fur coat with her, but not you. Not even a note to say goodbye?* Some nights she would choose one bottle to open, usually the opalescent pink, and take deep, deep sniffs of that sickly sweet smell, never once brave enough to pull the brush across her nail. Then or since.

AUGUST 2012

NIGHT SWARMED IN, and the twins were in their syncopated running rhythm: the middle leg launching them off, then a beat, then landing on their outer legs, hitting the pavement in unison. They preferred to run at night when there was more room on the sidewalk and fewer eyes on them. Neither was saying anything, their breath in sync now too. Bruce was focusing on the sound of their footfalls and the drone of cicadas. They both heard a few people running up behind them, probably starting out from the alley they had just passed. Dougie moved himself and Bruce slightly toward the inside of the sidewalk to let the group pass. He assumed they were one of those spandexed running groups of marathon trainees—upper-middle-class, bird-like ladies with their swinging ponytails. But the group wasn't speeding up to overtake the twins. Neither twin turned to look behind because once they had their rhythm, they were loath to break the comfort and ease of it. But they both noticed shadows lengthening in the street lamp's radius beneath their feet right before they hit the ground. The shadows were not bird-like, not a marathon trainee among them.

For a split second, Bruce had the sensation that they had tripped on the sidewalk and had lost their balance, but he quickly realized that something bad was happening and happening fast. A wall of hands shoved the twins down with an angry and uncompromising force. They were held face down. Someone had a fistful of Bruce's hair and was smashing his cheek into the ground. Dougie's head was bounced hard on the uneven ground twice before he was also held down. Their heads facing away from one another. Hard kicks to their stomachs and ribs. The twins each twisting and jolting in opposite directions, trying to protect themselves separately. Their smaller inside arms that were usually held around one another's shoulders remained interlaced but were strained, almost to popping out of joints, against unusual pressures, unable to put up any resistance or protection. Rather Dougie's nails were digging deep into Bruce's neck, and Bruce's arm was being pulled straight down. There was a knee pushing down on Dougie's back with such force that he couldn't press up with his good arm, though he tried. Bruce was trying to get his legs up under him, but something heavy was keeping the middle leg immobile, and he struggled to get free. And then suddenly nothing. The footfalls receded in the direction they had come from. Dougie and Bruce hadn't seen anyone or heard any distinguishing sounds other than the running toward and the running away. That was the eeriest part; the whole attack had been silent save for the incessant alarm of the cicadas. There had been no threats, no swearing, no robbery, no derogatory insults, no sexual demands.

Bruce and Dougie gathered themselves up to kneeling, examining one another's faces and arms and chest and hands, each wiggling their fingers and making fists with their smaller hands. Still neither spoke, just took quick shallow breaths. All across the plane of Bruce's cheek were cuts and scrapes, plus some gravel to be picked out later at home. His right side was bruised and aching. Dougie's head was bleeding quite a bit, and a nasty cut had narrowly missed his eye. His left side was aching and bruised. They were sore and in shock, but they decided there was no need for the hospital or the police, that instead they would finish out their almost-done route.

"Fucking Patrice!" they yelled in unison.

They both felt very sad. Their feet slowly found their rhythm again, limping, fighting the thick, dark night. Dougie was emboldened with rage, clearer now than ever before about his life purpose: to dominate inside that ring. Bruce was wounded and brittle and diminished. Being isolated for those long minutes (hours, each may well have said) not being able to rely on the other's outside arm had left both feeling exposed and vulnerable. Utterly helpless like their smaller, weaker arms.

Bruce knew the only reason this had happened was because of the boxing.

And he was done.

When they rounded the corner toward home at the end of their run, neither seemed ready to go down the few steps to unlock the door, peel off for a shower, and examine the other for further bruises or oddities in silent reckoning. They came up the lawn, but Dougie gave a quick glance and Bruce a slight nod, and then they picked up their pace and continued jogging past their house. Bruce didn't want to go inside and just carry on as normal; Dougie was seeing red and couldn't be confined to the walls of their apartment. The slight limp was getting easier to push through; nothing felt broken.

About halfway through their route, Bruce slowed them down to a walk. "I'm done."

"That's fine. Let's just go back." Dougie was rubbing his temple.

"No. I mean the whole thing. I'm done boxing."

"What? C'mon, like you were done a couple years ago? You just get in these funks, and then it passes."

Dougie remembered after they had turned thirty Bruce had started sabotaging their training sessions with Dom. There was a period when Bruce was unemployed and he was getting down about everything. Dougie was convinced that if they could focus on training, the discipline and the endorphins would buoy Bruce up until the next opportunity came along. But his brother was dragging around for what felt like months ("weeks," Bruce corrected). One morning Dom had gotten impatient with Bruce, who was unfocused and listless as they kept getting bested by three different sparring partners that Dom had brought in from an out-of-town gym. Dom had gotten really quiet—which was scarier than if he had been yelling—and told Bruce that he was acting like a spoiled brat. He said that Bruce had a gift; the gift wasn't the fact that he was a decent boxer; rather it was that they had far surpassed any and all expectations of being conjoined. That the Reuben Beast could physically do something that would inspire anyone out there, no matter their lot in life. Dom told Bruce to get his head out of his ass and get to work or neither of them would be welcome to train with him anymore.

They had stopped in front of a narrow entrance to a bar and now stepped back a few paces to let some smokers out. Bruce felt like he had been having this conversation with Dougie his whole life.

"What just happened was—"

"Insane. Yeah."

"—insane."

"We should probably go home and get cleaned up now."

Dougie noticed the smokers getting a closer look at them.

Two guys of average height and build, skewing toward lanky, both in sneakers, one in shorts. Dougie was observing them closely, getting his eyewitness account.

"Everything okay?" It was the smoker farthest from the twins asking. He brought his hand up to touch the corner of his eye.

"It's nothing—looks worse than it is." Dougie mirrored his gesture then rubbed his thumb across his fingers, which were smeared with more blood than he had expected.

Bruce spoke up. "Some fucking guys just jumped us from behind."

"Where? Just now?" The smoker closest to the twins was looking up and down the street.

"Thanks, guys." Dougie started them walking ahead. "I'm going to fuck Patrice up at that match."

"Dougie, I'm serious."

"What a little shit-for-brains."

"I don't have more of this in me. I'm tired. We've done enough boxing." Bruce did feel extremely tired now that he had said the words aloud. "We're middle-aged men. Patrice is in his twenties. We're fighting kids. It's fucked up if you think about it."

Dougie had his head turned, staring his brother down. Silently.

"Our agreement was that when I wanted to stop, we'd stop."

"You need it as much as I do. I know you."

Bruce could feel his brother picking up the pace of their walking. He pulled back a bit. During their tenure as boxers, even before they'd begun fighting in the amateur league, there had been times when Bruce had tried to get them to quit, starting about six months after their first lesson. He had felt that he'd put in the required time, that they could move on and try something else. His mother informed them that their lessons had been paid up for the year—end of story. He had to stick it out. Six months after that, Bruce had tried again and Dougie promised he'd do the full share of their chores.

"I'm dead serious this time, Dougie. No more. Fuck the Patrice match."

"It's tomorrow. It's too late to back out." Dougie was incredulous.

"We should get him disqualified and banned for life or something."

Bruce had always ended up doing his half of the chores anyway because he was standing right there. He was determined not to roll over this time.

"We can talk about it later, but you and I need to teach Patrice a lesson tomorrow. You're not pissed?"

"I'd rather get my revenge by getting him banned. Isn't that a better way to fuck his life up?"

"I'd rather punch his face. Make him look me in the eyes. I'm not just going to roll over. Plus, what evidence do we take to Boxing Ontario to get him banned?"

Dougie was rubbing out some blood that had dried in his eyebrow. He continued, "If we don't fight back, he's going to keep pulling this shit with every opponent."

"He's already pulling this shit on everyone," Bruce hissed. "So we win the bout tomorrow, then what? We take a fucking break, okay?"

Dougie was imagining knocking Patrice out in the first round.

The cicadas gave up and called it a night.

At home, before they got into bed, they both took ibuprofen. Bruce's neck and shoulders were painfully tensed up; Dougie's head was pounding. Dougie fell asleep quickly, but Bruce couldn't shut his mind off. He was angry that Patrice would probably get away with acting like some second-rate mob boss ordering his goons to take all his opponents out. He was frustrated that someone like that just bullied his way through the world, that now they were getting beat up on the street, not just in the ring. The thing he had never enjoyed about boxing, since he was a kid, was feeling physically exposed during a match. That his performance, his skill, his stamina, his strategy, his half of the Reuben Beast was under intense scrutiny from everyone. And he never felt like he had things under control. And after tonight he was feeling this lack of control more acutely than ever. He was disgusted to realize that Patrice wasn't a bully, but rather a big coward, attacking them from behind instead of coming at them honestly, face to face. His mind's eye kept replaying the vertigo of being pushed down from behind, of the sidewalk at his eye line. He flicked his bedside lamp on and grabbed his book to try to distract himself. He was irritated that Dougie wouldn't hear him out about reporting Patrice; he was aggravated about having to admit that Dougie was right that they had no evidence that it was actually Patrice. And he would have to wake up tomorrow and fight again. He forced himself to concentrate only on the words on the page until his breathing deepened and slowed, his eyelids fluttering and heavy.

> There was no gigantic, toothy eel oozing beneath the boat, inky and supernaturally patient, waiting for M to succumb, to give up and jump overboard. The real monster wasn't out there lurking beneath

the waves of a pitch-black sea; it wasn't some soul he'd betrayed long ago that was now haunting him, its accusations and hurt volleyed at him in the wind. There was no ghost out there. But he certainly couldn't get comfortable. That creature in the water, and in those dark skies pressing down, had staked its ground in M's imagination. In this moment even, it prowled at the curled edges of each of our own imaginations. But that didn't make it less dangerous, less cruel, less honest. There was no adventure out there. There was only a battle to keep that monster from raising a mutiny within. There were no heroes on that ship. There was only one small being standing vigilant and alone in the dark. Where no one could hear him mutter those low, involuntary whelps; no one could see that the spray on M's cheek was not from the sea, but from his own tears of fright. There were no heroes there, alone, in the dark. No master but what lay beyond the wind and water.

You, yourself, are no hero; you are a tiny flash in the dark. You persist until the sun rises and either finds you still here and engulfs your sputtering spark in his fierce warmth...or doesn't.

The ref pried all the boxers apart for holding too long. Patrice had his sinewy arms spanned across the width of Bruce and Dougie's shoulders, rasping through his mouth guard, "You fucking freaks. You're both dead."

The bell sent them back to their respective corners. Dom was there with two towels and water. Dougie's whole world now consisted only of the glowing white square of the ring. The ropes. Patrice's shiny red shorts. It had been two rounds. He hadn't been able to knock him out yet. Patrice was fast, circling around the twins quickly, hitting hard, spitting venom.

Dom was doing some last-minute training. "He's gonna dance around you. Stay focused. Force in your body shots—even if the judges miss them—it'll open him up for a head shot."

Patrice glared at them until the bell sprung the boxers free for the final round.

Bruce couldn't believe that he was here after last night. That as a grown man he had to sacrifice a day's pay in order to take and deliver body shots. His ribs were sore before he even stepped into the ring, but Dougie was not going to let Patrice get away with being a cheating little shit fucking half-assed bully. Dougie hadn't listened to a word that Bruce had said after they got home from their run. And Bruce—now back in the ring with his hands wrapped, his helmet on, and his shirt off—did have to begrudgingly concede that yet again Dougie had been right: Patrice wasn't even that big a deal. He was wiry and shorter than them. Even if he had gotten some hulking guys to beat up Olivier and attack them last night, the friends he had with him this afternoon were clowns.

The twins let Patrice close the space between them; Bruce blocked a jab to his face, and Dougie lunged for Patrice's liver. Patrice recovered and answered with a hard hit to Bruce's side. Patrice punched Dougie in the face, then jabbed Bruce's side again, hard. Dougie's head had blown back with the punch, but Bruce kept him on his feet. Bruce was still always a second too slow at protecting his side. The twins absorbed all of the blows that were landing and barrelled forward and wide, trying to overtake all of the available floor space, cutting the ring down to the size of a placemat; they managed to dance Patrice into the ropes. Dougie and Bruce alternated swings left, right, left, right, until Patrice slid clear through the ropes, a marlin wriggling off a stretched line back into the sea. The bell clattered like spoons in a bowl. Dougie leaned over the ropes and roared at the nerve of this snivelling dirtbag.

Patrice had a group of his guys huddled around his corner, mouthing off opinions and strategies after each round. Through the whole match, Bruce and Dougie had had only Dom there that afternoon. Standing on ceremony for the official decision from the judges, Bruce's chest was heaving and Dougie wiped his neck with a towel. Now Dougie could take in the larger scene beyond the ring. They were in a gym they'd never fought in before, the ring taking up most of the space with only a few rows of chairs on three sides. A small crowd was gathering around the twins' corner, trying to get pictures, assuming the Reuben Beast would be declared the winners. He could hear the murmur of many conversations as people moved around the tight space, shuffling the black folding chairs. A woman in her late seventies was seated alone by the door. In the post-match commotion, she didn't get up but rather sat almost trance-like, smoothing down her thin, wavy, pink hair, palm pressed flat to her head. She wore sunglasses and a fur coat.

A new excitement started to build in the crowd below, and they all suddenly migrated, squawking and snapping photos, over to Patrice's corner. He had climbed back into the ring with both arms raised high in the air, showboating in his shiny red shorts. Dougie couldn't believe what a chump Patrice was. Poor guy had been debased in his home club and didn't even realize it; the audience had witnessed his utter defeat to the Reuben Beast. The ref gathered up the score cards from the judges and passed them on to the official who made the call. At the centre of the ring, the ref grabbed hold of Patrice and Dougie and threw up Patrice's hand. All three judges had awarded top points to the red corner for clean punches landed. Patrice had won by unanimous decision.

Dom was deeply hurt by this. "Fucking hell?"

The crowd immediately dispersed, a flock startled by a gunshot, as Dom's tirade continued unabated and largely ignored: "Fucking goddamned SHIT for brains, none of you ever been INSIDE these goddamned ropes. Fucking hell? Dougie, Bruce, FUCK—that was a shit call—you boys DON'T DESERVE that, that match was YOURS. It's so obvious. Both of you, you knew it in there—you were BOTH on point, you TOO Bruce, even YOU were RIGHT FUCKING THERE in your body."

Dom seemed to be on the verge of tears, panting to a near-empty room, with Patrice and his entourage clamouring loudly as he made his way to the change room. Dom let out a helpless yelp, but the judges merely jostled themselves out from behind their table, which was wedged in under a row of windows. Bruce surprised himself by feeling robbed. They hadn't been knocked off their feet; he wasn't bleeding all over himself. Disappointment spread slow and thick through his tightened muscles like molasses. Dougie smacked his fist hard against his helmet two times, then ordered a mousy teenager down below to take his picture. The boy took out his cell phone and climbed up into the ring at Dougie's insistence. He got a shot with neither twin smiling.

"Save that picture. You just got a picture of the real winners here. Honest champs."

"Oh. Okay. Cool, cool. I'm just waiting for my dad. He works here at the club."

The boy tucked his hair behind his ears and hopped down out of the ring. Easing his headphones on, he loped out of sight like a fawn on a dew-drenched morning.

The twins showered without saying a word. Water streamed over Dougie's left shoulder, while Bruce was turned out in the mist. There would be no recourse, no understanding or justice from the judges who had made their choice clear. The win had been denied them for no discernible reason. They changed into their street clothes, trading the blue boxing shorts for the grey ones that their mom had fashioned from some old pairs of sweats. By this time the gym was empty; even Dom had disappeared without waiting for them. The chairs around the ring were in mild disarray, the room now dense with humid silence. Their punched-up, aching bodies were the only indication that anything had just occurred in that tiny room, that something rotten had just taken place. The room had been full of complicit witnesses with only Dom screaming and being ignored. They decided to walk back to their apartment.

Dougie kept thinking of the old woman sitting stone-still with her sunglasses on, that fur coat in the middle of summer. The colour of amber. He thought she must've been a mirage.

"Did you see that lady? In the seat by the door?" Dougie was hoping Bruce had more insight.

"What? No, what lady? Just now?"

"Right after the match, when everyone was out of their seats, I saw a lady in shades and a fur coat sitting by the door. Pink hair, but like a grandma."

"Weird. It's so hot out."

"Yeah, it was weird. She was like out of a movie. I wonder if she knows Dom. They were both gone when we left."

"Whatever."

Dougie looked askance at his brother. "Why're *you* acting so weird?"

"I'm not. I'm just not sure why you care about some stranger."

Bruce was prickly. Resentful that he'd been dragged into the ring just to be robbed and rejected. Frustrated because he hated boxing and confused because he was proud that he was actually getting better at it. "Why does it feel like we're always rolling a boulder up a mountain? Even when we show ourselves to be the better fighters. And what the hell was last night? All for nothing. It's not worth it."

They continued their march. Dougie was tired now; for once he didn't have an answer for his brother. They still had another twenty minutes until they'd be home. To add insult to injury, a scheduling conflict had required the bout to be an afternoon match, so now the twins had to fight their way through busy sidewalks. They had to continually pause for families with strollers and frozen yogurts and iced coffees and shopping bags, and sidestep around trees planted in the sidewalk, and get sniffed by a million dogs. Finally they both wordlessly agreed to cut up a quiet residential street where they could take up all the room they needed.

"She was an omen, Bruce. I just can't figure if good or bad."

Bruce shook his head clear; he had other things to focus on now. He didn't have to give any more energy to Patrice because, though he had been forced to put it out of his mind during the bout, he had been sitting on the delicious thrill of a letter he had found in their mailbox that morning.

Bruce had been the one to check the box before heading to the match, and he had spied an envelope without a stamp, addressed to him. Dougie hadn't noticed because he was busy hyping them up, going on about demolishing Patrice in the ring. Bruce quickly tore the envelope open, a corner of it in his mouth, and slid out the letter. He shoved everything into the pocket of his shorts to keep it from Dougie, who had been waiting for Bruce's response to something. Dougie had shaken his head, frustrated, and kept them moving.

The whole way to the match, Bruce had been dying to see what she had written, but he wanted to read it in relative privacy if he could manage to. There was a chance that she had written something along the lines of *Fuck off, you creep*, and he preferred to face that embarrassment while Dougie was otherwise occupied.

It wasn't until after the match and after they had showered that Bruce had finally snatched a moment in the change room to read the letter quickly while Dougie was busy stuffing gear into his bag.

August 27, 2012

Dear Bruce,

Thank you for your letter. It was very kind of you to be neighbourly. A letter is not the type of thing you see a lot of.

Today I decided it was time to start a new project. I am knitting a rug that is a map of the city's underground rivers. It will take over my entire apartment. Obviously it won't be to scale.

I hope this finds you well.

Your neighbour,
Priyanka Ramratan

And now, as they walked in that gloomy silence of defeat, Bruce could also allow himself to relish in his own private victory. He thought about the woman from the library, who had now become the woman who had written him back, who had told him her name and something about herself. He couldn't believe his letter had worked. And that maybe it would be okay to write her again. He wanted to share his success with Dougie while they walked, but the time didn't feel quite right. Dougie was stewing; he said nothing but smacked the side of his head every now and then. Bruce knew that nothing he said would register with his brother, so he just ignored Dougie's silent raging as they made their way through the grid of residential streets.

For the rest of the walk home, a jumble of sensations, feelings, and thoughts churned through Bruce's body: soreness from the match; an aching shoulder and still-healing scrapes across his face from the attack; excitement over the letter; humiliation from having their bodies thrown and pinned to the sidewalk; anticipation about what to write next; a delicate understanding that Priyanka had not explicitly asked him to write back; resentment about still having to box; exhaustion about having to train, and make an effort, and remember to punch right through, and yet still lose the match. Bruce knew he had to slow his mind or he'd likely have an aneurysm, so he tried to conjure an image of Priyanka's face. It was hard to latch onto, blurry and approximate, but beautiful, and so he just rolled her name around his mouth until finally they were home and Dougie unlocked their front door.

In the kitchen Dougie went straight for the fridge and grabbed two bottles of beer, which Bruce took as a window of opportunity. He accepted one of the bottles. "She wrote me back."

"No shit?" Unsmiling, Dougie clinked his bottle to Bruce's in cheers. "That's great," he said flatly.

Bruce could tell that Dougie wasn't all there.

Dougie took the lead toward the living room. "I need to sit."

On the couch Dougie propped some cushions up to rest his head and perched his outside leg on the coffee table. He closed his eyes and brought the bottle up to sip at regular intervals.

"You okay, Dougie?"

"Yep."

Bruce didn't push it, mostly because his notebook was there next to Dougie's foot on the table, and he decided that with Dougie off in his own world, now was the perfect chance to write another letter.

August 28, 2012

Dear Priyanka,

I'm sorry I didn't address my first letter properly—please forgive me. That is a lovely name.

You're a knitter—that's great! Your project idea sounds wonderfully ambitious. Sadly I'm all thumbs. I can't say that I have many hobbies, though I do have a twin brother, Douglas—Dougie. He's been an amateur boxer for as long as I've known him. He's made of steelier nerves than I am. But enough about me.

Priyanka, is your project going to be a copy of an old city map with streets laid out, or will it just be the rivers and tributaries? I would assume that it's critical to decide this early on. There could be so many implications... Is it this city or somewhere else?

Bruce was relieved that Dougie wasn't paying any attention to him. He was embarrassed by the stiffness of his words; he knew that Dougie would've teased him mercilessly over his sudden interest in knitting, but he couldn't help himself. It was astonishing that there had been a letter waiting for him in the box. He knew it wasn't fair that he already knew what she looked like while she had absolutely no idea who he was. At least he had told her about Dougie, in a way. He took her letter out of his pocket, basking in the possibility of this new connection. He read the words over and over in the soft, darkened space around him. Dougie began to snore quietly. He put the letter and his notebook down, picked up *The Life and Art of Being M*, opened to a random page, and tipped back the last of his beer.

Eventually both twins woke up on the couch and agreed to get food and some drinks at the bar. It was already dark when they headed out along the familiar path. Dougie was still furious about losing to Patrice, and Bruce was still frustrated that Dougie hadn't listened to him about fighting Patrice in the first place. As they passed by an alleyway, Bruce shuddered, still rattled about the previous night's ambush. Bruce wanted to take a break and hole up in bed for a week, but Dougie reasoned that they had to do what they would normally do or they'd be admitting defeat on many fronts and would thus be forever fucked. In spite of himself, Dougie had been glancing over his shoulder, tense and at the ready.

They took the same path back at the end of the night, and just as they were nearing home, Dougie—mid-whistle—crumpled forward and jolted Bruce off-kilter.

"Dougie? Doug...what—?"

For the second time in as many days, Bruce found himself pitching forward toward the ground. Bruce's first thought was someone had come at them from behind again, but this time he was able to catch himself and correct his balance. Supporting his brother, who was out cold, he whipped around and saw they were alone. Maybe Dougie had tripped over the middle leg. But Dougie wasn't righting himself, wasn't whistling or speaking anymore. Bruce had never known Dougie to black out, and they certainly hadn't drunk enough tonight to warrant it. Bruce staggered to keep them both on their feet; Dougie was slack and slumped forward, and Bruce was afraid if he succumbed to his brother's gravity, they'd both end up like an overturned bug—wriggling and helpless—alone under another streetlight.

"Can you hear me? Shit. Dougie?" Bruce was at a loss, but he had to overcome the encroaching panic. "What's happening, Dougie?"

He tried to stack the brunt of Dougie's weight onto his side and keep his brother standing. Dougie's head bobbed, his lips parted, loose. Bruce took comfort in the fact that he wasn't foaming at the mouth or anything. He figured he could drag Dougie the rest of the way to their place and probably manoeuvre them down the few steps to their apartment, but he wondered if Dougie should get to a hospital instead. Bruce felt exceptionally sober all of a sudden. He had his outside arm around Dougie's chest, holding him up under his armpit, wondering how best to get at the phone in his back pocket.

"Shit. Someone's bound to drive past soon and stop to help. Okay. Forget it. Let's not waste time. Dougie, don't worry. Can you hear me? I'm gonna take us back to the bar and get some help, okay? Don't worry. You're going to be fine."

Bruce strained to support his brother's weight and ignored the bruises that felt tender and smarted from that day's and the previous night's bouts. He'd never experienced this with Dougie. To have him just tap out. Unresponsive. Quiet. Just this solemn dead weight tugging on his left side.

He swung them around, back in the direction they had just come from, their shared middle leg keeping Dougie mostly upright. And very slowly and gently, Bruce stepped right, then left, then dragged Dougie forward. And again: right, left, drag. It was the strangest sensation, willing that middle leg onward by himself. When the two of them were consciously moving in tandem, the leg felt no different than his own outside appendage, but now without Dougie's consciousness at work, it was unwieldy and enormous and rickety. Bruce stopped to re-distribute the weight.

"What the hell's going on in there, Dougie?"

Bruce debated ringing someone's doorbell, but it was so late, the street so hushed and still. A skunk crossed up ahead, oblivious to the twins.

"It's okay. We're okay." A bystander would've assumed Bruce was politely refusing help from the skunk.

Bruce wondered what Dougie would've done if the tables were turned, if Bruce had passed out, mid-stride, without warning. He turned to face his brother and jostled Dougie's head toward him a bit. Drool was collecting at the corner of Dougie's mouth, and Bruce slapped him as hard as he could. Twice. And then once more, leaving a splotchy handprint. Dougie's eyelids fluttered. Bruce started clapping his cheek and then stopped to shake his shoulder. "Doug. Dougie. Wake up."

Dougie gasped as though he'd been underwater for a long time. "Holy shit, Bruce. What's going on? Why're you slapping me?"

"Jesus, Dougie. You scared the shit out of me. You passed out. What the fuck just happened to you?"

Dougie blinked hard and shook his head. He pressed his hand against his ear.

"C'mon. Let's get you to a hospital."

"No hospital. I'm okay." Dougie wiped the corner of his mouth. "My head's killing me, but I'm all right. It's just from when I hit my head last night."

"What if you have a concussion? We should see a doctor."

"In the morning. I'm too drunk."

They turned around again, back now in the direction of their apartment. Still no car had driven by. Bruce still took the brunt of their weight and guided them home, the middle leg noticeably lighter.

Bruce worried about letting Dougie sleep, wondering whether it was smarter to wake him periodically through the night. Dougie threatened to punch Bruce in the nuts every time he got woken up. "I'm fine. Maybe I just drank too much tonight."

Bruce didn't buy it. He listened to his brother's breathing eventually lull into something rhythmic, then silently listed off medical conditions to look into. He got to brain cancer, and his stomach lurched, so he stopped listing and began listening instead to his own breath, trying to match his brother's rhythm.

The next morning, Dougie and Bruce ate toast with marmalade before shaking out a newspaper. Bruce had let Dougie sleep uninterrupted and was immensely relieved when Dougie woke up and seemed normal again. Bruce held up fingers and asked how many. He asked what day it was, what year, who the prime minister was, their mother's maiden name. Dougie insisted that he was fine, not even hungover, and threatened to punch Bruce if he continued to fuss over him.

Sitting on their couch, each twin held a page of the newspaper open; their basement apartment was like a submarine submerged, with a slim portal of light jimmying in near the ceiling. Each concentrating on different stories, the physical newspaper was a comfortable, weekly ritual that they had shared since they were kids. On the weekend the whole family would sit together reading with the sections spread out on the floor. The twins only read the comics then, but as they grew up, they extended their reach through Sports and Arts and the national headlines. It was something the family always did together silently—unless someone was mad about something and raucously read bits and pieces out for the others to hear and add in their two cents. Even now they kept up a weekend subscription.

The air was hot and still, with the lamps already turned on this early in the day. Dougie coughed, stretching his outside leg to rest on the coffee table, and the pages rustled. Bruce made the choice to accept that maybe nothing serious had happened to Dougie last night—nothing serious, just unusual—and he released some of his worry. He was always the twin who worried too much, according to his brother. The smell of toast and coffee lingered. Bruce half-read a story about an American toddler who had accidentally shot and killed his nanny, but his mind began to wander. His mind floated back to a passage he had read about M:

> The ocean lolled in its own depths and luxuriousness. Glassy, persistent waves. M never failed to be surprised by how loud it was. Alone with only the wild noise of everything that the world is really made up of: wind, clouds, and an incredible volume of water. Fear, beauty, and faith. All of it screaming around him. This is what M wanted; this is where

> he knew himself best. The sheer mass of open atmosphere would leave a person feeling deranged if they put up even the slightest resistance to it. It was M's test of authenticity not to panic: to trust, to relax and fall back. To mix with the atoms of the air and waves, of the boat. To dissolve into nothing and yet to become everything. Wind continued to pummel the surface of the sea from one side of the world to the other.

Bruce held up his side of the newspaper so that his brother could keep reading, but he was in his own world now. He quietly shifted his weight, trying to relieve the discomfort that had begun to swell in his back, under his thigh, in his tailbone. He was never completely able to surrender or to trust like M, and he fought against the feeling of being caged in this silent and dim apartment dug below the earth's surface. He felt every inch of distance between himself and Dougie—and that space between their apartment and all of the other apartments and houses and condominiums in this city, all breathing with a pulse of their own. And there was Bruce, stymied, able to see but unable to feel a part of that same roiling mass.

Unbeknownst to his brother, Dougie also couldn't concentrate on what he was reading, re-reading, on a loop—the same two-sentence paragraph about a filibuster. His head was still throbbing, and his stomach felt unsettled. He kept reassuring himself that nothing was wrong. Even though he had never blacked out in the past, he was fine and didn't need to worry. He told himself that he wasn't the first person in the world to black out, that it was nothing; maybe a break from the booze was all he needed. It was possible that Patrice or his friends had somehow managed to loosen a screw. Dougie was grateful, though, that he always had Bruce looking out for him. He was spooked by the idea that had his life been different, he could've passed out in the street at night, alone, not coming to for hours, probably having pissed himself. He let his mind prod around Patrice's surprise attack. It felt dangerous to poke too insistently into what he was feeling, that being splayed out like that on the sidewalk—incapacitated without being bolstered by his brother's half, another strong arm and leg—meant that without Bruce, Dougie was too weak, too soft, too much like the raw underside of some amphibious creature. This fear surprised him. He could sense a vulnerability skirting the edge of his consciousness, one that he'd never noticed before; it felt like something ghostly breathing down his neck. He cleared his throat, feeling ridiculous considering that he was literally the size of not one but two men. For a brief moment, he considered all of the women he knew. All of the people in his neighbourhood, in his city, who were feeling unsafe. He wondered how people lived their lives without a built-in buddy system. In moments like these, he wondered if he and Bruce were really on the leading edge of evolution. Were two always better than one?

Before Dougie's next shift on the lot, the twins made the walk over to deliver Bruce's letter, with Dougie grumbling that his brother should just get this girl's email address. Dougie was feeling grumpy, dealing with a somewhat strange and persistent nausea that he was trying to ignore, not to mention irritation at how diligent Bruce was about checking the mailbox any and every time they left and returned home. And Bruce's vigilance was quickly rewarded.

August 30, 2012

Dear Bruce,

It's true—I spent the better part of a week thinking about how to design this thing. I have to say, it is nice to actually be able to talk to someone about all this. It's possible I don't get out enough.

There's a lady who always comes in to the laundromat where I work who I call "the Marchesa Casati." She comes in every few days with piles of extravagant clothes to wash. She yelled at me because she ruined some sequined thing in one of the dryers. Ordinarily I'd really enjoy having someone so eccentric and oblivious always hanging around, but she's actually just mean and not that cool. In my version of her origin story, she was orphaned and left to be raised by jackals. She's bloodthirsty and on the hunt. Glistening red claws.

Your neighbour,
Anka

PS. You can call me Anka. My parents were the only ones who called me Priyanka, and I always introduce myself with the name they gave me because... Well I'm not sure why. But Anka is fine, Bruce.

That night Bruce waited until Dougie was asleep before scratching out his reply. He had a feeling that his brother wasn't telling him something, and he assumed it was that Dougie thought he was wasting his time writing these urbane little notes that he and Anka were now passing back and forth like grade-school classmates. But Bruce found, for the first time, that he wasn't bothered by what his brother thought. It didn't matter that they were doing the opposite of taking a break from boxing and instead stepping up their training sessions for the Golden Gloves. Neither that nor Dougie's blasé attitude could stop Bruce's heart from beating like a kettledrum each time there was a new note waiting for him, each time he set his pen to a fresh page in response, each time he bounded down Anka's front steps in absolute astonishment.

August 31, 2012

Dear Anka,

I hope you've had a good summer. I'd say mine's had its ups and downs.

I read an article about a sinkhole that swallowed up an entire house with the whole family still inside. It's terribly sad.

Forgive me if this is odd, but it's also quite lovely, don't you think? To be taken up by the earth when it decides that it's time for you to go. And all together like that. No other house on the street even moved an inch.

I apologize for this maudlin letter. I'm just feeling a little beat up tonight, but I still wanted to drop you a line.

Anka, thank you for writing me back when you received my first letter.

Bruce Reuben

ANKA RAMRATAN
SEPTEMBER 2011

TWO WEEKS AFTER Anka had gotten that devastating call from the police, after taking care of all the administrative horrors that were required, she had found herself back in her apartment and crumpled her body into her bed. The sun had been streaming in until she flipped the Venetians closed. She could smell her bedding, her hair, Auntie Sab's perfumed laundry detergent on her t-shirt. Everything in her shoebox of an apartment so hopelessly familiar and intact. Every glass perfectly containing the air within their smooth, quiet lines. It was cruel, the mundane morphing back to normalcy after everything had been torched, a burn left in the middle of a page, both of her parents just yanked out of matter. Only the blackened edges of Anka's life were now left in the middle of that fragile paper. Her mind on fire, her heart a hole.

She was so angry today. She hated who she was—who had she ever been? A loser. She had no ambition, no interests, no one close now, save for Diane. She was punching her stupid chest for being so sad and so pathetic and so fucking dramatic and so lost. Scratching, clawing at herself—she felt feral. Trying to get to some balance. Waiting for her body and brain and heart and spirit to sync. But they all hurt with different frequencies.

She had no parents. No Mama, no Dad. The police told her that a man, age forty-eight, had been reported driving erratically for some distance, deliberately trying to run up onto sidewalks, hit signs, and the like. They had found a note amongst his possessions. He had swerved at the last minute into their lane.

She stopped. She absolutely would not let her mind veer into that imagined crash site. She rolled to one side, gulped in some air, and held it in tight, blowing up her cheeks and chest until her heart beat up into her throat, bursting out and forcing an exhale. Her head was light and woozy for a moment. She did this three more times. *Okay. Priyanka, it's okay. It's okay. You're okay.*

She cradled a pillow and used it to wipe her face. She didn't do anything except listen to her room. Her very normal room. It told her that whenever she felt like getting out of bed, she could do something with her hands instead. Her knitting needles were tucked up on her closet shelf. She imagined using them to poke her eyeballs out, but they weren't offering to perform any kind of cruel medieval torture. They weren't doing jack shit; they were happy enough to wait. They were ready to knit and give her hands something reliable, something singular to do. They would still her mind for some of the time.

She had to turn the pillow over eventually to find a dry patch to wipe her face.

ANKA RAMRATAN
SEPTEMBER 2012

ANKA SAT AT THE BAR BY HERSELF. She waited for ten minutes before her phone died. And then twenty-five minutes and then forty-one minutes, and then she accepted the fact that Diane was a no-show, unbearably mad with herself that she a) always forgot to charge her phone before she left the house, and b) never once thought of throwing her charger in her bag. She ordered her third double vodka soda (*Fuck*) and an extra side of courage, walked over to a table of twenty-year-old students, sat down, and interjected as if she'd been sitting there all night: "What the hell? I can't believe you're going to let him say that to you."

Anka had silenced the whole table.

The boy next to her shuffled closer and hitched his arm to the back of her chair. "Whadd're you gonna do about it?"

"Me, personally? I'd challenge him to a duel, a fight to the death. But he didn't just call me a liar, so I dunno... What are you going to do?"

Two girls across from Anka rolled their eyes in silent conversation with one another about this crazy bitch who had just sat down, uninvited, and started talking shit. The words they spoke out loud were about how out of control their bangs were.

Anka heard every word, spoken and otherwise, and ignored them. Today was the first day that she had made eggs without talking to her dad. Instead she had been thinking about what she'd write to Bruce Reuben next. It was the first time that she hadn't said *gesundheit* after cracking an egg like her dad used to do after he started teaching himself how to cook. It was the first time that she had so callously let the memory of her parents slip from her mind, if even just for a few moments.

She needed to get wrecked and fuck a lukewarm twenty-year-old. But the last thing in the world she wanted to do was get trashed and have sex with someone she didn't know. She was feeling too sad to give a shit about these yahoos. Anka stewed inside her army jacket. She finished her drink and emptied her pockets of gum wrappers and streetcar transfers, rolling them out like dice where she imagined the bill would sit in a puddle around the pitcher. She had taken a gamble to go out and have fun, and she had gambled wrong.

Outside she hunkered down for a long walk home, piloting her body though the dark city looming before her: couples taking up the entire sidewalk, a dog barking at nothing; the bass of stereos booming, cars pulled over and hunched, waiting for fire truck sirens to wail past. The smell of fleeting cigarettes. Bright bus shelters. Garbage bins. Pylons. Manhole covers. Shawarmas.

When she got home, she wrote Bruce a three-page letter. She wrote to him about the girls at the bar that night, about her favourite jacket; she made a pros and cons list about working at the laundromat. She wrote to Bruce Reuben about what she imagined he did on the weekends. She imagined that he was the kind of kid who never ate the crusts of his sandwiches.

She read the whole thing over and could see how obviously drunk and lonely she was. She tore the letter up, feeling foolish, suspecting that he had been a figment of her imagination this whole time. Anka figured she was just the kind of girl who couldn't get a grip on reality, spending large swaths of her day in reverie. Her so-called pen pal was just a composite of bits of data stored in her subconscious. She remembered that Bruce was the name of the man who'd lived next door when she was a child. And then she felt mortified for thinking that Bruce's letters were sincere—it was obvious that he was preying on her, making fun of her, waiting in shadowy corners for the right moment to leap out and hack her into tiny pieces. Anka knew that she was going to have a hell of a time being hungover and feeling sorry for herself in the morning. She crawled out of her jeans and under the covers. A moment later she hauled herself out of bed, the room tilting under her feet, and scribbled a note in the dark to herself: *remember to murder Diane*.

After Anka left the bar, the two girls at the table started telling a story about some guy they had seen on their way over that night, trading the details back and forth. They had cut through the alley and through the grocery store parking lot—"You know, the one up at Bloor, by the subway?"

"A real-life two-headed man, we shit you not."

"He was just, like, pacing around the lot. It was seriously trippy."

"He seemed kinda cute actually."

The first girl swatted the second girl's arm. "You would, you animal," she said, and the whole table laughed and ordered another round.

It seemed to Bruce that Dougie had been picking up too many extra shifts at Everest lately. Tonight they were working again on the lot back by the loading dock, chatting with Nikki while she took her smoke break. Dougie had plucked her a tired geranium from the sparse planter by the store entrance and presented it to her in exchange for the gum she had pilfered for them. Bruce marvelled at how easy it always was for Dougie to casually flirt, to be lighthearted, even when he was probing about someone's fiancé.

Nikki had tucked the drooping flower behind one ear. "We've been together since high school."

"Holy shit. Wow."

"Yeah. We're planning on getting married. Eventually." She held up her left hand so he could see the ring while she took a drag from the smoke in her right. She shook the armloads of bracelets back down to both her wrists as she lowered her hands, tinkling and jangling. "Actually when we first got together, I was dating one of his friends. But I guess he just swooped in and swept me off my feet."

At this Nikki did a little *ta-da* type of thing with her hands, making eye contact with Dougie.

"Sounds like fate." Dougie was grinning, and Bruce looked at the familiar lines that had gathered on his face.

Nikki turned to Bruce. "Martin—his friend—was actually my first boyfriend. He was nice, but at the time *nice* meant the same as *boring*, I guess. But after we broke up, he was kind of a dick to me."

Dougie seemed genuinely interested. "How so?"

Bruce didn't have much else to offer, and so he just kept nodding. Dougie had his hand on his hip; Bruce didn't know what to do with his. He couldn't decide if he was more comfortable with it in his pocket or out. Maybe out, on his hip like Dougie's? Bruce could hear two of the stock guys coming out for their break as well.

"He wrote me a letter informing me of all the ways I was a shitty girlfriend, and then he outlined how his new girlfriend was hotter and better than me in every way. It was pretty fucking detailed too."

"Teenagers suck. I'm sorry."

"Nah, whatever." She shrugged. "It was a long time ago. We were all shitty, I guess."

Dougie: "Have you and your fiancée set a date?"

Bruce, at the same time: "How long have you worked at Everest?"

"No date. We've been engaged for three years though. I think my parents have given up on us actually going through with it."

"What about you?"

"What do you mean?" She exhaled one last plume.

"Have you given up on it?" Dougie was inching away from shore into some dangerous waters.

Nikki dropped the butt of her smoke and ground it down with the ball of her foot. "I started here right after we got engaged."

She popped in a piece of gum and applied some lip gloss. "You guys are cool. What do you like to do outside of work?

"We're boxers." Dougie comically flexed his bicep.

"Fuck off? That's rad."

Bruce groaned while Dougie told her about the Golden Gloves tournament.

"Bruce, you seem stressed." Nikki tilted her head.

"Don't ask." He was glaring at Dougie.

"He just gets nervous, but you should see him in the ring." Dougie was patting Bruce's shoulder as though soothing a baby.

"I'd love to see you guys box sometime."

"The heavyweight championship bout will be one to see, for sure. It's the first of December."

"I'll be there."

"Come say hi before the end of your shift. We'll be ensuring the peace out here."

Nikki laughed and flashed the twins a pair of peace signs before heading back in. Her bracelets jangled and twinkled some more. The parking lot still had the exact same number of cars as when she had come out for her break. The stock guys were still out, sitting on milk crates and eating from small bags of chips.

"December first is the final round of the tournament. You're feeling that confident that we'll win all our matches?"

Dougie gave him a peace sign, and Bruce wanted to punch his stupid lights out. He balled up both hands, his outer fist and the smaller inner bulb. Dougie noticed the tiny knuckles pressed against his neck and arched away to take in a wider view of his brother. "Tell me you're not a boxer."

Dougie wrapped his outside arm around Bruce in half a bear hug. Frustrated, helpless tears clouded Bruce's vision. Bruce realized that he actually felt jealous of Dougie—it was so natural for his brother to be around Nikki; he knew what to say and how to be. A familiar foolish sensation, the taste of brine and char on his breath. An interminable rash crawling across his skin.

"It's always so easy for you, Dougie."

"What's that?" Dougie released his brother from his grip. "What are you talking about?"

Bruce was too ashamed to admit that he resented his brother's easy nature. His charm. Bruce felt he'd cycled through the same thoughts since he was ten: *I don't want to, I'm not allowed, I'm tired, I'm fine, I don't want to.* He had made an effort to think of boxing the way Dougie did, and it was certainly true that he was in far better shape than he ever would've been in if left to his own devices. As kids Dougie was always upbeat, but once he started boxing, he seemed settled and sure of himself. But Bruce's muscles constantly ached, his wounds were always tender, his nerves rattled. Anxiety thrummed in his stomach.

He didn't know how to even begin. "Never mind," he said, dragging a roughened finger back and forth across his eyes one at a time. For as long as he could remember, even before boxing, he'd always had to force this frenzy down. Tamp it down to something low and contained.

Dougie had let Bruce sink into his thoughts. He was practising his left jab repeatedly, and the effort was rocking his brother forward and back slightly.

Bruce started picking through his memories, looking for the earliest instances of that fearful fluttering in his side of this shared body, that high-pitched drone that drowned out everything else around him, that Dougie said he had never experienced. Bruce now traced a path back through some of the obvious triggers in his mind: kids at school, teachers, misguided strangers—run of the mill teasing, one real bully, undeserved scolding, thinly veiled judgments. He remembered himself at various ages throughout his childhood sitting at the big table with Dougie, doing homework while their mother cooked dinner. There was a feeling threaded through the DNA of the farmhouse that home was the only place in the world to feel safe; it was the barricade each of them spent their day running back too, breathless, sweaty, haunted as the world hid land mines and threw up hand grenades. And yet, despite the perceived threats out there, Bruce had felt his own restlessness ricocheting against the farmhouse walls, firing his impatience and unease right back at his unarmed self.

Dougie was really going for it with shadow boxing now, and he caught Bruce off guard, jolting him forward, making him scramble to catch his balance. "The fuck, Dougie? Quit it."

"Oh, sorry, Brucie." But Dougie didn't break his rhythm or alter his speed.

Bruce was livid. "How many hours do you have left out here?"

Dougie seemed right at home wherever he went, and Bruce didn't belong anywhere.

~

The alarm went off at 5:15 a.m. for the fourth time this week. Dougie had successfully cajoled yet another extra run into their schedule.

"Mornin', Brucie. You awake?"

"Morning, Dougie."

"You shouldn't scratch at that thing. It'll just get worse. We should get you some ointment."

"Remind me again why we have to run."

"Up and at 'em, buddy. On three."

Dougie propped himself up, and Bruce reluctantly followed suit, the muscles along his spine complaining loudly, and clamped his arm around Dougie's neck. Bruce was on the outside, so he kicked off the wad of blankets and swung out while Dougie scuttled around to the edge of the bed.

"I hate running, Dougie."

"No, you don't. When you get out there, the sun just up, the air fresh in your lungs, you love it. When we get into that zone, man, don't say you don't love that."

"I don't. Truly, I don't."

Bruce and Dougie presented themselves to the bathroom mirror. Dougie grabbed the toothbrushes, and Bruce worked the toothpaste.

"We really should go to a walk-in clinic for your rash. After you're done work."

"Maybe later—if it doesn't get better by the end of the week."

"Why would you let yourself suffer another week, Bruce? That makes no sense. It looks really rough... It must be killing you." Dougie spat into the sink and looked at the rash in the mirror.

Bruce changed the subject: "You think I should grow a beard? I think I'd look good."

"You know you can't keep it for matches, right?"

Even though Bruce was technically considered the first-born, Dougie was the more sizeable twin.

"Does what I do really matter?" Bruce spat.

Dougie spoke into the mirror: "Okay, hold up. What's gotten into you? You've been kind of crusty lately, and I haven't said anything about it. But Christ, you don't have to be an asshole."

"Who's being crusty now, Doug?"

"You just deal with whatever it is that's got you feeling shitty before our match next Friday. We need to bring our A game. Cranston's a bulldozer. We gotta be ready. Both of us."

"Yeah, yeah, I know."

"We'll go to the pharmacy later."

Bruce continued to watch his brother, his best friend, in the mirror. It was impossible for them to keep anything from each other for long. Bruce knew how lucky he was to know someone so fully, to support and be supported in ways that were not just obviously physical. They had been a witness to every single moment of one another's lives; who else on earth could have that intimacy and, frankly, data on another single being? Bruce knew that Dougie's adventurousness had lent some boldness to his own meek spirit. Although they were side by side, they didn't always talk about everything. And so Dougie's instincts were right; something was bothering Bruce. Dougie had brushed aside the whole incident before the Patrice match—like he had brushed aside passing out on the way home from the bar. Like he had brushed aside Bruce's requests to spend less time boxing. Bruce had vowed to himself that the Patrice match would be his last. But how could he stop boxing when Dougie was gunning for the title? At this point Bruce could see only one way out. There was only one way for Dougie to do what made him happy and for Bruce to have the opportunity to freely find out what would do the same for him.

Bruce wanted to separate.

Bruce cleared his throat and noticed that he could continue brushing his teeth without the threat of a coughing fit. The possibility of an operation, the potential of starting a new life, meant hurting the person he loved the most. But not having his own life was becoming painful. These were the things making Bruce feel shitty lately.

Walter Reuben picked his sons up from the train station and drove nearly an hour down a two-lane highway that sliced ever northward through rolling fields bound by trees changing season. They made a left before the causeway, onto that narrow road that snuck them onto their farm. Once inside he poured himself and his sons a scotch, and then they rooted themselves in front of the picture window that overlooked the acreage. A *V* of geese honked insolently overhead.

Bruce looked out and was six again, remembering when he and Dougie had gotten stuck in the mud out there after a big rain. They were happily squelching along until they sank in too deep and the land had pervertedly grabbed hold of their ankles. When they lifted either of their legs, just tiny feet in white tube socks came up for air, with three yellow boots holding fast in the mud. They held on to each other and yelled, "Mommy, Mommy, Mooooommmmyyy" until she appeared to unmoor them. She had two flattened cardboard boxes, and she laid one square out after walking the length of the other, over and over until she reached her shipwrecked sons. They hopped out of their rubber boots and slid back to the house across the cardboard.

Bruce came back to his scotch while Dougie and their father considered the possibilities of adding a hot tub to the deck.

"All right, boys. Here comes the bird." Jane set the Thanksgiving turkey down in the middle of the table, then sat and poured herself a glass of wine. "Hi Père."

Walter's dad had let himself in and was standing with his son and grandsons by the window.

"It smells wonderful, Janie," Père offered.

"I know it does. I've spent the last five and a half hours of my life with the thing."

Dougie laughed, and he and Bruce settled in at the table.

"Boys, go on, make sure you eat your fill. You both look a little pale."

"Mom, we're fine. But this all looks great."

"Well, thank you, Brucie. Here, take the Brussels sprouts. They're fresh. Take more. Dougie, you need to eat carbs. I don't care what Dom tells you. Eat."

Walter passed the sweet potatoes to his dad. "Guess who I saw today."

When nobody offered any guesses, he just went on: "I ran into Dr. Halpern in town this morning. That man always catches me when I least expect it. I was buying tubing for the irrigation system, and out he springs from behind a trowel display. Except he looked like he had seen a ghost." Walter was making himself laugh with the memory of it. I told him I was picking you two up today, and he asked after you."

"Tell Halpern to mind his own business. They're doing just fine. Without him."

"Mom, relax!" Both Dougie and Bruce chorused. Every visit home caused Bruce to feel like a child.

"Well, it's a mother's prerogative to decide what she wants for her family." Jane topped up her wine glass. "What mother needs a doctor to tell her what she should and shouldn't do with her own children? Every woman's got her intuition to tell her. What's Halpern got? A piece of paper and a string of divorces."

"Mom, don't worry about it. Halpern was just making small talk with Dad. He didn't mean anything by it."

"Like hell he didn't. He was always a vulture. He cared more about making a name for himself than about anybody's health and well-being."

Bruce was chafing under a bristling urge to ask his parents more about Dr. Halpern, but it was obviously still a thorny issue for his mom. However he didn't want to pass up the opportunity that arose now. "So. Um. Tell us again why Halpern never referred us to any specialists in Toronto?"

"When?"

"When we were born. My impression was that he didn't really do much or suggest any options with you and Dad, right?"

Bruce was looking around the table, searching for any foothold; Dougie was looking at him with his eyes screwed in confusion.

"I'm just curious why Dr. Halpern didn't really pursue—"

"There was no need. Right, Mom? We didn't have any other medical issues that needed attention."

"But why...?"

Walter cleared his throat. "We did take you two to a specialist. He said pretty much the same thing as Halpern. At the time they were concerned about the dangers of operating, about how much you two shared internally. He said that there was no guarantee that once they operated you would both make it."

"The risks just weren't worth it, Brucie. For us," Dougie said through a mouthful of potatoes.

For a long moment there was nothing but the sound of food being forked around plates and wine glasses clumsily returning to their tight spots on the table. Dougie and Bruce had been privy to as much information when they were younger, that an operation to separate wasn't medically in the cards. In the past this had been enough to satisfy the curiosity either twin had had about their early days. But it wasn't enough for Bruce anymore; these answers felt pat and didn't offer new insights. Dougie was suspicious of Bruce's choice to get into this now, when they were neck deep in training for the tournament.

"Boys, save room for dessert. Your mother made her world-class pecan pie."

Beyond the picture window, the air was lovely and crisp. Jane looked around the table into the faces of the men who were hers and took a generous gulp from her glass.

When the laundromat door flung open, there was simultaneous ringing out of Anka's name and the chiming of electronic bells. It was Diane.

"Anka, I lost my phone. I have no idea where. It sucks." Diane came around the counter to give Anka a hug.

Anka, still hugging Diane, let herself wilt a bit. "You were supposed to meet me at the bar."

"I'm so sorry. I blanked. I spent the whole night trying to retrace my steps looking for my asshole phone. Anka, I'm so sorry."

"It's okay."

"My parents send their love; they wished you had come to my grandma's for Thanksgiving."

"Yeah. I needed to get a bunch of stuff done yesterday."

"Okay."

"What? My knitting. It's practically a full-time job."

"You weirdo. Let me see this thing."

Anka pulled some pages out from under her knitting and showed Diane a sketch. "It's the rivers beneath the city, but abstract."

"I get it—a grid. And these blocks? With all these squiggly bits all over? And this big blob is the lake?"

Anka took her sketch back, feeling naked somehow. "It'll make sense in the end. I think. The only thing is that the actual waterways have been filled in or re-routed into the sewage system."

"So you'll have a map of the city's plumbing."

"It's more like remembering what used to be here before."

"How romantic. You're a romantic, Anka." Diane was twirling a strand of her hair, head tilted sweetly.

Anka became suspicious of what Diane had up her sleeve. She knew Diane was adamantly against writing any letters in response to Bruce.

"I might reverse the colours on half of it—rather than a white background, make it black, and the lines white—to better hide the dirt if it's a rug."

"Let me take you out this week to make up for my flakiness. I know someone I think you should meet."

"Ungh."

"He's cute. His name is Dylan." Diane was rooting around inside her tote. "I made us some sandwiches. Leftover turkey."

"Dylan? The guy you met online and went on a date with?"

"Listen, as soon as I met him, I knew he was the one for you. I spent the whole time singing your praises. There was more of a sibling vibe between us. So no worries. You're welcome."

Anka moved her knitting aside to make way for the picnic Diane was laying out. The foil-wrapped sandwiches, a Tupperware of pie, napkins, plastic forks.

"Why didn't you like him for yourself?"

"I found him a little pretentious, honestly. For me."

"Dude. Seriously? What the hell?"

Diane was squeezing Anka's cheeks like a granny would. "You're too cute and smart. And you can dish any pretentious bullshit right back at him. He's a hunk. Kind eyes."

Diane let go of Anka's face because they were laughing.

"What is my life?"

"I know, right? The rug's gonna to be cool. You've got a vision. I believe in you. Look, there's no obligation, so just meet him. Have some fun... You're allowed to. He's a real person."

"What's the difference between writing letters on paper or messaging online?"

"Pictures, Anka."

"You can get catfished."

"Dylan is normal and seems cool and legit. No catfish here."

"Thanks for lunch. This is amazing." Anka took out some change from the till for the vending machine. "Drinks on me."

Diane and Anka met Dylan and his friend Anthony at the same bar that Diane had dropped the ball on. She was right—Anka needed to live her life again. The world was not going to swallow her whole. Dylan was chatty and exuberant and had a lot of stories to tell. Anthony had a dry sense of humour and worked in film. They were nice. They had everyone laughing much of the time. Dylan was ambitious and didn't understand why Anka was working at the laundromat. He kept teasing her about it all night. He was a graphic designer and on top of the world. Anka was doing her best to keep up, to slip back into her old self. The drinks were making her tired. Diane suggested shots that tasted like cinnamon hearts. Anthony said that if she knew how to sew, he could talk to his buddy in props about some piece work. Anka said she didn't. Dylan launched into an epic story about people that Anka and Diane didn't know. At the end of the night, Dylan asked for Anka's number. She suggested he give her his before getting into a cab. Anka wanted to lean back, close her eyes, and be driven around in the backseat of a car forever, but instead she struggled to keep her eyes open, barely answering the cabbie's sparse questions. She remembered this was what it was like to have fun.

October 13, 2012

Dear Anka,

I'm sorry if my last letter was a bit overwrought or if it upset you in any way. That wasn't my intention at all. I hope that all's well.

For some time now I've been interested (Dougie would say "obsessed") with something called the Golden Globe Race. Have you ever heard of it? (I'm going to assume here that you would say "no.") It was 1968 in London. The Sunday Times newspaper held a race to see who could sail around the globe—solo and uninterrupted. Can you imagine that? To be alone on a ship circling the earth itself? It knocks the wind right out of me every time I think about it. This kind of non-stop voyage had never been undertaken before, and so the race was on to make a go of it alone without stopping even once.

The things that befell many of the sailors were downright eerie, but I won't get into another sad letter now! But one French sailor, M—he was something else. He was nearly done the voyage, just weeks away from getting home after battling stormy seas and all that isolation. And you know what he did? M, mere inches away on the map from his wife and children, turned his boat around and decided to circle the world again. He turned his boat around! He made it halfway around the globe again until he finally came to land in Tahiti.

At any rate, Anka, I just wanted to share this with someone who might revel in it as much as I do. If you want me to cease and desist with the letters and strange tales, then simply mail this letter back to me. You have my gentlemanly promise that I will never bother you again, and I only wish you (and your knitting) well. I've enclosed a self-addressed, stamped envelope.

Yours at sea,
Bruce Reuben

Bruce tucked this letter into an envelope he had taken from the storage cabinet at work. Lana was hovering over Dougie's shoulder, and they were using Bruce's computer to look up restaurant menus for the wedding. Bruce was writing his own address onto another envelope, bracing himself for the moment when he would be faced with it again, when sometime in the future his knotty handwriting would reappear in his own mailbox, mocking him. He couldn't be sure that Anka didn't have a boyfriend or that she hadn't figured out who he and his brother were. Maybe she had only been humouring him, taking pity on a pathetic little puppy dog. She probably had a string of charming, handsome men vying for her attention. Self-assured but soft-spoken men who could play the electric guitar. Men with assorted high-quality leather goods who owned beach-front property. He licked the sour back of a stamp and hoped against hope that Anka had just been very, very busy knitting the end of the summer away.

The dawn was just starting to brighten the edges of Bruce and Dougie's window in an easy, slow way that would belie the sweeping winds predicted to come in before noon.

Bruce was having a dream that he was a bear, a tawny-coloured bear sliding headfirst down a steep slope. His thoughts and sensations and fears as he hurtled down the vertical descent were his own, but he knew that he was a Syrian brown bear living in Egypt. He opened his eyes and realized that for the first time in a long while, he was up before Dougie. He closed his eyes again and remembered the bear: the feeling of fur edging off a finite boundary around his body. Four legs, his neck, his head, his ears. Also the feeling of dirt and grit and sand against his belly as he slid down, picking up more and more speed. So strange. Strange, too, that Dougie was still asleep and not hustling to go running.

"Dougie?"

Nothing.

"Dougie. Are we running today?"

Bruce kicked the sheet off his outside leg and shifted to lean over Dougie. He was so quiet, his breathing barely perceptible, his forehead cool. Bruce was rough in trying to jostle Dougie's outer shoulder, but he was cradling his brother's cheek with the hand of his smaller limb. He could feel his stubble, the slackness of his jaw. He yanked them both up to seated, and Dougie's head lolled back and then swung out to the left. Bruce was yelling his brother's name and reaching for his phone to dial 911.

Dougie wheezed and started coughing, eyelids fluttering open.

Dougie wouldn't let Bruce call an ambulance. He convinced his brother that he was overreacting, that he was just tired. Dougie claimed that he hadn't slept well and had been up half the night. And so they went in to work at Ogilvie's, Bruce at a loss as to how to get Dougie to a doctor.

At Bruce's desk Dougie had his head lowered, snoozing while Bruce reviewed changes to the income tax legislation affecting the next filing period. Dougie refused to admit that something was going on with his health, and so he adamantly refused to mention either of the blackouts to their parents or Dom, let alone a doctor. He self-prescribed a routine of extra-strength ibuprofen at regular intervals. Bruce angled his monitor away from Dougie and opened a new tab. He spent some time typing combinations of the words *concussion*, *conjoined*, *ambush attack*, *headaches*, *fainting*, *unconsciousness*, *migraines*, *vomiting*, *boxing*, *causes of*. After scanning several articles fruitlessly, he checked to make sure Dougie was properly sleeping and not unconscious. When he was sure that Dougie seemed comfortable enough and asleep enough, he decided to indulge in one last search now that he had the opportunity. He googled Dr. Jonah Halpern and scrolled halfway down the first page, then clicked on a link. He didn't know exactly what he was looking for, but he felt certain he would know it when he saw it. He felt very aware of every small noise around him. His heart was beating fast, and he tried to calm himself quickly, to focus on steady, deliberate exhalations. His skin prickled. Bruce felt nauseous; he didn't know whether it was from nerves, stress, fear, anxiety, or betrayal. He scrawled a phone number on a Post-it note. There was a photo of Dr. Halpern in his lab coat and stethoscope, unsmiling, holding a clipboard. Bruce went back to Google. The cursor blinked patiently in the search box, waiting until he was ready to type again. *Blink. Blink. Blink.*

Lana was on the phone making a dentist appointment. The radio was off this morning. It was quiet out on the street. *Blink. Blink.* Bruce stopped fiddling with his pen and raised his clammy right hand to type. There was a kind of rush, that queasy but also thrilling edge as his hand pecked out the letters: *p-a-r-a-p-a-g-u-s c-o-n-j-. Blink. Blink.* He was doing something he didn't feel allowed to do. He felt like a kid with a contraband substance. He quickly closed the tab.

His armpits were uncomfortably damp.

He opened a new tab.

Blink. Blink.

S-e-p-a-r-a-t-i-n-g

Blink.

p-a-r-a-p-a-g-u-s t-w-i-n-s

Blink. Blink.

What was he even thinking? Seriously.

He held down the backspace key before closing the tab.

He cleared his throat. "Lana, sorry to bother you."

"What's that?"

"Could I ask you to grab me a glass of water? I don't want to disturb Doug, but my throat's really dry."

"No problem. You do look a little flushed. Here you go."

Lana came over with a paper cone of water from the water cooler, careful not to squeeze it during the handover. Something about Bruce made her stop for a second. She rested her hand on his shoulder. "Are you sure you're okay? Do you need anything else?"

"It's fine. Maybe I've just picked up a bug."

"You two really need to take care of yourselves. Don't let yourselves get too run down."

Bruce read a paragraph entitled "The Acquisition, Use, and Disposal of Depreciable Property" without understanding a word of it. He lowered his head to his chest and slowed his breath to match Dougie's until he felt centred. Anchored.

At the top of the stairs leading down to the twins' basement suite, Walter had staked an old tin mailbox he had unearthed in his barn. He had wanted to save the twins some grief by not having to climb a whole set of extra stairs up the porch of the main entrance and then back down, and then down once more to their apartment. However what happened was that the mailman put everyone's mail in the box marked BSMT to similarly avoid an extra round of stairs on his route. Dougie flapped the maw open while Bruce shuffled for the right key. Bruce stopped to watch Dougie examine the contents. A month had gone by since Bruce had dropped his last letter off to Anka. Every night when they got home, it was with both dread and a barely contained excitement that Bruce peered into the box. He was immensely relieved with every day that passed without his self-addressed letter returned to the box. But still. There was nothing. Radio silence.

"It's all for upstairs. Bills. Oh, let's keep this one—it's a flyer that gets you twenty percent off a dine-in meal at Thai Swan, and it comes with one free appetizer."

Dougie happened to notice Bruce's expression slacken for a second. Bruce felt dejected but tried to push it aside quickly. Dougie shifted so he could lead them down the concrete steps to their door.

"Don't worry about it too much. Let's get this Thai food tonight. You gotta let her go, get your mind on other things. We'll watch a movie, but nothing too depressing, okay? What about a documentary? Your favourite."

Bruce wanly nodded. "Yeah. Right, it doesn't really matter. Thanks, though."

When the twins were bunking down at the end of the night, Bruce kept his light on for a little while.

"Dougie, are you into anyone?"

"Like a crush?"

"Like Nikki?"

"Ha! Shit. She's a sweetheart. She'd never go for it. I wonder what the deal is with the fiancé."

"Do you ever think about the future? What our life is going to be like years and years down the road?"

"Honestly I can only see what's right in front of me. Winning the Golden Gloves. I can only see as far as the next match and what we need to do to get there. Even thinking about us living our days out as the provincial champs is a stretch."

"Do you honestly think we have a chance? Age-wise, aren't we at the end of this thing?"

"It's not about having a chance. I know that the heavyweight title already belongs to us. It's laying there for us, right there in the ring, waiting for us to go scoop it up."

"Oh really? Even with what's been going on with you?"

"What do you mean? Going on with me—what?"

"The passing out? The headaches? The nausea?"

"It's just migraines. I've always gotten them. You know that."

"Are you fucking kidding me? You've always just passed out in the middle of doing shit?"

"Okay, easy. That was once when we drank too much."

"What headaches have you always gotten?"

"From the weather—you know the humidity kills me."

"Are you fucking kidding me? Dougie. Stop pretending that I haven't spent my whole life right fucking here. You need to talk to a fucking doctor. Fuck. Talk to Dom at least."

"What are you yelling for? Relax, Bruce. You're getting all worked up. Shit."

Bruce threw his arm over his eyes to black out the room. He wanted to yank himself off the bed and out of the room and out of the basement and out into the night. A bear beholden to none.

"C'mon, Bruce. Don't be like that. You want to know how I really feel about Nikki? I joke around with her all the time. I get that she's engaged, but I think she's incredible. I'll settle for being any kind of friend to her. She's tough, and she gets it. She's a lot like us, Bruce. She's got drive. She's not going to be at Everest forever."

"'Night, Dougie."

Bruce lay awake, his eyes pressed shut beneath the weight of his forearm. He knew deep down that Dougie wasn't feeling right, no matter how his brother tried to play it off. Should they even be boxing? Was it irresponsible for Bruce to let Dougie keep getting into the ring? These headaches had started after that Patrice match, had gotten more frequent anyway. He really should talk to someone about this. What if something serious was happening to Dougie's brain? How could he witness these maybe serious, but possibly minor, changes in his brother and just do nothing? But what if he was overreacting?

What if he refused to fight in the tournament unless Dougie paid a visit to Dr. Halpern, both for Dougie's health but also to have a conversation about the possibility of separation? Bruce wondered why it had taken him so long to realize he had had this leverage the whole time. He didn't sleep. This shot felt low. Below the belt.

ANKA RAMRATAN
NOVEMBER 2012

ANKA WAS TAKING CARE of the day's laundry-service orders, heaving wet clothes out of one of the washing machines. The TV was playing a cooking show, onions screaming for dear life in a wok. She liked being here during the day when it was basically dead, but she hated that it was always so cold.

An elderly man came in, took off his cap, smoothed the hair over his crown, and took a look around. He didn't have anything to wash with him, but Anka was rarely surprised by anything that happened at the laundromat. This had turned out to be a place where people invariably brought their secrets. When doing laundry one could choose to face themselves deeply, to clean the grime and wear that was evidence of the particular life they were living. Anka had very specific theories about the type of person who paid someone else minimum wage to wash and dry and meticulously fold their intimate garments and linens.

Unwrapping his scarf, the elderly man grabbed one of the fashion magazines that were up at the front counter. "I'm not going to buy it, but is it okay if I just glance through it?"

"Whatever. Sure."

"I like to see what comes down the runway every so often—as a strictly professional interest... Well, a former profession, but still a current interest, you could say. Over the decades you see that there isn't anything terribly new, but the clothes you see around you nowadays"—he gestured toward the sidewalk beyond the wall of windows—"are so coarse and shabby. There's no spirit in the stitches."

"I can see what you mean."

"I just needed to take a quick break from home. My grandsons are wonderful, but God help me—they're going to kill me."

"How do you think they'd do it?"

"Of course I originally—unimaginatively—assumed it'd be a scare-induced heart attack. But they're light years more sophisticated than that. If they weren't so lazy, I'd say poison. But they'd never have the will to mete it out slowly over a prolonged period of time."

"Maybe it'll be a banana peel left on the stairs."

"That's it exactly. Only the younger one will think to also loosen the screws on the banister railing."

As he took a seat, Anka noticed that the man was wearing a well-fitted wool coat and sharply creased pants. A cashmere scarf. The only other patron was a middle-aged man with tangled blond hair, wearing wire-frame glasses and dirty jeans. He was standing with his arms crossed over his unzipped puffy green jacket. Standing directly in front of his dryer, watching its every rotation.

Behind the cash register, Anka flipped on the electric kettle and produced two lumpy but functional mugs her mother had made long ago in a weekend pottery class. "Let me make you something warm."

Since the beginning of this year alone, the Reuben Beast had competed in thirteen matches, when they generally would have averaged about ten. They stood balanced between six wins and seven losses. They approached the gym, which was a converted autobody shop. The doorway was flanked by statues of oversized boxing gloves. Seeing the statues every time they approached the gym gave Dougie the same feeling he had had when he was a kid reading his first boxing magazine. He opened the gym door and stepped into a different universe.

"The trick is to keep moving forward. You guys are no underdogs here, but we're still running uphill so we gotta pick up speed." Dom quickly swiped one palm across the plane of the other to indicate speed. "All right, the tournament starts in fourteen days. Right now your biggest competition is twenty-four-year-old Hugo Farroz. Patrice is also competing, but who gives a shit about that weasel?"

Dougie and Bruce had just walked up the stairs and into the gym. They still had their jacket on, and Dom was still going. "Farroz, though, man. He's sharp. Apparently he rarely says a word outside of the ring, but when that bell sounds, phew, he's a goddamned poet. Fast? Man, he's fast. Graceful, like. He's lean but packs a powerhouse punch. And tall. He's built more like a ballet dancer than a boxer, but watch out! Those fists'll rain hellfire down on you."

Dom was miming the jabs and dreamily swaying his hips like a ballroom dancer.

"Jesus, Dom. Whose side are you on here?"

"C'mon, Dougie. I'm telling you all this because it's my responsibility to make sure you two are as prepared as humanly possible. I couldn't live with myself if I didn't give it to you guys straight. He's in a showcase match tonight in Mississauga so we've gotta leave now."

A few months back, Bruce had read a small feature about Farroz in one of the daily commuter papers. Bruce liked the look of him: clean-cut, big searching eyes, pock-marked cheeks. The reporter made a crack about boxing helping the young man with the ladies, and the response he'd received read something along the lines of:

> *Every opponent I've been pitted against has been a mirror held up for me to face myself. Boxing has taught me how to focus my mind. With a focused mind, you can see what people are thinking before they even know they're thinking it. You know exactly what to do to protect yourself. Or when to make an offensive strike. The irony is that boxing in the ring has kept me from getting into any fights in the neighbourhood.*

His mother was widowed and had raised her two kids alone—him and a younger sister—and she was most proud of the fact that he had graduated high school at the top of his class and had done so much for their community, volunteering with kids and seniors. Bruce had no real desire to take the title of Golden Gloves champion from a good guy like Hugo Farroz.

By the time they got to the boxing club in Mississauga, the room was packed, more so than for any bout they'd fought. It was clear that Farroz was beloved; he entered the ring to a hearty welcome from the crowd, cheers rising as he lifted a glove in acknowledgement. The spectators were not solely boxing enthusiasts. There in the crowd, Bruce saw a woman he immediately took for Farroz's mother—because of the undeniable resemblance—clutching the hands of her sisters, more than likely, on either side of her, all three already on the verge of tears; a team of middle-school boys wearing baseball tees emblazoned with Farroz's face under felted letters spelling out *Mavericks*; and a larger-than-usual percentage of single women of every age. Meanwhile the other boxer's name barely made a ripple in the crowd when he was introduced. The match was fast, and Farroz was in top form. It took Bruce until the end of the first round to recognize that he was thoroughly enjoying it, mesmerized along with the adoring crowd.

Dougie was similarly entranced but taking careful note of how to best Farroz when their time came. He was giddy; he knew that if they could beat a fighter of Farroz's calibre, the Reuben Beast would prove themselves to be the absolute best. Dougie never took his eyes off Farroz. When the boxers went back to their corners at the end of the second round, Dougie watched as Farroz's trainer got right in close to the boxer's face, yelling and pointing at the twins. And then he spat in disgust. Dougie raised his middle finger in the coach's direction. He noticed that Farroz had sat with his eyes closed the whole time, totally Zen, while his coach had stormed around him, red-faced and vile.

Dougie and Bruce were coming back from a morning run. The sight of their three legs galloping up the sidewalk caused a man to pause at his car door, mid-unlock. He was trying to take in as much detail as he could in order to impress his jaded receptionist later. Summer had relented, and by now the trees were dropping their leaves, suddenly exposing globular nests high above in the branches. As they came up the walk, one of the young professional upstairs tenants was coming down the steps on her way to work.

"Oh, hey, guys. Sorry, one of us has been meaning to drop something down for you for, like, ages. Hold on."

She clacked up the stairs and bungled around with the key for a bit before dashing inside. She left the door open behind her, and a calico cat tore out and trotted down the street. Dougie was checking his pulse. Bruce remembered they were out of coffee.

Their neighbour finally re-emerged, wearing a different coat and her hair up. "Sorry I took so long. My outfit sucked; I had to change. Here you go." She thrust her hand out to the twin closest to her. "We must've grabbed it by mistake."

"Thanks. Enjoy your day," Dougie offered. He had one hand squeezing his temple again. He didn't understand where this headache was coming from, but he needed to get inside before he threw up on his neighbour's shoes.

Bruce was totally preoccupied with a postcard. "Oh. My."

It was exquisite. On the back was written: *For Bruce Reuben*. On its face was an artist's etching of a nighttime schooner gliding alongside a towering, crystal iceberg. In the water the boat's quiet, silver reflection shimmered icily.

November 17, 2012

Dear Anka,

I sincerely apologize if you've been waiting a long time for a response. I just received your postcard this morning (don't ask). It's stunning and marvellous—thank you!

M was of the mind that to do anything properly, you had to become one with the very action or object itself. When he was growing up in Vietnam, he used to spend his summers in a small village where an old man taught him how to repair boats. The best way to make the strongest, most lasting vessel was to actually become the crack in the wood. To see with the wooden plank's eyes where the water would seep in, to see with the water's eyes where it could ingratiate itself. I'm going to try to do this today. I am going to become the numbers on a spreadsheet. I'm going to become the almonds that I eat this afternoon. I will become my sentinel mailbox waiting against the wind for another lovely surprise. I am the sun that shines down today.

See me there sailing above,
Bruce

PS. How rude of me... How have you been? How is the knitting coming along? Are you a person who likes the changing seasons, or do you forever miss the summer? I hope you're doing really well, Priyanka.

Bruce wondered when the timing would be right to broach the subject of a meeting with Anka. He wasn't ready today. It may have been selfish on his part, but he was so thoroughly enjoying just simply, slowly, going back and forth with the letters. It was him alone coming up to the surface of the page. Not yet the clunkiness of him and Dougie, tethered. He was also nervous that these careful exchanges would vanish altogether if Anka knew the truth about his life. From where he stood, he had no idea how he could possibly proceed, but he was certain that he didn't want to risk this new thing that had begun. He flipped the postcard over and traced the lines of Anka's curlicue handwriting spelling out his name.

Dougie wanted to buy new shoes for running outside in the winter, and Bruce thought they may as well buy some sponges at the dollar store, so that afternoon was set aside to hit the mall. They rode the escalator up from the entrance and stepped into the organized chaos. The twins added themselves to be counted amongst the herds of teenaged boys in sagging pants, toddlers stubbornly struggling to push their own empty strollers, care workers navigating frowning seniors in wheelchairs, and everyone else in line for coffee and a crueller at the donut shop's walk-up counter.

"Wanna grab a bite first?"

Stepping across the threshold, Dougie had become inspired by the spirit of spending time and money.

"Sure," replied Bruce, who was similarly willing to walk the circuit of long, interconnected hallways.

"We shouldn't eat any junk this close to the match though. Salad bar or sushi—your call, brother."

Settling on sushi for lunch, Bruce and Dougie loaded up their plastic orange tray with the mall's finest sashimi and miso soup and set it down at an available table.

"Maybe we should start thinking about Christmas gifts," offered Bruce helpfully.

"Let's decide that after we buy what we came for."

It didn't take long before the novelty of the mall crumbled into the drudgery of actually shopping. Before the twins finished their lunch, they were approached by an elderly man wearing suspenders and a fedora, his shirt sleeves rolled to the elbow.

"Excuse me, gentlemen. I don't mean to intrude on your meal, but I couldn't help but notice you, and I wanted to introduce myself. My name is Kristof Verhoeven." He offered his hand to Bruce, which connected solidly in a handshake;

Dougie simultaneously poised his left hand for Verhoeven to take in a type of mid-air arm wrestle.

"I am a tailor by trade, and I noticed you two have an ingenious type of coat."

The jacket they had been wearing was an amalgamation of two pea coats their mother had fused together with a Frankenstein seam down the back and extended panels in the front for the buttons.

"Yes, hello," Bruce cut in, unsure of exactly what was transpiring.

"Gentlemen, it's just that I would be honoured if you would consider allowing me to make a suit for you. Tailored precisely to serve your specific needs."

"A suit? What kind of suit?"

"The formal kind. Every man needs to have one—ideally three—good suits at the ready in his closet. You know, for job interviews, funerals, weddings, baptisms, court appearances, whatever it is—I really don't judge. But regardless of the occasion or venue, a fine suit that fits like a second skin is crucial to success. Consider it a good luck charm of sorts. To feel good in an impeccably crafted garment, made to measure, is to be able to stand tall. And well, that's everything right there, isn't it? It's the most, and yet the very least, any of us can do for ourselves in this life."

"I don't think we can afford anything like that," Bruce demurred.

"Mr. Verhoeven, it's a pleasure to meet you. My name is Douglas Reuben, and this is my brother, Bruce. And I have to tell you, what's impeccable, right here, is your timing."

Bruce was still unsure of what they were about to get themselves into when Dougie turned to him. "Lana's wedding. This is perfect."

Dom wasn't about to hold anything back in training. "Sons, if you think you're leaving here tonight with the desire or the energy to grab a bite, hell, to even take your shoes off before bed, you've got another thing coming. Because this afternoon you're both going to leave every ounce of yourselves in this gym. And then some."

Bruce could only imagine the pontificating that Dom's wife had to endure any time talk came up of doing a bit of yard work, repainting a bathroom, or changing a light bulb. Dougie felt he needed this. He needed to channel the intensity of his migraines and work it out of his body. Physical exertion was the only antidote to anything that had ever ailed him.

"Start with the heavy bag. Don't stop until I tell you to."

Dom went back into his office and shut the door.

"All right, you heard the man." Dougie was windmilling his left arm back to loosen up.

Dom emerged half an hour later to find Bruce and Dougie diligently drenched and battering away at their combinations. "Sorry, boys. Lost track of time there. Oh, wait a minute, who am I kidding? It's not as if we're fighting for a title here. Look alive, Bruce."

Dom went back to his office and shut the door. Farroz's trainer had left an unwelcome message on his voice mail yesterday. He had gotten wind that the Reuben Beast would be competing in the Golden Gloves, and he had called to inform Dom that he was a washed-up hack and that the twins were an affront to the men who worked hard to earn their place in a world where nothing was handed out freely. Dom didn't listen to the whole message, but there was something about the twins turning the boxing ring into a circus, and that the trainer would make sure that Farroz made a devastating example of them if they managed to con their way into the finals. And then something about a petition to get them kicked out of the league. Something. Whatever. This wasn't the first call like this that Dom had received over the years. He'd never met Farroz's trainer but had been eyeing him the whole time they were at that showcase match in Mississauga. He noticed that when the trainer spotted Dougie and Bruce in the crowd, he had spat, grabbed Farroz's face with both hands, and pulled him close to emphasize something. Dom had also seen Farroz swat his trainer away in annoyance.

Cigar smoke filled the six hundred square feet of Dom's office as he sat behind his desk, his eyes never coming off the second hand of his watch.

Bruce had fallen into the rhythm in time with Dougie, pivoting the leg, the arm like a piston. For the last thirty minutes, his mind had stopped all its chatter for once and he had succumbed to his body's lead. The fluorescent bulb crackled like a bug zapper, causing a sickly, flickering haze in the gym.

After their training Bruce scrambled to dredge up a bit of courage before he missed his chance to talk to Dom. "Wait. Before you go..."

Dougie perked up at his brother's urgency between breaths. He was hopeful that Bruce wanted some last-minute pointers since his balance and timing were still shit, but lately he couldn't be sure what was going to come out of his mouth.

Dom yelled at a young boxer sparring in the ring while he waited for Bruce to catch his breath.

"Dom, wait. I need to tell you something. I'm worried about Dougie."

Furious that he was being ratted out, Dougie reared up. "Dom, I'm fine. I just drank too much after the Patrice match."

Bruce pushed through, though he suddenly felt that his ears and cheeks were flushed, his voice shaky. "Dom, he passed out—we can agree that's not normal, right? Especially for a boxer, getting bashed up all the time?"

Dom studied Dougie's face. "How many fingers am I holding up?"

"Three."

"Any persistent headaches?"

"Nope."

"The doctor already signed off on your pre-bout medical forms?" Dom looked back and forth at the two boxers for confirmation.

"Yeah, no problems."

"Stop drinking. If anything changes, go see the doctor again."

Dougie dragged Bruce out of the gym and to the streetcar stop. "What the fuck was that, Bruce?"

"I'm worried about you."

"I feel fine. Haven't I been fine for the last month? I haven't taken one sick day off work or missed a day of practice."

Bruce had to admit that was technically true. "Yeah, but do you think you would've passed the medical last week if you hadn't withheld some pertinent details on your form? Maybe we should just go see the doctor. Like, separate from the Golden Gloves."

They got to the stop just as a streetcar was opening its doors.

"I didn't lie on my form. I asked myself the same thing for every question on there: *Has this negatively impacted my skills?* And every answer was a no."

November 19, 2012

Dear Bruce,

I like M's theory of getting inside the heart of things. They should teach kids how to do that in school.

Have you lived in this neighbourhood for a long time? I imagine that when I'm in line for coffee up the road, I've just missed you by a hair. Or that we've unknowingly waited at a crosswalk together. Or that you've come in to the laundromat and I was none the wiser.

I should knit you a bright orange toque to wear.

Anka

It was three o'clock in the afternoon when Anka dropped the letter off at 44 Hudd Street, BSMT. She let herself consider the possibility of going to the door. She reasoned with herself that it was unlikely that anyone would be home in the middle of the day, particularly a bookkeeper. At her feet in the mud was a baby leaf burning gold with its own fire. She pried the mailbox open, slid her envelope in, and bent to pocket the leaf. She would be early for her shift but decided to head to work anyway.

Anka decided to mop the floor of the laundromat to give herself something to do. A bright, sharp day exploded through the windows. As she vigorously mopped, a knock on the glass snapped her attention up. It was the elderly man she had made tea for. They waved at one another. When he came inside, he wiped his boots on the mat before he made his way over to Anka.

"Hi there. It's nice to see you. Unfortunately no new magazines have come in."

"Ahh, no matter. I thought I'd take my chances and see if you were working today. This may sound strange, but I've got a small favour to ask."

Anka twisted the dirty water out of the mop and rolled the bucket into a corner. "Shoot."

"First off, where have my manners been? My name is Kristof Verhoeven. I am a tailor."

"I'm Priyanka—Anka. It's a pleasure."

"Anka, lovely. Perhaps you remember from the last time I was in here that I've got two...spirited grandsons. Yes, well, I've recently taken on a tailoring job, and I'm going to need someone to watch them while I'm working on this project. I haven't begun yet, but I need a plan in place in order to allay my daughter's impending frenzy. She won't be happy if I'm preoccupied for large chunks of time while her sons are terrorizing the neighbourhood. I will pay you, of course."

"I'd be happy to help you out, Mr. Verhoeven. When do you need me?"

"Well I'll work around your schedule. Tomorrow afternoon the gentlemen are coming to be measured, and then I'll buy my materials right away once Mimi—my daughter—gets home. Ideally we can start the day after, if you are able."

"Perfect. That should give me enough time to gather ammunition and get all my vaccines."

"I suggest you notify your next of kin of your whereabouts. Let someone know what time to expect you home."

"How old are your grandsons?"

"Damian is eleven, and Devon is nine. We're just over on Preston, at 6781."

"I can come that day at noon. I'll stay as long as you need."

"Anka, you're an angel. You're helping an old, tired acorn to sprout. Believe me."

Anka's smile did the work that the frozen sun had obstinately refused to do, finally warming the laundromat.

KRISTOF VERHOEVEN
NOVEMBER 2012

KRISTOF VERHOEVEN SAT ON THE EDGE of the double bed in his daughter's guest bedroom. He raked his bare feet back and forth mindlessly, enjoying the plush of the rug beneath them. He was old now. He had ferocious old feet, the feet of alligators or dinosaurs. Verhoeven had been a tailor in Montreal for more than fifty years. He was retired now apparently. He was retired, and nearly a year ago Mimi had sent him a one way VIA ticket to Toronto. She had said it would be perfect. Now that she was a single mother, he could watch the kids after school. And they, in turn, would keep him occupied and young. Mimi had thought of everything.

Verhoeven had come into his room for his tape measure and had somehow gotten distracted. This room with none of his own furniture and its palette of taupe and dusty rose distracted him; nearly every time he set foot in it, some bland feature—the small sliding window, the bulk of the dresser, the wicker chair in the corner—sent him somewhere else. As a boy his family had had a neighbour who everyone called Rosetti. Rosetti ran his backyard garden like a general, and year after year he was rewarded with an unrelenting bounty. Rosetti had a lemon tree planted in the sunniest corner of the lot. He had planted it the same morning that his wife had given birth to a stillborn child in 1919. The two events were unrelated. The lemon tree died when Rosetti died. Verhoeven was just starting out as an apprentice when it happened. He did not consider the lemon tree to be consequential when his mother delivered the news that morning. He was practising a blind hem on a scrap of gabardine. She had laid breakfast out for him and told him that the lemon tree was diseased, suddenly covered in fungus. It had only been two weeks since Rosetti had passed. She crossed herself.

Verhoeven's peripheral vision was filled with the red gingham print of his mother's dress as she hovered about him. He kept snaking the needle through the fabric and offered up a kind of a "Hmmm. Mmm. Unnghhhmmm" that trailed off behind her.

But his mind's eye was wilfully deceiving him here in the guest bedroom. In fact he could not remember his mother having a red dress like that. For his entire life, he had known her to be much more dour and navy. An impossible red gingham print and a lemon tree unbelievably surviving all those Montreal winters.

The truth is Verhoeven's business had trickled away. His eyes were still sharp, his hands still steady, his suppliers all still living. But how many men now wanted a handmade suit to mark an occasion? He couldn't keep pace with blue jeans and sweatshirts with machine-embroidered logos. But as luck would have it, he'd procured himself a new job. Mimi didn't like it—he could tell when she opened the door to them standing on the porch, exaggerating the need to tightly wrap her sweater around herself. The men couldn't walk straight through the front door; they had to turn not quite ninety degrees and sidestep their way with all three legs over the threshold into his daughter's home. Verhoeven knew that Mimi protracted an exasperated huff for his benefit alone when she closed the door behind the men. He always chose to make everything so difficult. To be so difficult and stubborn. Unable to just take it easy and watch the kids. Watch TV and watch the kids. That's all Verhoeven was supposed to do.

Well too bad. Once the scarves and shoes and coat had been shed, he had ushered the men into the front room, brushing past Mimi, and told them to stand in the middle if they wouldn't mind pushing the coffee table to one side for him. And then Verhoeven had realized his tape measure was still upstairs.

Verhoeven heard Mimi calling up the stairs for him now. He knew she would be standing with one foot on the bottom stair, both hands on the railing, neck craning up to the ceiling. She called for him the same way she called after the boys.

Verhoeven had seen the twins at the mall. He had seen the way some people gave them a wide berth, some looked away, and some did not. He saw that the men were nothing more than men. They talked, they ordered food in the food court, they smiled, and they drank bottled water. He had seen how they had to manipulate separate items of clothing in a sort of ramshackle patchwork to cover their bodies. He watched them for some time while he drank his paper cup of coffee before he approached them, Mimi's address carefully penned onto the margin of a newspaper page. He didn't know if they would be open to his proposal, but he just had to ask; he couldn't let himself leave that day without at least making an attempt. To be able to sew something again, to craft a beautiful suit for two men joined at the waist. He itched with the challenge of it, the technicality required. The promise. It could be like magic.

NOVEMBER 2012

WHEN VERHOEVEN HAD INTRODUCED HIMSELF at the mall, Dougie had reached for the narrow rectangle of paper that the man had offered with his name, phone number, and address. Dougie had been eager to get started. And so the twins now found themselves in the living room at 6781 Preston, waiting for the tailor to return with his tape measure.

"What if we can't afford this?" Bruce knew what their budget was.

"We'll be okay. We definitely need something to wear to Lana and Gary's wedding. I mean Mom's outfits are great, but c'mon. Let's splurge. We're moving up in the world; we gotta dress the part."

"Yeah, that last pair of pants where my half was corduroy and yours was denim was—"

Verhoeven returned, whistling. "Gentlemen, stretch your arms out for me."

The tailor then went through the process of taking measurements: around the neck, around the chest at the widest part, across the shoulders, outside shoulder to wrist with the arm at ninety degrees, inside shoulder to wrist, natural waist, high hip, low hip, waist to knee, inseam, around all the thighs, around all the calves. "It helps if you can tell me a bit about how you get about in your day-to-day activities."

"We're pretty in sync, left and right. Mostly," Dougie offered. He shook his head and shot Bruce a stern look, which Bruce didn't see.

Verhoeven took one twin's full measurements top to bottom before moving on to the other, and when he measured the second twin, he re-took all of their shared measurements, in effect considering the shared leg from each of their perspectives. It was a small detail, but he took Bruce and Dougie each on their own terms.

"Our non-dominant arms are always out of the way, so we share all of our responsibilities." Bruce breathed out the trepidation he had been feeling about spending the money on a bespoke suit. As Verhoeven stood to his side, the tape measure snug around his chest, he instantly felt like the tailor would make a good doctor.

"Yes, yes. It's those arms, and the shoulders—smaller here. My thought in terms of the blazer design is to create something structured and yet not restrictive. To accommodate those arms, such that they aren't just hidden under the fabric. That would be lazy. The trousers will actually be a cinch to whip up. Your shirts will be two separate garments, but with a minor adjustment so no skin is left exposed."

"Excellent, excellent. Can we also discuss your fee?" Dougie was feeling a bit like a celebrity, indulged and important.

"Well to be perfectly honest, I will only accept money to cover the materials. My labour is pro bono."

"But why? Isn't this going to be an enormous amount of work for you? In such a short time?"

"You see, Bruce, it may be hard to understand, but I'm at a point in my life when I need to create one last piece—nothing frivolous, but rather something meaningful, beautiful, masterful."

"Please let us do something for you in exchange, if you won't accept payment," Bruce offered.

Verhoeven shooed him off. "We'll worry about all that later."

He folded the yellow notepaper with the twins' measurements into his pocket. "There's just one last thing. Close your eyes and picture yourself on the day you intend to wear this suit. Feel how it feels. Where are you? Who else is there? How do you see yourself in your best version of this? Got it? All right. Follow me into the kitchen. I'll make us some coffee, and you're going to write down exactly what you're envisioning. Don't leave anything out, even if it seems odd or embarrassing. Describe the smell of the room, the time of day—anything. Everything. Those uncensored thoughts are the nuggets that lead to the best creative solutions and innovations."

Verhoeven clapped his hands and began whistling an Ennio Morricone theme.

The twins finished their cups of coffee and each had a refill; Verhoeven assembled a plate of arrowroot cookies and a cluster of seedless red grapes.

When they left he went up to his room to sit on the edge of the bed and read the assignments, scrawled on pages torn from a legal pad, that Dougie and Bruce had taken the time to complete. Downstairs Damian and Devon barged through the front door, panting, wearing dollar-store gorilla masks, and wielding nearly empty Super Soaker water guns.

KRISTOF VERHOEVEN
FEBRUARY 1992

WHEN KRISTOF VERHOEVEN HAD BECOME A WIDOWER, Mimi had been twenty-one years old. She had been living in the dorms on campus but announced that she would be moving back home. He didn't want her life to be put on hold; he didn't want her to feel burdened with the mistaken responsibility of having to parent him through his grief. She insisted however, so he gave her the bigger bedroom, which he and his wife had shared for decades, and moved himself and his sewing machine into the spare room. He needed a more contained, confined, anonymous space. His wife's warmth still emanated from all of her effects, but he suspected that this was precisely what Mimi needed. She rearranged, put posters up, and eventually changed the blinds, but for years she kept the collection atop her mother's dresser intact. The silver hairbrush and mirror set, old perfume bottles, a pair of diamond earrings. A black-and-white photo of a young man on a horse.

Verhoeven spent all of his time sewing and having one-sided conversations with his wife. He asked her how she thought Mimi was really holding up; he explained how to alter a blouse if the shoulder seams drooped too low; he asked her where he should send Mimi to get better cuts of meat. He asked his wife if she had been happy with her life and their life together.

He got his answers through his sewing. Bunched and knotted bobbin threads clearly expressed the extent to which Mimi was frustrated and holding onto something too tightly; they just didn't tell him what. Scissors slicing silk into perfectly frosted ribbons assured him that if she had had to choose again, his Helen wouldn't have chosen any other path. The pristine silence that was exposed every time his sewing machine stopped taunted him with the cruel fact that Helen was not busy in the other room.

Verhoeven sewed with a fury in those few years until one night when the motor quit on him. No amount of stomping on the pedal, flicking the switch, or tweaking the plug could rouse it.

Fine. You win. I'll take a rest now.

An entire month went by before Verhoeven dragged himself from his bed and took his machine in for repair.

NOVEMBER 2012

SNOW WAS FALLING FROM AN OVERCAST SKY in the way children understand snow to be: big, lacy, riotous flakes. The twins had walked over to Everest for Dougie's afternoon shift and gone down to the grocery's basement lunchroom. Dougie slipped his timecard into the machine to punch in. The twins threaded their arms through their reflective vest. When Dougie had first been hired, he had routinely made jokes about being able to moonlight as a school crossing guard.

Nikki came down to change into her Everest t-shirt before counting her float. "Hey, guys. What's shaking?"

"Hi, oh, hey. Nothing much. Just, you know, that this will be the last time you'll talk to us before we become the Golden Gloves heavyweight champs."

Nikki was impressed. "Guys! Wow. I can't wait. I'm really excited for you," she said warmly, stretching to give each of their outer biceps a squeeze.

"Thanks, Nikki. It's all Dougie, though—you can focus your squeezing on him."

She lightly punched Bruce's arm in retort. Bruce felt the engagement ring. Dougie leaned back slightly and winked at his brother over Nikki's dark roots.

Nikki treated the twins like she would other men—her flirting, although it was gathering steam, was indiscriminate. Bruce could appreciate her including him, even if it left him feeling more lonely. He honestly didn't know what was worse, pretending that there was nothing different about them or seeing only what was different.

Out in the parking lot, a black lab tied up near the entrance was barking at everyone exiting. Dougie was translating for the dog:

"The end is nigh! Save yourself!

"You forgot to buy toilet paper!

"My owner's an asshole!"

Bruce was bored but not bored enough to play along, and then he noticed Anka coming up the sidewalk toward Everest wearing a hoodie and an army jacket and a huge scarf, her long hair blowing furiously in the wind.

"Dougie. Quit it. Quick, duck down." Bruce had pulled them both into a walking crouch in order to sidle between two cars.

Dougie thought Bruce was finally getting into the spirit of his game, though he didn't see where it was going. "Are you hiding from the dog?"

"Shush for a minute."

Bruce peaked through the windows of the car as Anka bent to let the lab sniff her hand.

"Hey, wait. Brucie, isn't that your pen pal? You should go talk to her."

"Keep your voice down."

"Get a grip, man. I know you're dying to talk to her. This is perfect—she's on our turf. Just go say hi."

"She doesn't know who I am."

Dougie shook his head. On the one hand, he knew he didn't have the right words to offer Bruce. On the other, he wanted to smack him.

"I don't believe it. You're afraid to be yourself."

"No. It's not that. Just give me a second here." Bruce was panicking.

"Dude, we were raised to be better than this. Hiding? Seriously?"

Bruce forced them to remain crouched until Anka had been inside for a good minute. Twenty minutes ago he had delivered a letter to her mailbox before the start of Dougie's shift, at the time feeling emboldened by her last letter. He could barely get over the line about her knitting him a toque, so thoroughly warmed was he by the notion that she thought about him, wanted to know him, somehow. Bruce had woken up each of the last three mornings feeling like maybe there was a possible world in which he could reveal himself to her. That he would not get rejected. That he could take a step toward being his own man. The good feeling had stayed with him up until this moment, but now it twisted into something sharp and paranoid without warning. He wondered if she had seen them through her window while they were on her porch and had followed them to Everest. Maybe she planned to publicly confront him about his dishonesty. He was embarrassed by the earnestness of everything he had written, and he knew he couldn't just casually walk up to her now: *Hey, surprise. I'm Bruce. I've been pouring my heart out to you, but I forgot to mention this one thing. Meet Dougie. My literal better half.* He wanted to crawl into a hole and stay there through the winter, the world above a shaken snow globe.

But Anka had not yet checked her mailbox, and so Bruce's letter had not yet been discovered. She had no idea who was working and who was hiding in the Everest lot. She just needed a sleeve of crackers and a container of hummus for dinner, which she'd later eat standing at her sink, only then reading the letter that had been waiting for her—absolutely none the wiser that Bruce was losing his marbles a few blocks away.

November 21, 2012

Dear Anka,

I hope this past week has been a happy one for you, filled with things you like to do and delicious things to eat. I'm reading a book that I bought at that second-hand bookstore on Wilber—it's on the second floor, above the convenience store. It's a slim volume, an imagined account of M at sea, filled with the author's own ink sketches. A rare find. I'm predictable, I know. Maybe you can recommend something new for me?

Anyway, I'll leave you with a little taste. At this point he has decided to enter into the Golden Globe race, even though he was unimpressed by how gimmicky it was:

> M was living in Paris in 1968. He thought the whole idea of a race around the world was unfounded, that for the man who ventured out inspired only by the monetary reward and the prospect of getting his name in the paper, having never before made a mistress of the sea, the journey would be treacherous folly. When a reporter proposed the idea that he enter, he laughed in the man's face and then left the cafe, leaving him to finish his drink alone and settle the bill. But when M

> returned to his apartment, he could do nothing but pace its length for a week straight. He smoked and argued with the ocean, who was jealous that he had left her for a pedestrian life on land. A life of paying bills, and walking the streets, and eating croissants. It was said that he told his wife some version of, "I cannot cleave myself from that fresh light which filtered through the forest canopy of my childhood and beckoned me ever onward out into the open." But she knew why he had to go. She had sailed around the world with him once already. She wouldn't hold him back. Neither would she embrace him before he set sail, knowing deep in her heart that he had already gone.

Anka, this may be a bold question, but have you ever felt that way about anything? My brother feels this way about boxing. I look at the ocean, and it feels magnetic but terrifying, a siren unto itself. I feel that I should know by now what my passions are. Do you think that maybe not everyone is born blessed with something they're good at?

Bruce

"Brucie, I know something's—"

"Nothing's—"

"—bothering you."

"—bothering me."

The twins were waiting for the subway on their way to Ogilvie's. Dougie had waited until the next morning after Bruce's freak-out in the parking lot before pressing any further. Somehow a pigeon had flown down past the collector's booth, over the turnstile, and down the stairs to the platform. Following a path that was the opposite of its natural, wild trajectory.

"I'm all right. I don't know. Maybe I'm just a bit confused about Anka, I guess."

"Well, you gotta talk to me." Dougie was watching the pigeon who had strutted out to the edge of the platform as if to wait for the train. "I know you think about this girl all the time. But if you're not gonna talk to her, what's the point?"

"I'm not like you, Dougie. It's not that easy for me. I just don't see any way that it could work out with her."

"Well she's already agreed to write you. I mean, you were upfront about our situation from the start, right?"

The train's horn was blasting as it pulled into the station; the pigeon flapped and stepped back, suddenly unsure about its place underground.

"And frankly, Bruce, right now you need to focus. You're gonna have to put her out of your mind. We have to keep our eyes fixed on the Golden Gloves."

As the twins jostled onto the train, Dougie didn't say another word. He couldn't get distracted by Bruce's lovelorn moping at the moment. The first thing he had to do when they got to Lana's was grab an ice pack and some more ibuprofen. The allotted time between doses wouldn't have elapsed yet, but that didn't matter. The tournament started next week. He was ready; he just needed his cranium to chill out.

Lana handed over two wedding invitations to Bruce and Dougie once they had settled in at Bruce's desk. "You're both welcome to bring someone," she offered.

"Thanks, Lana. These look great." Dougie brought his up to his nose. He expected the paper to smell like French perfume or cotton candy. "New Year's it is. So, Brucie, you going to invite anyone?"

Unnerved, Bruce scratched at the rash along his ribs. "Umm, well, what about you?"

Lana swivelled all the way around to get the full, uncensored scoop. "Douglas Reuben! Any special ladies in your corner, then?"

"Honestly, Lana, who has the time?"

Bruce gave in to imagining himself at the wedding on New Year's Eve with Anka by his side. He imagined standing up from his chair and asking her to dance. He felt the warmth of her hand pulsing there on his ribcage, her breath on his neck rather than Dougie's. He pretended that he had made some clever observation that made her laugh, the sound of forks twinkling against delicate glasses. He bent to kiss her.

"Hey, Bruce, you think I could actually get away with asking Nikki? Ha! That'd be something to stir the pot, for sure!" Dougie was tempted by the devilish idea of it.

Bruce took note of the fact that he had imagined this moment alone with Anka without having an out-of-control coughing fit.

Later that afternoon Dougie sat next to Bruce on the deacon's bench trying to devise a scheme to get to the painkillers in the cabinet without his brother knowing. His head was throbbing and had been for days now. He had an extremely high threshold for pain, which he had inherited from his mother, and so he had been able to carry on as normal since the last time he had passed out. But sitting under the fluorescent light at Ogilvie's was making him feel nauseous, and he needed to nip that in the bud because he most certainly could not hide from his twin the matter of losing his lunch again. Yesterday afternoon as they were getting out the door on the way to Everest, Dougie had had to beeline to the bathroom in the midst of getting his shoe on, yanking Bruce behind him. He had then spent the whole of his shift unsuccessfully trying to convince Bruce that he suffered from acid reflux. He texted Lana in rapid fire:

> Could you do me a favour? Don't turn around.
> Could you grab me some pills from the cabinet?
> But pop them in the water before you bring it over?
> I don't want to disturb Bruce.
> I'll ask you for some water in a minute.

> Lana responded quickly. Are you feeling ok?

> Yeah. I feel a sore throat coming on, and I don't want Bruce to worry that I won't be ready for the tournament. You know how he is.

Dougie's plan went off without a hitch, in that Bruce was too busy to pay him any attention. He tried to breathe into the pain jackhammering inside his head. While he waited for the pills to take effect, he forced himself to face the intensity of the pain he'd been feeling. It had only gotten worse after that attack from Patrice's guys. His brain rattling at the bars of its cage. Pressure behind his eyes. Ever-present nausea.

The white-hot pinprick centre of pain in his skull. *Breathe.* He tried to pay attention to what his body was feeling, and despite all of it, to feel calm. *Breathe.*

What he felt was pain and panic and cold sweat and fear and weakness. *Breathe.*

Anka was knitting her rug with enormous needles behind the laundromat counter. She was alternating between white and blue yarn, which was lapping up all around her. The only customer at that moment was the Marchesa Casati.

"Could you help me grab something out of one of the top dryers? My item's too far back for me to reach it, and I really shouldn't be straining myself according to the doctors."

"Of course. There is actually a step stool next to the big sink at the back. You're more than welcome to use it."

The Marchesa wasn't budging, but she finally conceded when it became apparent that neither was Anka. "What do you get paid to do around here? I'm sure it's not to knit your little afghans."

Anka turned the volume on the overhead TV up to an uncomfortable level. She changed it from a soap opera to a local community-issues show in Urdu.

The Marchesa re-approached after scrambling in the dryer for her polyester-blend kimono. "Listen, love, I could use your expertise here. I've deposited a dollar twenty-five worth of coins into my third dryer, and I pressed the button, and nada. It's broken."

As the woman came close, Anka felt guilty. She noticed the liver spots on the Marchesa's deeply wrinkled cheeks, and though her nails were manicured, her hands were shaking and brittle. Anka knew better than to be spiteful. But then the Marchesa snapped, in a voice that was very much still strong, "You useless cow. Call the owners or a repair man." Anka held a finger up to the Marchesa while she counted stitches out loud. "I'm sorry. I'm under strict orders never to call the owner." She mimed slitting her throat with her raised finger. "Just give me a second—there's a trick to it."

Anka wrote a number down and dug herself out from under the mound that was Garrison Creek. The Marchesa had no less than four dryers on the go and one load still in the wash. Anka opened and slammed shut the door of the suspect machine, then hit the power button. Nothing. She hit the button in rapid fire. Nothing. She opened and closed the door again. She peered in through the glass. The Marchesa's clothes sat in an unhelpful, soggy clump. Anka got five quarters out of the till, transferred the clothes into another dryer, and reloaded the change. Inside the dryer something mauve and feathered started tossing around and around and around.

Anka went back to her knitting and considered what she would write in reply to Bruce. Her hands moved in a smooth, satisfying way: holding the left needle still with its row of patient loops, gliding the right needle through the top stitch, harnessing the needle with the yarn from below, shaking out some more slack from the ball, pulling the needle back through with the yarn secure, sliding the old stitch off with the right needle's tip, fluid, easy. Again. She enjoyed working with her hands, but she didn't consider knitting her passion. It was a balm, a method of healing, a simple way to use time in order to carve out a refuge in the space around her. She understood passion to imply enthusiasm and forward motion, a compulsion that could not be denied or curtailed. She posed the question to her parents: *What makes me happy?* She couldn't feel any answer coming. She was still holding on to both knitting needles, the left one free of all its loops; she gripped them both like an upright knife and fork about to be banged on a table in demand of a meal. She tuned into the energy pulsing in her arms and her chest and her legs, but she strained to feel her Mama and Dad. *What is my purpose?* Nothing. Anka didn't see the Marchesa eyeing her from the other side of the laundromat, smoothing down her hair, trying to will the wiry curls into something sleek. Anka exhaled audibly. She searched for some kind of sign out the window. No one walked past, no cars pulled in or out, and no birds came to land in her view. *I can't even make myself a decent curry yet—how am I supposed to be a grown up?*

With the mention of food, Anka now heard her dad speak up: *Man, dat's the easiest t'ing in the world to make.*

And then she heard her mom: *I always blend up my onions and garlic first, but I suppose you don' have to. Get yuh'self a food processor.*

Anka instinctively thought about all of the reasons why it was utterly impossible for her to buy and find room to store a food processor. *My kitchen's too small.*

Stop mekin' excuses, Priyanka

Anka could feel her dad laughing at her unwillingness.

Guess what, my dear. You're already a grown-up. At your age your dad and I were married and you were already five years old.

Anka didn't feel like she was going to start crying, so she kept going. *What am I supposed to spend my life doing?*

A calico cat came up to the door and looked in for a brief moment. Anka held her breath. The cat dashed across the quiet street. Anka dropped her shoulders. That first snow had quickly melted, leaving just its chill behind. She couldn't feel any answers coming and finally released her needles.

She wrote a number down in her notes and interlaced her fingers to stretch her hands and arms. She carefully tucked all of her knitting into her bag and pulled out her notebook.

November 23, 2012

Hi Bruce,

That's the million-dollar question, isn't it? I'm not sure if having hobbies means the same as having passions. I guess I've never thought about it before. What if some people don't have one major thing that's theirs? What if most people have lots of little things that buoy them through the day? Through the years? What if passion is more like an attitude, a willingness to keep going? M's thing was obviously the sea, sailing, but what about his wife? She would've had to find what made her feel active and alive in his absence. She didn't ask her husband to be anything other than what he was. (Can I be honest? He sounds a little... How do I put it? Um... selfish. Anyway.) We have an accepted notion in our society that passion is loud and singular, but maybe passion can also be quiet and multiple? A way to be and not just a thing to do? I have no idea. I can't answer your question because I haven't felt about anything the way M felt about the sea, so my answer to your question is, like you, not yet.

Anka

Dougie woke up and declared that he was going to get a tattoo. Bruce was surprised by this spontaneity because Dougie didn't think about anything other than boxing these days. Nikki had told Dougie about a place on Yonge that did walk-ins, and so they headed in that direction later that afternoon. They detoured through Chinatown for barbeque pork buns and sesame balls with red bean paste.

"What's with the sudden need for a tattoo today? Especially so close to the tournament. You know it's not going to heal in time."

Dougie considered this between bites. "I dunno. I'm feeling really restless or something. You have been too, right?"

Bruce knew the source of his own malaise: it was most likely coming from his swirling indecision over the past months, swelling but held at bay, ever mounting in pressure. He finished his bun. "Yeah. I have."

"I figured I'm gonna get it on my thigh so it'll be hidden under the shorts, out of the way. It's strange—the other day I just really started feeling like I badly need to make a change. It was either get a tattoo or pierce something."

"I see."

Bruce tucked his chin into his scarf, which was tucked under Dougie's small hand, as he and his brother joked.

"Am I a skull and crossbones guy?"

"Nah, more *MOM* to me," Bruce teased.

"Dragon? Hmmmm, phoenix?"

"Snake fighting a phoenix. On fire."

Bruce was using all his faculties to be light with his brother in order to force down the jitters in his chest. He had also woken up determined to make a drastic change. He felt deeply ashamed of how he'd let his anxiety make him behave at the mere sight of Anka the other day, and he knew it was time to take a stand for what he wanted.

Dougie smiled and wrapped his outside arm around his brother, pulling Bruce's shoulder in tight. "I've got it. I know what I'm going to get."

Standing at the counter of the tattoo shop, Dougie explained to the guy working what he was thinking. The guy opened a huge binder of plastic-sheathed samples of photos and illustrations and flipped to a divider near the middle before offering Dougie a look. Dougie made his choice. Bruce approved. After a short wait, the twins were perched on a table. They'd changed into shorts, and Dougie had pushed his side all the way up. They went through all of the prep, and then the needle was going, and they were going to be a while. Bruce was reading a magazine featuring a French chanteuse and her tattoos on the cover. He had been debating how exactly to bring up what he wanted to say. He was mad at himself for not doing it earlier on their walk over. He was getting hot and shifted his weight. He didn't think he could sit with it the whole time this would take. But Dougie was basically trapped, and Bruce knew it wasn't fair to his brother to spring this on him now. *Fuck.* Both his palms were clammy; he wiped the right one on his shorts, turned a page, and blurted out: "I'll only fight in the tournament if you agree to a consultation with Dr. Halpern."

"For what? Your rash? About time."

Bruce closed the magazine on his lap. "Separating. To see if—"

"How about you give *us* the match, and I'll help *you* with Anka."

Dougie hadn't missed a beat, nor did he break a sweat.

"What?"

Bruce was dying. He thought he was being a heel for laying out a bear trap, and somehow he had stumbled into it himself. The needle stopped buzzing. Dougie was so certain, so confident. How was he thinking of helping with Anka?

"Girl trouble?" The tattoo artist looked up from her work. "Maybe I can help?"

Dougie explained about Bruce's letters while Bruce opened the magazine to a random page. Bruce was always the one to bend. He still had not learned how to catch himself in time to right his course. Although maybe it *was* possible that Dougie could give him some pointers on how to get over his nerves and self-consciousness about approaching Anka.

"How does it usually work when you guys date? Do you date? Is this rude to ask?"

"No, not at all," Dougie piped up. "I've dated. Bruce has chosen not to yet, but something about his new crush has gotten under his skin."

"Do you guys have any rules between you?" The tattoo artist pushed her glasses up with the back of her hand and kept working.

"Well, to be honest with you, the relationships I've had have hit the fast track to…" Dougie was looking for the right word. "Unghhhhhh…."

"Companionship," Bruce clarified.

"And they sort of fizzle out from there. Fun for a short while, and then time to move on."

The tattoo artist lifted the needle again and made eye contact with Dougie. "Funny, that's exactly my problem too."

"Oh yeah, that whole 'easy to catch, hard to keep' thing," Dougie and the artist shared a laugh, and Dougie continued, "Honestly, I'm too committed to my ambitions for anything serious."

"I get that." The artist was bent over Dougie's leg again.

Bruce couldn't handle it. Dougie had no qualms about flirting with Nikki or even talking so openly with this tattoo artist. Bruce felt ridiculous about his crush on Anka, about never knowing what to say. About only having been kissed once in his life. *Fuck.* He was exactly right back where he started. His face was on fire.

The tattoo artist was checking in, asking if the pain was okay and telling them to just let her know when they needed a break.

"Do you mind if we stop so I can use the bathroom?"

"Really, Brucie?"

"Sure, no problem." The tattoo artist rolled her chair back to give them some room.

The tiny bathroom was tiled in white from top to bottom and was a tight squeeze for the twins. Dougie admired the work that had been started on his thigh, lifting his leg for a better view of an outline of a tiger's head, teeth bared, and half of a rose.

"Ummm, so for real, I think we should talk to Dr. Halpern." Bruce was talking to his reflection.

Doug stared at Bruce in the mirror, blank for a moment.

Bruce turned on the faucet, cupped some water in his palm, and lifted the water to his face, rivulets sliding into the neck of his shirt. He turned off the tap. Dougie handed him a paper towel.

Bruce caught Dougie's eye in the mirror. "Um. I've been thinking."

Dougie sensed his brother's heart racing, and his own sped up to match its rhythm.

"There's so much you can do in boxing. Without me. You shouldn't have to drag me around. You could find a way to make the national team, probably."

"What the hell are you talking about? Less than a week before the Golden Gloves? Really? You don't want to go up for the tournament? Fine. If you really want to pass up this opportunity, then fine. Fuck it."

"Really?"

"Spit it out, Bruce. Tell me whatever is really going on with you or I swear to God I'll clock you."

"Um. I've been thinking about this a little bit, and I think we could be happier?"

Dougie gasped as though he had been sucker punched. "Is this about Anka?" Dougie felt like he was the last one in on a secret.

Bruce wasn't looking into the mirror anymore. He stared at the water stains on the faucet instead and finished his thought. "If we separated."

"You'd be happier? Christ, Bruce. Listen to what you're saying. You can't be serious. You just want to—I don't ev—Bruce!" With his strong arm, Dougie was wrenching paper towels from the dispenser and shoving them at Bruce.

Bruce was left clutching an armful of crumpled rectangles of brown paper. Dougie warbled out a frustrated yell.

"Dougie. I'm sorry. I really am. But I'm sure it's right. Even if it doesn't—

"Brucie, if she can't handle us—you—the way we are, just forget her. You'll find another girl."

Dougie yanked them out of the men's room. Dougie's hand hanging around Bruce's neck was balled up and knocking against Bruce's collarbone. There would be a sore spot there in the morning.

Bruce woke up the next morning with an awful pit in his stomach. Dougie hadn't said another word to him after they had left that bathroom and continued with the tattoo. He regretted the way he had approached the whole conversation. He was still pretty sure it was what he wanted, but he desperately wished for a do-over. He should've brought it up before the tattoo shop. He could've tried to inspire Dougie's sense of adventure with passages about M on the open ocean. He should have definitely assured Dougie that they would always be there for each other. Not every second, but they'd still be roommates. They'd still be brothers. They'd still be twins.

"Dougie?"

Dougie didn't answer. He covered his eyes with the crook of his elbow. Under the covers, stage one of his tattoo was sheathed in plastic.

"Dougie, I'm sorry that it came out the way it did yesterday. But if you think about it, I think you'll see that it could be for the best."

Dougie pretended he was snoring.

"C'mon, Doug. I know you're awake. You can't ignore me forever."

Dougie swung the pillow from under his head and propped it in the space between his and Bruce's faces.

Bruce was left staring at a lumpy, grey-striped wall between them. It was the first time in his life that he had felt so thoroughly lonely. What was he doing? He couldn't believe that after all this time he'd actually pulled the plug on this grenade and that he hadn't spent any time considering what the immediate aftermath of the conversation would be like. It was a stalemate. He had no more moves, and he honestly wasn't sure what he really needed. He eventually reached out for M.

> M had been through the Roaring Forties on his first time around the world. That didn't make his second trip along these menacing latitudes any easier. The winds made the ocean illogical

> and irate, and there were few land breaks to talk it down. He hadn't slept the night before; a gale was predicted to come in, and he had wanted to get ahead of it. M was dragging his exhaustion behind him, lagging to secure the sail, feeling too diminished to replace the jib with a larger one. Water collected on deck, and it was up to his knees by morning. But M wasn't getting involved in this fight between the winds and the seas. Irrespective of the high winds, when the salty Indian Ocean butted against the frigid Antarctic waters, the collision of two opposing and equal elements resulted, more often than not, in both boats and spirits being chopped to the quick.

Even though it was impossible to have an actual conversation with his family about the possibility of separation, Bruce decided he needed to take a real stab at it and made arrangements for his father to pick them up later that day at the train station. Walter didn't ask any questions on the way back to the farm, but his radar was up; there was something cumbersome taking up space in the back seat along with his sons. He knew it would reveal itself on its own. He turned the radio on, and they all listened to a report about a town where dogs outnumbered humans at a ratio of two and a half to one.

When they arrived home, Jane set her book aside, made her sons hot chocolate, sat down across from them at the table, and waited.

Bruce addressed the mug in his hand: "Mom, Dad. Um. I would like for Dougie and myself to talk to Dr. Halpern." He could feel his mother ready to pounce. "I wonder if science has progressed and if maybe there's a procedure for us now."

"Do you see this drama I'm dealing with?" Dougie was hoping his parents would be able to talk Bruce in off the ledge. "Right before our tournament."

"Dougie, there's nothing wrong with us having a conversation. I don't think I'm being unreasonable here."

Walter took his wife's hand across the table. "It's okay, boys. What's on your mind, Bruce?"

"I just think we owe it to ourselves to see if Dr. Halpern can do anything for us. We owe each other a chance at that—"

Jane abruptly got up from the table and went upstairs. Bruce watched her walk away feeling an indignant heat in his cheeks, his heart sounding an alarm. He had opened his mouth to call for her to come back when Dougie spoke up and Bruce turned, letting her disappear up the stairs.

"Bruce, you're feeling ashamed of who we are." Dougie was trying for the last drop of his hot chocolate. "Mom and Dad taught us to be more authentic than that."

"Dougie, there's a difference between feeling ashamed and feeling trapped," Bruce snapped. The words came of their own volition, and it amazed him that he had never before been able to name how he felt so precisely.

"I'm a trap? This isn't my fault, you know."

"Of course I know that. You're not a trap—"

"Because I never think of you like that."

"That's because I do everything you want me to." The sooty mounds of coal that had been accumulating in Bruce's chest over time were now pressurizing under the heat of this taboo conversation into diamond-like clarity. His mind had gone still; the words were just coming.

"What? Brucie, how can you say that?"

"The Golden Gloves? Obviously it's happening no matter what I say, how I feel. I never truly have a choice. It's always just one more thing, one more thing, just this one last four-day tournament until the next thing comes along."

Dougie blinked. And then blinked again. He was trying to do a review of their entire lives in his mind. "Bruce, this is who we are. Who you and I have been our whole lives. Us, this family—that's what's real."

"Boys, listen. Your mother might be thinking all this over, but I want you to know that we support you. We trust you to find your way. Your mother made a trifle this afternoon—any takers?"

Bruce and Dougie didn't want any trifle.

"Dougie, I've boxed for your sake for as long as I can. Just give me one appointment with Halpern. Then we'll go from there. One hour."

Walter took a bowl full of dessert up to Jane, who he found cleaning the upstairs bathroom. "What are you doing?"

"I need to think."

"Here, have some trifle."

She took her yellow rubber gloves off and received the bowl. They went into their bedroom and sat on the bed to eat.

Walter dug his spoon in through all the layers of cake, cream, pudding, and fruit. "Where'd you get blueberries this time of year?"

"Is dessert the only thing you ever have on your mind? They were frozen. I bought them at the grocery store."

"I know you're worried."

"We made the right choice back then, didn't we?"

"There's never one right thing. Our sons are healthy and happy and able now to make decisions for themselves. That was the job we had."

There was a picture on the dresser of Bruce and Dougie as four-year-olds. They were in the bath, pretending to be a scary monster, all four chubby arms of theirs reaching out for the camera and photographer alike. Their wet curls slicked back, Dougie's little tongue sticking out, Bruce trying his best to be menacing. In the family it had always been taken as fact that Dougie took more after Jane and Bruce took more after Walter. But her sons had each seemed so self-possessed to her. Confident as a team. Safe because they would always have one another. But Jane wondered now if one of her sons had spent his life feeling like a monster. Had she dismissed any subtle signs of Bruce's unhappiness this whole time? She quickly pushed aside the notion that maybe Bruce had felt that it wasn't him and his brother on the same team, but rather that one team was her, Walter, and Dougie. And the other team was Bruce.

All these years she had never seen anything but four very huggable arms reaching for her through the frame.

On day one of the Golden Gloves tournament, Dougie woke up before Bruce and lay unmoving. He was tired from dreaming; a headache had yanked him awake, and he knew he should get up early for their big day, but he just couldn't convince his body to follow through yet.

He had been dreaming that he and Bruce were on the lot and a black car with dark-tinted windows was slowly, menacingly, following them through the lot. It went up one row and slowly down another as he tried to awkwardly guide them through what had turned into a labyrinth of parked cars. Eventually the car was chasing them down the street, gaining speed, bearing down, the sound of the gears shifting up, closing the distance. Dougie and Bruce were pumping their legs as fast as they could when Dougie heard a shot and felt a searing pain in his left temple and woke up. He felt upset and uneasy and groggy as he blinked awake.

He threw an arm over his eyes and visualized himself and Bruce in the ring later today for their first match up. He skipped forward to the end, to a familiar visual, when the ref would raise his arm up to signal victory. He felt the sturdy grip around his wrist above his glove, both hands hot and encased to different degrees. The helmet pressed to his temples. His breathing slowing down. He made himself smile to make it feel more real. The first win secured, two to go.

He imagined checking in at the registration table in the lobby of the sports complex. The tournament would be hosted in the suburbs just under an hour's drive northwest of the city. The weigh-in would be the usual gong show, particularly if the official wasn't apprised of their legitimate status as competitive boxers in good standing with Boxing Ontario's heavyweight division.

"Morning, Dougie." Bruce had decided to be there for his brother through the tournament. He had no intention of sabotaging anything or making things difficult.

"You ready for today?"

"Yeah, don't wo—"

"I hope you've got your head screwed on for the next four days," Dougie interrupted. He scuttled out of bed. His tone came out sharper than he had intended. He led them to the medicine cabinet.

"You feeling okay, Dougie?"

"Unghhhhhh. Hmmmm." Dougie was gulping down water from his cupped palm.

Bruce knew that the closeness between them had slipped, that his brother's trust in him had bobbed and dipped beneath the swell.

November 30, 2012

Anka,

The last few days have been exhausting. I think I have to tell you something. It seems as though this past week I've been putting it all out there, so I figure why stop now—in the spirit of action and forward motion.

Right. Okay. I will just punch right through the bag. Bear with me.

The first time I saw you was one afternoon at the library in August—that big one on College. I don't know if you remember seeing me and Dougie in line behind you. You couldn't have missed us—we're joined at the waist. Dougie and I are what is known to the medical community as parapagus conjoined twins. Side by side. We have three legs between the two of us.

I recently broached the topic of talking to our childhood doctor about the possibility of separating. Dougie isn't keen on it. I'm just feeling really tired. Today is day three of a four-day boxing tournament we're in. We won both of our matches so far—fairly easily, actually. We have the day off today. Tomorrow we're up for the heavyweight title. It's Dougie's dream, so I'm happy we're actually within reach of it.

I don't know how you're feeling, especially in light of what I've just mentioned, but just know that this week, reading all of your letters again (and again) was what kept me from falling apart.

If you see me around, I'm the one joined at the hip with my brother. In an orange toque.

Bruce

He was too tired to think too hard about what he'd written to Anka, but he'd drop the letter off tomorrow after their match. He hadn't a clue how Anka would feel about his confession, but he knew he'd prefer she found out that he and Dougie were conjoined because he told her and not because they accidentally crossed paths in the neighbourhood. Either way Bruce felt hollowed out. He wanted to lumber into a deep, dark, narrow cave and sleep until the spring.

Anka was helping Mr. Verhoeven make grilled cheese sandwiches for his grandsons and would walk them back to school in half an hour. Damian and Devon were sitting at the kitchen table. Devon's top lip was stained with fruit punch, and Damian was trying to balance his chair on its two back legs.

"Why's she here, Grandpa?" Nine-year-old Devon had his eyes trained on Anka as she stood at the stove using the wrong spatula.

"*She* is Anka. And Anka has kindly agreed to spend time with you boys while I do some important work."

"Damian, if you crack your skull open, I'm going to make you clean up your own bits of brain off the floor," Anka reasoned with the eleven-year-old.

"Eww. Gross. That's child abuse." But Damian squared his chair back to the table and dipped his triangular sandwich half into ketchup.

Devon was slyly picking his nose. Anka handed him a paper towel.

When she got back to 6781 after dropping the boys off at school, she helped Verhoeven spread suiting fabric over his daughter's dining room table.

"Thank you for helping. I need to make sure I get most of the pieces cut before the boys are back at quarter to four."

The fabric was a charcoal linen–wool blend with the faintest traces of navy through the weave.

"What are you making?" Anka was straightening out an end that was sliding off the side of the table.

"It's a men's suit. But it's a bit more challenging than what I've forged in the past. The parameters and measurements are more, well, nuanced and dynamic than the average garment."

"How so?"

"Unhmm. Mmm. Hrunggg." Verhoeven was putting some straight pins between his lips.

Anka didn't press him, afraid that a pin would slide down his throat.

Verhoeven was concentrating, following a path alone. Anka thought she could be more helpful if she started on dinner. Verhoeven had explained to her how hard his daughter worked and how she viewed his tailoring as a nuisance—Mimi thought it was too stressful on his body and that he'd be better off relaxing and keeping an eye on her sons. Anka didn't want Mr. Verhoeven getting in any trouble, and she thought a meal might get him off the hook or at least buy him some time.

She considered the contents of the fridge. On the freezer door was a drawing of a large robot that was being controlled by a tiny figure inside its mouth, with the words *I love Mommy* in uneven, belaboured printing. *Devon* was scrawled across the bottom third of the page in a mix of upper- and lowercase letters. An oversized *E* backwards and charming.

Two days later, after school, Anka hid one gummy worm somewhere in Verhoeven's house. She told the boys that she'd give five dollars to whoever found it and that whoever didn't would still get a baggie full of worms. She could hear them running all over the basement. They eventually agreed on a systematic search from the bottom up.

Verhoeven was sitting behind his sewing machine at Mimi's dining-room table, surrounded by piles that did not yet resemble a suit. He was whistling, which Anka could only hear when the machine stopped trundling. She was stretched out on the sofa panning through a cookbook. Verhoeven mentioned that Mimi had nearly passed out when she saw dinner warming in the oven and the table set that first night.

Pretend machine gun noises ratcheted up the basement stairs. "Anka—we can't find it!"

She figured she could keep them going for another half hour tops. She turned to a recipe for a cabbage and sage panade and quickly flipped the page.

It was too late. Anka was now hostage to her memories. Her father had once called her asking for a cabbage recipe other than coleslaw. The only way he knew how to cook it was to fry it and eat it with dhal and rice ("my favourite!" her mother piped up), but he didn't feel like eating that. Anka had given him one for a panade, a slight variation of the recipe she was looking at now. He had invited her to come eat with him and her mother, but she was going out with Diane and so turned him down. He had put her mother on the line, and they had talked while her father scrounged through cupboards gathering ingredients and pulling out pots and measuring cups and the sharper knife. Anka's mother had told her about a West Indian grocery store they had discovered, about what a good cook her father was becoming, about what the weather was doing to her skin. She had asked if Anka wanted to come home for dinner, and Anka had turned the invitation down a second time. Her mother told her to bring Diane over, but Anka informed her that Diane was on an all-meat diet. Except for maybe avocados. They had hung up with the promise to talk again soon and wishes for each to enjoy their evenings.

Anka wished that she had gone home for dinner that night. She wished she had taken over a bottle of wine and a fresh pie and stayed the whole weekend. She wished. She wished. She wished.

She turned the page. She couldn't make a cabbage and sage panade for Mimi and her family.

Damian and Devon were dismantling the kitchen. They were so loud; when they weren't running through the house, they were stomping instead of walking, their voices always urgent, either demanding or whining. Right now they were carelessly plowing through the cutlery drawer, metal ringing out, arguing over who got to dig through this one because the other had hogged the Tupperware cupboard. Anka wanted to wring their necks, one in each hand, and shake them until they shut up, these ungrateful and uncompromising little turds who still got to keep their mom and their grandad, insensitively taking them both for granted, allowed to just be brats with abandon in the safety of their mother's love. Not fair.

Two very bright lights had gone out, and it was a constant struggle to adjust to the world's new dimness. She plunked the open cookbook over her face, listening to Verhoeven's sewing machine prattle away. She curled herself into the tight slice of light that had washed up on the sofa and counted her slow inhalations and her careful exhalations until she trusted herself again. When would that be? She was pained by the sheer force building up in her throat because she refused to let herself cry.

They wouldn't find the jewel-coloured worm in the kitchen; she had hidden it in Damian's right shoe.

It was the fourth and final day of a strangely subdued tournament. Bruce couldn't be sure if the muted tone was coming from the outside—just the vibe of that year's Golden Gloves—or from within, from the strain between himself and Dougie. The twins had seen Patrice only once, during weigh-ins, but they were in different brackets and never faced off. Word was that he had lost his match on day one. All of the tough opponents the twins had faced that year had sharpened them. The Reuben Beast had easily ascended to the top of their bracket, and Farroz had done the same in his. Dougie was not ignoring his brother outright, but there was none of his usual dynamism, and the whole affair just felt like business as usual. Bruce wondered if Dougie was just focusing all of his energy on the title match. What Bruce was mostly focused on was the letter in his coat pocket back in the change room. A letter that told her everything. He would deliver it before they went home that night. He wasn't all that concerned about where they would place by the end of the tournament, now that they had made it to the final bout: first or second place, he'd done his part. He was at the end of this thing. Soon enough he'd be upfront with Anka and maybe be at the end of that thing too.

Bruce and Dougie met Hugo Farroz in the centre of the ring to tap gloves before the first bell. The twins had to look up ever so slightly to make eye contact, and then the ref sent them to their corners. The ref already looked tired; he thought he'd enjoy this bit of part-time work through his retirement, but now he really wanted to do nothing but be retired. To eat dinner with his wife at a Red Lobster. He readjusted his bow tie.

Dom was wiping the sweat from his hairline. The twins had never seen him actually nervous. "Well we're all here now," he said. "There's nothing more for me to pass on. Remember everything you've learned..."

The bell rang and Dom was left, yet again, finishing his speech to an empty corner.

Bruce and Dougie's parents were together in the front row, and Lana and Gary had also come out and were madly cheering before the action had really begun. Nikki had slipped in and was sitting near the exit.

In the ring Dougie and Bruce were steamrolling Farroz, combination after combination making satisfying contact. Farroz didn't lay a hand on them.

Farroz's trainer stood with his arms folded, nodding his head, *Good boy.* The strategy he had hammered into Farroz was to take the force of all blows, tire out the Reuben Beast, and then attack in the last round.

After three minutes the boxers simply stopped what they were all doing when the bell politely asked them to. Bruce was suspicious that something was up. Farroz was making this altogether too easy for them. He assumed that the famed ballet moves would show themselves in the next round.

Ninety seconds into round two, it was no different than what had come before, with Farroz letting the twins run the ring.

And then it began.

Farroz blocked a jab from Bruce and almost simultaneously got Dougie with a fierce hook. The crowd exploded. This was what they had come to see. Farroz's trainer tensed. He raised his chin and clenched his jaw. He wouldn't blink again for the remainder of the round.

Now Farroz began to dance. But erratically. For a good minute, he was bobbing and ducking punches that hadn't even been thrown, jumping around like a rabid animal. Bruce and Dougie were barely able to keep their eyes on him. Bruce managed to land a punch that went through Farroz's chest, and the kid immediately went back to taking hit after hit like a dead fish. Dougie split Farroz's bottom lip, and then the bell interrupted to as if to say, *That's it. I've had about enough of this sideshow. Get back to your corners, all of you.*

The twins were giving everything they had. Dom watered them down and reminded them to keep their arms in close. They looked at each other without saying a word. Fighting Hugo Farroz was like fighting three different boxers. They had no idea which man would meet them when the bell ordered them to resume their play: the lax punching bag, the frenetic jackrabbit, or the solemn heavy fists.

Bruce thought Farroz's strategy was ingenious.

Back in the middle of the ring, Dougie took a test jab, mindful to bring his elbow back in quick. But Farroz still got into Dougie's face. Hard. Now they were boxing with the kid that Dom had told them about, a force to contend with. Once he started Farroz didn't let up. He stayed on the outside edges to spend some time working Dougie over, and then he lunged into Bruce. Farroz was only a few inches taller than the twins, but at this moment he loomed over Bruce; Bruce was trapped on all sides between the ropes, Farroz's fists, and his brother. Bruce knew they had never fought a boxer like Farroz in their career. Bruce didn't have time to predict when the next hit would land; he could only acknowledge its force when it arrived. Dom's hands were shaking. He kept his eyes on the ref in those seconds when he couldn't bear to look at his boys struggling.

The twins took a chance with a jab-cross-uppercut. Dougie threw the punch, but he couldn't see exactly where it landed, and if it *did* land, he couldn't feel it. The headache that had been with him day and night for the last few months was now strangely, blissfully absent. A giant bubble had popped, Dougie was breathing clearly and easily, and for a moment time stood still. Farroz's body in front of him. Blue shorts. But with Bruce's head atop his shoulders. Dougie quickly shot a glance over to his right. Bruce's little arm around his neck: check. Bruce's shoulder pressed slightly behind his own shoulder: check. That middle leg: check. But when he looked at his brother's face, Dougie found himself staring deep into Farroz's beautiful, puppy-dog, cocoa-brown eyes. Farroz opened his mouth. Dougie turned back to where Farroz should've been—across from him—but instead there was Bruce alone, solo, his head attached to a body in cerulean shorts. Then Bruce clocked Dougie in the jaw. Hard.

He didn't feel like he went down. The ref wasn't on bended knee slapping the mat as he counted. He was somehow slumped back on a stool in their corner with Dom.

He searched Dom's face. Dom's nose: check. Dom's scar above the top lip: check. Dom asking him what the fuck: check. He didn't dare look over at Bruce for fear that Farroz would be there, and instead he buried his head into his glove. He couldn't stop himself from laughing hysterically.

"I feel confused. I honestly can't do this."

The ringside physician appeared, and the ref escorted Dom to another corner of the ring. Dougie was still laughing so the doctor shone a light into Bruce's eyes first. He waited for Dougie to calm down. He checked his watch, at a loss for what to do. He took a step back. He wasn't sure what could be wrong if Dougie was laughing so hard. He felt everyone in the room staring at him. He cleared his throat and asked Bruce how many fingers he was holding up. He decided to end this and yelled out for the ref to call an ambulance, which wasn't the way things were usually done. Eleven minutes later, no less than six paramedics were crowding into the ring. "Wow. I've never had conjoined twins. Sweet," one said to Bruce.

For the first time in his life, Bruce actually wanted to punch someone.

An orderly in Emergency had created a contraption out of hospital beds in order to accommodate the twins and two sets of monitoring equipment. He was proud of his creativity and ingenuity. He made some notes on his phone to add to his résumé. The twins were not comfortable, but not for a lack of the orderly's care and attention and ability to take initiative while also working well as part of a team.

Bruce had been awake for everything. Dougie had not—he had been out cold since the ambulance started driving, like a baby tricked into nap time. Both were now hooked up to monitors and IVs. Dougie had an oxygen mask; Bruce had taken his off. There were a series of tests being run, endless amounts of blood being taken, and already every resident was crammed in around the doctor at any and every chance. Bruce found his mind and body eerily silent; he had no idea what was going on mere inches away. He couldn't imagine that something serious was happening to Dougie when his own body wasn't registering anything out of the ordinary. In those last seconds of the fight, Dougie had been about to throw a punch but instead went slack. Dougie had stood there looking at Bruce like they were waiting to catch a bus, and then his eyes rolled into the back of his head. Suddenly Bruce was alone against the ropes with the grim weight of his brother threatening to drag them down to the mat. Bruce had hoisted Dougie up, leaning all of their collective weight to the right so as not to let the ref start counting Dougie out. He knew that was his one responsibility out there tonight. By the time he had lugged them to their corner, Dougie was back.

Hours passed before the twins were admitted to the hospital and deposited into a room. More time passed, but Bruce was still unclear about what was happening. By now Jane was able to see her sons and was sitting in a chair next to Dougie's side of the bed. Walter was buying coffee downstairs. Jane came over to Bruce's side of the bed—the window side of the room—and tucked some stray hairs behind his ear. She was saying something, but he closed his eyes and listened to the rhythmic inhale from Dougie's oxygen mask, trying to find something like the sound of waves in it.

"Brucie, how are you feeling?"

Jane held onto his hand and reached up to clasp Dougie's small hand stretched across Bruce's shoulder. It felt cold and boney. Bruce squeezed hers for a moment and relaxed.

"Fine."

"Has Dougie been okay lately? Did anything happen before tonight's fight?"

Bruce put his oxygen mask on.

"You've got to look out for him when he's boxing."

A very young doctor came in. "I'm Dr. Chen. I've read through your charts, and everything looks stable—no underlying conditions, I understand."

Bruce shook his head. He was shocked that she had come in without an entourage.

"Have you ever had any issues with motor skills, numbness, pain, anything?"

"Um. Dougie. Well, headaches lately. And he's passed out a few times."

Jane tightened her hold on Bruce's hand again. "What? When? You never once mentioned."

Though Bruce had told this story about three times already since the paramedics arrived, this was the first that Jane had heard it.

"Mom, ouch. Let go."

Dr. Chen gave Bruce a reassuring smile. Her own mother had left her four messages during her shift last night: to leave detailed instructions on how to use a Crock-Pot, to give a weather report, to inform her of the death of a second cousin, and to ask if she had gotten the last message.

"Can you tell me more about the incidents?"

Bruce shifted and repositioned his leg under the sheet. He raised the head of the bed slightly, which left Dougie sloped down at an awkward-but-not-unmanageable angle, and concentrated only on Dr. Chen, her face open and patient and present. It was dark outside, and the blinds hadn't been shut yet; the whole sterile room was twinned in the glass, reflected over top of the city lights stretching out below. Bruce relayed to Dr. Chen and his mother the two times, plus tonight in the ring, that Dougie had been momentarily unconscious. He told them that he had suggested going to a doctor but that Dougie wouldn't cooperate.

"You should've called us," said Jane.

"I'll come check on you guys in the morning when you're both awake, and we'll chat some more," said the doctor.

The window of their room didn't overlook the parking lot, and so none of them could've known that Dom had been sitting in his car for almost an hour, unable to come inside. He had driven behind Walter and Jane's car as they followed the ambulance to the nearest hospital. Dom hated hospitals, but more than that he hated the guilt that was smacking him upside the head. He knew he'd only be in the way if he went in to see Dougie. He knew he owed Bruce an apology. He knew their parents would have every right to give him an earful. He knew all of this and started the car.

Walter came back to the room with two coffees, and seeing him with his jacket on reminded Bruce that all his and Dougie's stuff was still at the sports centre, or maybe with Dom. They had only had on their boxing shorts when they were whisked away in the ambulance.

Walter reassured his son. "We'll go get everything. Don't worry."

They agreed that it would be easiest for his parents to stay at the hotel next to the sports complex rather than drive all the way back home.

Eventually the hospital room was empty, and with Dougie asleep, Bruce was alone until morning came.

"It was the most bizarre thing. I couldn't stop laughing, or maybe laughing was just happening to my body. I can't explain it exactly, but I was in the ring as normal, then bam. Bruce wasn't next to me; he was out in front. Farroz was here beside me. Or rather Farroz's head was where Bruce's head should've been."

Dr. Chen had returned as the twins were finishing their breakfast. Dougie was awake and itching to get out of their hospital bed and clear his head with a run, but instead he was trying to describe what he couldn't understand.

"Their heads were switched, but their bodies still looked normal?" Dr. Chen was not taking notes anymore.

"Yeah, yeah. Bruce's arm was still here, and his torso. Across from me was Farroz's body with Bruce's head."

"Any pain?"

"No. At that point nothing. It was a total relief actually. It had been a couple of months, I guess, of a constant, very intense headache. Unrelenting."

Dougie felt Bruce gently squeezing his shoulder. They both reached to scratch an itch on the middle leg. Some nurses walked by, the sound of their conversation filling the space; one cheerfully greeted a patient who was struggling to walk, dragging their IV, coughing a greeting in response.

"Okay. Thanks, Douglas."

"You can call me Dougie."

"Okay. Thanks, Dougie. It sounds like your vision is okay now, but we'll run some tests to get a better picture. What you're describing sounds like a stroke. I'll be back to check on you before my shift ends."

"What?"

"Normally we'd get you in for an MRI. But given your physicality, I will review your case in consultation with my colleagues to determine next steps. We'll chat again before you have dinner."

"Stroke? Really, I'm fine now. I can walk outta here no problem."

"Get some rest."

"What?"

Dougie was shifting his weight and fumbling with the bed guardrail, attempting to shimmy off his side. Bruce stared at him, unmoved. Bruce was the one who started laughing once they were alone again.

"What the fuck, Bruce?"

"Shit, I know. I had no idea. A stroke. I'm so sorry. I don't know why I can't stop laughing. I'm so sorry."

"Ungggggggggghhh. What does this mean?"

Dougie flapped back onto his pillow, shaking his head back and forth. Bruce's laughter had shifted into crying, and he had to wipe the tears from the corners of his eyes.

While Dougie was laid up with his eyes closed in his half of the double hospital bed, he took himself back to the ring: Farroz was bearing down on him. The white mat gleamed to a fluorescence; the crowd—packed to the rafters—was screaming to a roar. Dougie was breathing hard; a bead of sweat slid down the length of his nose and dangled for a poetic moment before dripping off. Backed against the bounce of the ropes, he looked into Farroz's deep eyes and saw that though he was determined, he also looked tired. Dougie knew he had a seconds-long window to turn this around. Farroz took a beat to look to Dougie's right, and before he could make that minuscule adjustment back to centre, Dougie thrust himself off the ropes and bounded forward. Hammering Farroz with body shots. Farroz connected with a left jab, but that didn't matter. Dougie was steamrolling, then holding, then pummelling when the two were pried apart. A vicious uppercut. Farroz dropped, and just like that it was over. The ref counted him out, slapping the mat with each count. Farroz was done.

Dom, Lana, and Gary were hugging, screaming, jumping—an octopus of limbs in the sea below the ring. His parents had their arms around each other, still seated. Silent tears streamed from his mother's eyes; his father clutched his chest with one hand, beaming in awe of the man he saw before him. Nikki had slipped off her engagement ring. Farroz was still prone, staring up into the light, as the ref threw Dougie's gloved fist high above his head. Dougie couldn't hear the crowd anymore, just his own heart knocking fast, getting ready to explode.

Sometimes when he replayed it, he switched out that last uppercut for a jab, or he skewed his comeback more dramatically, depending on how frustrated he was feeling. Perhaps he was down and the ref was counting him out before he stumbled back up to his feet, teeth bloody, eye almost sealed shut before a miracle shot took down Farroz at last, crowning the Reuben Beast the Golden Gloves heavyweight champ.

A shaft of golden light was slicing through the hospital window. Broad and distinct. Particles of dust and sloughed-off detritus were caught in suspension, floating, falling. The room was unusually hushed; the white noise of the nurses' station, fellow patients cruising the halls, and code blues over the PA had all fallen away. Bruce felt that this lull could last for as long as he focused on that light beam. If he could hold his attention there, everything would be paused: Dougie would continue to nap peacefully, and all the emergencies out there would hold. A moment of respite. He was doing it. It was working. No clouds were passing over the sun; no footsteps were approaching. He felt his eyelids heavy, threatening revolt. He'd allow just two slow blinks. Bruce didn't want to fall asleep in this beautiful afternoon light because he knew that when he woke up there would be three doctors and two residents at the foot of their bed, a nurse on Dougie's side adjusting the monitor and the IV, and their parents and maybe Dom or Lana standing by. And then next steps. Next steps for Dougie and whatever this new looming illness was.

I'm here, Dougie. I'm not going anywhere.

Bruce had never gotten the chance to deliver his last letter to Anka; it was still tucked safely inside his coat pocket. It was time to leave it. He'd tear it up as soon as he could get to it. Dougie had been right. Whatever that unease and dissatisfaction he had recently been feeling, this desire to separate, it was just that: a passing, floating, falling whim. A simple curiosity. Something he had never seriously entertained as a child or a teenager. This is what a midlife crisis probably was, he reckoned. Some silly, idle desires to occupy his time. Anka was the unfortunate collateral in his middling malaise.

And yet he couldn't believe she had ever taken the time to write to him. To find that postcard. To be so kind to him. He remembered how she had looked crossing the parking lot while he hid like a little shit. His stomach twisted with embarrassment. She was totally out of his league anyway.

And yet. She had looked so beautiful and vibrant in that tumult of wind and snow.

If the twins had gone home from the Golden Gloves tournament having won either the gold or silver medal, Bruce would have picked his book up that night and read the following passage where the page was dog-eared:

> M had sailed around the world and then almost around again. He could've kept going, a perpetual motion machine spinning around the spinning globe. Instead he made the choice to make landfall in Tahiti. Here he found he could love a life surrounded by people whose lives depended on each other like gears intricately locked to the next: a man without a neighbour would not eat so well. M found he was able to stay on the island for a time before the ocean made her jealousy known again. His home had no walls, and the wind blew through without censure or reproach.

"All right, gentlemen. Douglas, my colleagues and I have reviewed all of your tests, and the good news is that we don't see anything out of the ordinary. The bad news is that we have yet to do an MRI, which would show us what we really need to see. Which, honestly, I very strongly recommend we do. The problem is that our MRI machines cannot accommodate you. And so before we think about an MRI, we have to consider a possible separation. I'm not sure if—"

Bruce's ears had perked up involuntarily; he swallowed but ended up choking over Dr. Lars's suggestion. Dougie passed him the plastic cup of water from the tray table. Bruce's whole body burned under everyone's stare: there was this new Dr. Lars, Dr. Chen, his parents, and Dougie. Bruce felt exposed, as if an X-ray of this secret wish had been plastered up on the wall—evidence of his narcissism. No one could believe that he would manifest an illness in his twin just to get his own way. Bruce was afraid to look at his mother. He imagined that she saw him as the real culprit behind Dr. Lars's recommendation to separate, that his mother could read his mind and was disgusted by what it harboured. He could sense the lightning bolts shooting at him from her neon laser eyes.

Walter and Jane were flanking the bed, Walter with his feet planted, anchored, his entire body tense and alert, open and vigilant. Jane was on Bruce's side in the only chair. She didn't entirely trust this doctor because she didn't trust anyone but Walter and herself, really, but she reminded herself to listen to, and remember, everything.

Dougie cleared his throat when Bruce finally finished coughing. "If all the other tests have come back clean and I feel fantastic, which I do, then why don't we put a pin in the MRI for now?"

"Well, Douglas—"

"Call me Dougie."

"Well, Dougie, the MRI would give us a better picture of your brain activity. We could see if any extensive damage occurred as a result of what we must assume was a stroke, and if there is a possibility of another stroke in the near future. And Bruce, though you've not had any issues to date, I would like to examine you as well."

Dr. Chen broke in here before Dr. Lars prodded for a quick decision. She smiled, a genuine smile that Jane noted. "I know this is a lot to take in for the both of you. Can I ask if you've ever had any consultations around the possibility of separation before? Mr. and Mrs. Reuben, was there much in the way of medical support when the boys were infants?"

"Not really."

Walter could sense Jane strapping her armour on, and so he stepped in. "Back then there wasn't much, especially out in the country. And we saw that the boys were thriving as they were."

"Of course, of course. This is obvious to see. And it was clearly the right choice. From where I stand, your quality of life is very high, and your lives are full."

Dr. Chen said all of this to Jane.

"I can appreciate that this is not an easy decision. But from my perspective it's worth exploring every avenue in order to ensure you both have long and healthy lives."

Jane relaxed her shoulders and unclenched her jaw.

Dr. Lars jumped in: "My concern is that this is time sensitive. A surgery to separate is in itself a long process and can't happen overnight. So I'd like to get the ball rolling on that. We'd need to assemble a team of doctors to take on your case."

Dougie let out a frustrated cry.

After Dr. Chen and Dr. Lars had left Bruce and Dougie with a lot to think about, there was a knock at the door. Farroz stepped tentatively into the room, wearing a hoodie over a button-up shirt and holding a vase of flowers.

"Hi, Doug. Bruce, hi. I just wanted to check in and see how you guys are. Dom told me where to find you."

"Farroz, the rumours are true. We are, indeed, not in Ibiza." Dougie put on a voice to say *Ihh-bee-thaaa*.

"That was some fight, huh?" Farroz offered.

Bruce noticed that his brother had not invited Farroz to call him Dougie.

"It's not over, Farroz."

Bruce broke in. "Thanks for coming. You didn't have to."

Farroz was looking down at his shoes and rubbing a knot out of the back of his neck. "I know. I just was feeling—well, I feel, like, somehow responsible. Being there, you know, that maybe I—"

"You didn't do this. This has nothing to do with fighting you." Bruce felt compelled to console Farroz.

Walter and Jane shared a concerned and not-so-convinced look.

Dougie wanted to poke the bear. "What about you? We banged you up pretty good—how were you after the fight?"

"Yeah. You guys are a beast, for sure. I've never fought an opponent so strong."

"Your strategy was unpredictable. And very effective," said Bruce.

Farroz gave a little nervous chuckle. "Yeah. Thanks, Bruce. My trainer was not happy at all with my improvising." Farroz widened his eyes in mock terror at the words *not happy*. "We're not really seeing eye to eye so much lately."

Farroz made some small talk about the weather, wished the family well, and offered his help with anything. He was sorry to see the twins laid up and wished them a swift recovery. He mentioned that Dom seemed like an amazing trainer and that he had also sent his best.

When Farroz left, Walter and Jane were quick to sing his praises, which was a testament to Farroz's gentle manner and very much in spite of the fact that Jane felt like boxing, and boxing Farroz specifically, was the sole reason they were all holed up in this room.

The card on the flowers read: *To the Golden Gloves Heavyweight Champs, 2012. Respect.*

All things as they were, the doctors couldn't find any reason to keep the twins in the hospital, especially given that they needed the bed for a teenage patient presenting with meningitis in the ER, and so Bruce and Dougie were happily discharged after six days and five nights. Walter drove them all back to the farm. That night they crept as quietly as they could back to the kitchen after their parents had gone to bed. Before they left the city, Walter had picked up Indian food from a restaurant across the street from the hospital. Bruce was spooning the last of the rice into two bowls while Dougie divvied up the lamb vindaloo and saag paneer. They stood at the counter underneath the microwave to eat, the kitchen lit only by the light over the stove.

"How are you feeling? You seem better?"

"I'm fine. I feel totally normal—no more headache."

"Um. So. What do you think about Dr. Lars? I mean, maybe he had a point?"

"Separating? You must be over the moon."

"No, I'm not. Whatever I was feeling before doesn't matter." Bruce leaned forward to catch his brother's eye. "But what about getting you more thoroughly checked out. I mean it's pretty scary what's been happening to you."

"Okay. Yeah. Brucie, I get what you're saying. But I don't think that's the route to take."

"No MRI?"

"Look, we're still not done this thing."

Bruce had put his spoon down and scratched his rib cage, then desperately tried to get an elusive spot on his back, equally frantic to get Dougie to listen. "Are you serious right now?"

"Shhhhh, Brucie. Not so loud."

Bruce continued in a whisper-scream: "Dougie, you were just in the hospital for almost a week."

"Yeah, and they couldn't find anything actually wrong with us."

"They need the MRI."

"Okay, okay. Hear me out. We're still up for a re-match with Farroz."

"What the fuck? Why? Why do you want this so bad?"

Dougie was going for seconds. "I think we're in an even better position now. Farroz is a great kid, but now he's gotten too soft around us. His first mistake was coming to visit us."

"He's a decent human being. I don't want to fight him again."

"Shhhh—Bruce, you're losing it."

"I'm going to put you back in the hospital. You're driving me fucking crazy."

"Bruce, you're going to give yourself an aneurysm."

Bruce turned to drag them back up the stairs.

"Where are you going? I'm still eating."

"Unghhhhhh. Hurry up."

"Take some more of this lamb—it's so good. I think there might be some pakoras left too. Let me warm them up for you."

Walter came padding into the kitchen and turned on the light. "Why are you guys eating in the dark?"

"We didn't want to wake you and Mom."

"I heard the microwave. I came for some of that rice pudding."

Bruce grabbed it from the fridge.

"What's going on, Bruce? You're scowling."

"I'm fine."

"Dougie? How are you feeling?"

"I'm fine. Dad, there's nothing wrong with me or us."

"Your mother's worried. We both are. Do you think this is a result of all the boxing over the years?"

"Nah. We've got helmets on. It's not like the pros."

"But still. Most people don't get punched every day."

The twins responded in unison: "Dad, it's not every day."

"Plus that's why we train. We're equipped to handle it." Dougie couldn't believe he had to keep having this conversation.

"Dougie, your mother and I don't want to see you get any more hurt."

"What are you saying exactly?"

"Maybe it's time to step away."

As he said this, Walter scratched Bruce's back.

"I totally agree with you, Dad," said Bruce.

As soon as Bruce opened his eyes the next morning, he saw that Dougie was already alert and chipper. They were in their bedroom on the farm. Dishes were being clanked around in the kitchen. Coffee was percolating.

"Hey. Morning." Dougie was chomping at the bit.

"Hey."

"Good sleep?"

"Hmmmmmm."

"Yeah, me too, man. I feel great. Okay. I've been thinking. Just hear me out. I get everything you and Dad were saying last night. But you can't deny that I feel great, like a hundred times better than before we fought Farroz, so just think how easy it'd be for us to fight him now. We've already got a read on him. Cakewalk, right? Let's talk to Dom and get a date for the rematch."

"Jesus, Dougie."

"We were already so close to winning while I was getting the headaches."

"What if you—us—getting bashed around since we were kids is the very reason—"

"No. It isn't. Trust me. What the fuck are the helmets for? What are you and Mom and Dad not getting here?"

Bruce covered his face with his pillow and screamed.

"Please, Bruce. I'm begging you now. We need this."

"I don't."

Bruce was never going to tell his brother, but he was almost certain that when they were fighting Farroz there were at least two times where it seemed like Farroz lowered his block and then one time when he shifted his stance to give the twins a clear shot. He couldn't be certain, but Bruce wondered if Farroz had been up to something to throw that match. The benefit of fighting as conjoined twins was always having an extra pair of eyes.

"Brucie, please. What else do I have? I'm a thirty-four-year-old part-time security guard at a grocery store. That's not me. Truly."

"Dougie, what if something happens again? Something worse? It's just not worth the risk."

"We'll talk to Halpern—Lars, even."

"Dr. Lars would not recommend getting back in the ring."

"If you give me this re-match, I'll do the MRI. And everything that means. I don't want that; it breaks my heart actually. So either way my heart's broken, if I don't fight or if I do."

At that Bruce's heart broke a little too.

And they both wordlessly got out of bed to go downstairs for coffee.

They'd been out of the hospital for two weeks and were rounding their block, taking an easy stroll. Dougie was starting to get scruffy, having decided to grow the beard that Bruce had threatened at the beginning of the fall. He had started biting his nails on his outer hand, and he had also become jumpy and loud and outwardly too cheerful. As the twins were nearing their house, Bruce felt a jolt and a tug as Dougie tried to break out into a run.

"You can't be serious right now."

"Let's just do a quick spin around the block. What?"

"No way. I promised your mother I was going to watch you and take it easy. We are going inside to eat soup and watch a movie."

"Oh. Fuck. Me. I can't sit in that apartment for another minute. I can't watch another fucking movie."

"*Raging Bull*? Don't tell me you don't love it."

"Fuck off, Bruce. I'm losing my goddamned mind. Let me run. I won't tell Mom."

"Nope."

Dougie screamed.

Bruce heard some actual anguish, and then a split second of ringing silence, followed by six hundred small birds tucked into a hedge also losing their fucking minds.

"You won't let me run or cook or vacuum or take out the trash. I'm not a vegetable, Bruce. I'm totally fine. How many more times do I need to scream it?"

"You actually sound unhinged."

"The doctors didn't find shit. And I am feeling fucking fine."

"Mom will actually kill just my half if I let anything happen to you. And. Also. What if I suddenly have some crazy stroke mid-run? I would definitely never forgive you. And you'd be stuck feeding me soup the rest of our lives."

"You're actually having fun right now. You're loving this. You're the worst."

Verhoeven had called Dougie wanting them to come over. It was time for a fitting, and so they had returned to Verhoeven's living room where parts of a suit were now being pinned and assembled onto them.

"I hope you both like the colour—it's classic, but also fresh, which I thought was a good compromise."

"It's sharp; well I imagine it will be when it's finished." Dougie was mindful of holding perfectly still.

"Yes, Mr. Verhoeven. You picked out a very flattering shade."

"Mrrng. Mmmhhh. Unnng." The straight pins were at the ready in the tailor's mouth.

"Bruce, hold still, will you, or else Mr. Verhoeven won't be able to do his job properly."

Bruce shot an incredulous raised eyebrow intended for Dougie, but it didn't land since Dougie kept his head facing forward and readjusted his shoulders back.

"Try to keep your spine straight, Bruce. And relax your legs." Dougie was peacocking, which Bruce could've lived without.

"I could do that, Dougie, if you'd stop pulling so much to your side. I'm going to lose my balance."

"All right, gentlemen. That's good for me. As you can see here, I've devised a hybrid jacket: the outer sleeves are full, and the tailored inner sides are fashioned as a sleeveless vest. This way the look will be clean—no bulky fabric. And it won't get too warm in there for you."

Bruce noticed a child disguised as a gorilla peering out at them from behind a potted plant. He hadn't yet spied the second one squeezed beside the sofa.

"In terms of the shirts and ties, I initially saw both of you wearing the same colour, most likely white. But why don't I put that to you? Are you inclined to wear two different colours?"

Dougie and Bruce answered the tailor at the same time, but with opposing answers:

"Same."

"Different."

Verhoeven took a step back, blocking Devon's view from behind the fern.

"Hmmm. Interesting. Well you said you're going to a wedding. Generally I would've suggested you wear the same colour shirt; we could even go with a pale blue or a small check. But since you said the wedding's to be held on New Year's Eve—that changes everything. We can be so bold as to switch up the colours, go black. Even one of you in white and the other in black. Or one side lavender, the other gunmetal. Really, boys, all bets are off. A tie here, a bow tie there. Take a day or two to consider it. You can buy the shirts, bring them over, and I'll adjust them. I still have to finish the hem on the pants and the lining on the jacket."

The sofa sneezed.

Verhoeven clapped his hands and began to whistle as he reverse-engineered the suit off of Dougie and Bruce.

"Dougie, I reckon a monkey has escaped from the zoo." Bruce pointed to Devon scrambling to join his brother in the corner.

"You know I've always wanted a pet, Bruce. Let's take that one."

Devon and Damian blew their cover and started yelling, "No! We're not really gorillas! Nooo!"

Bruce saw the way the younger boy clutched at his brother's bent knee, the older one letting him scooch in close for shelter. The bigger gorilla with his arm slung around the shoulder of the smaller one. Bruce noticed how their young voices were able to crash into a type of harmony the longer they screamed at the top of their lungs.

"Why don't we meet again in a few days?" Verhoeven yelled over his grandsons' howling. "There's a store in Kensington where you can find some nice quality shirts. It might help to bear in mind that a shirt is a very temporary thing. Easily changed."

It had been nearly a month since Anka had gotten a letter from Bruce, and she was trying not to feel slighted. She had to remind herself that there were times when she hadn't written him back right away. A month wasn't really that much time. She had to assume he had a life and was busy with it. And they didn't even really know each other, so why did she care? Anka had to admit to herself that she cared. She liked getting Bruce's letters. She had to admit to herself that she wanted to meet him in person now. She knew this would totally freak Diane out.

> *December 20, 2012*
>
> *Dear Bruce,*
>
> *I hope all is well with you. If you have any time between Christmas and New Year's, I was wondering if you'd like to have a drink with me.*
>
> *Happy Holidays,*
> *Anka*

Verhoeven wanted to stop by the laundromat before he went back home. He pulled his jacket collar up against his neck to keep a bit more of the wind at bay. He had finished the suit, and the twins had had their final fitting that morning. All three men had been speechless when the twins stepped in front of the hall mirror. Verhoeven had just dropped the suit off at the dry cleaner's to be steam pressed. He had left it there with a sweet and bitter heart. He was proud of the garment he had fashioned. It had come together beautifully, and he had stitched his initials onto the lining of one of the sleeves. But he knew when he went home and packed away his serger that he probably wouldn't be pulling it back out of the guest bedroom closet again.

He came into the Fraser Street Laundromat and found Anka knitting behind the counter.

"You're a knitter! I had no idea. What's the project? It doesn't look like a sweater."

"No. It's a rug—well I suppose more of a series of rugs—to put down in my apartment. I'm essentially knitting up the floor space around my furniture."

"You're kidding! That's wonderful. It looks a bit like veins—is it a body?"

"No. I'm making a map."

"Let's have a look. Oh, that's smart to lay it out in panels."

"I'll connect all of the panels in a basket weave, sort of knit it into the apartment itself."

"Yes, yes, I see it." Verhoeven clapped his hands. "Anka, I really came here to thank you for helping me with Damian and Devon. The boys adore you, and Mimi thinks you're a great cook. I know you probably have plans with your family for the holidays, but if not, I would be honoured if you came over for dinner on Christmas Eve. It's our turn to cook for you. But if you're busy with your family, we could do lunch another day."

Anka was suspended for a moment in a perfect icicle of time.

"Dinner sounds nice." The hard, persistent lump was choking out Anka's throat again. "Mr. Verhoeven, my parents have both"—she exhaled as she finished her sentence, saying the words out loud for the first time in a long time—"passed away." She scrunched her shoulders up to her ears and then rolled them down her back. She inhaled through her nose. And felt her feet, hip distance apart, planted beneath her. Diane had been taking her to a yoga class.

She could not, however, bring herself to say the word that had been pinballing around her mind without pause for seventeen months now: *killed.*

"It's been almost a year and a half now."

Verhoeven stretched his arms out over the counter as if to hug Anka, but there was too much in the way. He put his hands on her shoulders and gripped them tightly. "They would be so proud of you, Anka."

"I haven't done anything."

"Nonsense. Kindness is the truest act of valour, my dear."

Dom had called Dougie and set up a time to come by and visit. Bruce thought this was a bit unusual, but Dougie took it as well intentioned. Dom stood at the landing outside their door with a potted jade plant inside a small plastic bag in the crook of his arm. "Apologies for not coming by the hospital to see how you both were doing."

"No worries."

"No, that wasn't right. Truth be told, I felt—feel—I feel terrible about what happened to you, Dougie."

All three men were standing in the open doorway, sun gleaming off the snow above their heads.

"Bruce, you tried to tell me something was wrong. But I didn't want to hear it."

"What happened to me wasn't your fault. It was just one of those freak things, really." Dougie didn't want to waste any time while he had Dom in front of him.

Bruce couldn't believe the extent to which Dougie could keep himself in denial.

"Come inside."

"I'm double-parked." Dom gestured vaguely behind him.

"Actually, Dom, I'm glad you could stop by. Quick question: I'm really doing great, never better, and I'm ready"—Dougie looked to his brother and demonstrated a slow, deep breath in and out to suggest his brother be chill about what was going to come next—"for a rematch with Farroz. How soon can we arrange it? Do you need to talk to the Golden Gloves people?"

"Right. Dougie, Bruce, that's the other thing I came to talk to you about. So—"

But Dougie wasn't quite done getting it all out. "It doesn't happen all the time, but I'm sure there's protocol for this, for extenuating circumstances. We didn't get to the end of the bout with a winner."

"Look, so. Yeah." Dom had prepared his speech and wasn't going to improvise it now. "So after the match, Farroz came to the gym to see me. He wanted to find out about your health and whatnot. And he decided that he's going to join our club. He asked to train under me."

"What? The Golden Gloves is still undetermined."

"That's great for the club, Dom. He's so good," Bruce offered.

"He's forfeiting?" Dougie scrambled.

Dom cleared the frog in his throat, but the words were still barely a whisper. "It means there won't be a rematch." The usual upfront, tell-it-like-it-is Dominic Silva was suddenly incapable of looking his boxers square in the eyes. He was a man who had never stepped out on his marriage ("I had plenty of opportunities, believe me," he protested), and he knew in his heart that this was a similar level of betrayal. It would appear to outsiders as though he were trading up for a younger model, but that honestly wasn't the case. Nonetheless he still felt disloyal.

Dougie was afraid that he had misheard and instinctively cleared his own throat as though it would help him hear more clearly. "I'm sorry. Pardon me?"

Dom repeated himself, but truth be told, Dougie didn't hear the words because a very high-pitched whine had started in his ears, drowning out everything around him. He squeezed his eyes shut and gave his head a shake while Dom was still explaining: "At any rate, the judges officially declared that final match a technical knockout. I'm sorry, Dougie. Farroz won the Golden Gloves heavyweight title."

Dougie's stomach dropped. Just like that, it was all over. A match blown out, smoke curling up briefly, the smell of sulfur. For Dougie there was nothing left except a hole burned clear through the middle of a page.

Before Dougie realized it, Dom was saying they should come by the gym when they were ready. The trainer awkwardly hugged Bruce first, and then Dougie, continuing to speak an uninterrupted volley of words: not to rush, take it easy, all the guys send their best, Merry Christmas. But Dougie barely heard a word.

Bruce was doing all the talking, receiving the plastic bag from Dom and peeking inside, thanking him for the gift, wishing his family well, saying something about Dom's new granddaughter.

Dougie suddenly found himself closing the door.

Once it was just the twins on their own again, save for one new jade plant, Dougie told Bruce he needed to lie down. He pulled the covers up over his head as much as he could and let his breath heat up the space around him. His entire life had come down to a TKO that he wasn't even present in the ring for. There would be no rematch with Farroz. And what the hell had been going on with his head? After all those months of pain, suddenly nothing. A stroke? Would it happen again to either of them? Or both? Was it happening now? Dougie exhaled sharply, then laughed at himself when he realized he sounded exactly like Bruce. *Shit.* He didn't cry, but he felt every inch of the tournament's defeat. He had been hit and run over by a force he could no longer outrun, and he had finally been bested by it. Dougie almost wished he could cry, but nothing was coming; he had nothing but time, not even Everest to show up for until further notice. He would've curled up into the fetal position if he could have, but he couldn't even do that.

The twins were meeting Verhoeven to pick up their new suit before going to the farm on Christmas Eve. They had wandered the aisles of the liquor store weighing their options for an appropriate gift; they wanted the tailor to understand how much they appreciated his attention and care, but they knew he wouldn't want anything ostentatious. A haggard liquor store employee in a green vest absently recommended a bottle of prosecco. They decided on two bottles given the double amount of work Verhoeven had taken upon himself.

As they waited in the long line, Bruce eyed the mini bottles of alcohol at the cash. If things had been different, he would've bought one of each to leave in Anka's mailbox. But he hadn't responded to her last two letters. He owed her some kind of explanation, but he had no clue how to launch into the whole mess of it. He remembered when Nikki had told them about the letter she had gotten in high school from her scorned ex. He was sure a forensic accounting of all of his own flaws could fill a few pages.

"Bruce, snap out of it. It's our turn. You're making us hold up the entire line."

"Shit, Dougie, ease up. No one in the line is upset but you." Bruce immediately regretted snapping at his brother. He gave Dougie's shoulder a pat, but Dougie swatted away his little hand.

Verhoeven was wearing a merino shawl-collar sweater over a plaid shirt, his hair slicked back. He clapped his hands and received their gift bag. "Gentlemen, season's greetings."

The twins could hear Mimi and her sons upstairs arguing about who still needed to take a bath and why they had to wear fancy clothes for Christmas dinner if they weren't even leaving the house.

As he led them into the living room, Verhoeven gestured toward the suit laid out across the couch in the dry cleaner's plastic garment bag. "Well, Douglas, Bruce, here it is."

"Honestly, we've never owned anything this beautiful in our lives." Dougie took the plastic sheath off the hangers and ran his hand over the fabric. He lingered over the precision of a buttonhole. "I still can't believe you made this from scratch." He held the hanger with his half of the blazer up against his chest. The suit was making him feel a bit like himself again.

"I hope that when you wear it you are able to feel a small amount of the pride that I felt when crafting it."

The doorbell rang.

Bruce had been nearly moved to tears when the twins had had their final fitting last week. And it was the same now. "Wow. Thank you." The twins had never owned any item of clothing that hadn't been cobbled together by their mother.

And here was a perfectly tailored suit that would fit them exactly right. It wasn't an afterthought or an adaptation.

"Wait right here. We've got a guest coming for dinner."

Dougie and Bruce draped the suit out once again over the couch and sat alongside it, waiting for the tailor to return. Dougie checked his watch. "We should probably get going soon to meet Dad."

Bruce heard Mimi bribing Damian and Devon with the promise that they could each open one gift after dinner if they agreed to wear their ties and let her take a photo of them standing by the tree.

"Let me introduce you two to—"

"Anka," breathed Bruce.

Dougie slapped his knee and made to stand, while Verhoeven continued without missing a beat.

"—Anka. This here are Bruce and Douglas Reuben. They are my clients who I've been sewing for these past weeks."

Anka's hand was trembling as she offered it to shake Bruce's own.

"Bruce?" her voice came out strained, but she looked intently into his eyes. "Reuben." She turned. "And you're Dougie? It's nice to meet you. Both. Finally."

Bruce's heart was rattling. He ran his sweaty hand through his hair. He didn't know what to say. His mouth was desert-dry. He looked at Dougie. He looked at Mr. Verhoeven. He looked at Anka. She hadn't taken her eyes off him. She had an expression on her face that he wasn't sure how to read.

Anka reached a hand up to her earlobe, where the weight of a golden bell was pulling, vying for her attention. She turned to Dougie. "Mr. Verhoeven has been working so hard."

The tailor piped up. "Mr. Verhoeven sounds so formal. Call me Kristof."

"Indeed. Have you seen it yet? Our suit?" Dougie gestured back toward the couch. He decided against bringing up the letters, squinting to make out what the play was here.

"No, not yet." Examining the suit, Anka grabbed the tailor's elbow. "Mr. Verhoeven, this is incredible."

Bruce wanted to disappear.

Anka laughed. "I don't feel right using your first name, Mr. Verhoeven. I'm sorry." She landed her gaze once again on her pen pal. "I've seen you guys around." She was choosing her words carefully, leaving room for Bruce to wade in or not.

Bruce opened his mouth to try offering something suave. "I was in the hospital."

"What?" Anka's eyes filled with concern. "Are you okay?" She looked to Dougie for more.

Dougie rolled his eyes. "We work over at Everest."

"No way. That's probably where I've seen you."

"We're hard to miss."

"I work at the Fraser Street Laundromat."

"Cool." It was Dougie's turn to look from Anka to Bruce to Mr. Verhoeven.

Mr. Verhoeven was zipping the suit into a garment bag, oblivious to the painful awkwardness filling the room.

Bruce wanted to explain everything about the library. He wanted to tell Anka that he had written her another letter, but that he had had to tear it up. He wanted to apologize for the last month of silence. He wanted to tell her how beautiful she looked. He remembered that he had sworn off the idea of having a crush on her. He wanted to be the one to pass out. Where was that aneurysm, already?

"We should get going." Dougie tried to smooth over his brother's palpable unease. "Mr. Verhoeven, we'll send you a picture of the suit when we wear it to Lana's wedding."

"Gentlemen, please, don't be strangers. This one knits—who knows, maybe you can arrange to get something cosy for the winter!"

After another chasm of anguished silence, Bruce managed to stammer barely a greeting card of a goodbye: "Hap—happy holidays. Thank you."

Damian and Devon were a herd of elephants coming down the stairs. "Anka! Did you bring us anything?"

When the twins got outside, Bruce grasped at his chest. "What just happened?"

"You dropped the ball, brother." Dougie was shaking his head.

"That wasn't supposed to happen."

"What do you mean? Were you just going to write to her for the next twenty years? Bruce, she lives in our neighbourhood for God's sake."

"Ungghhhhhh."

"But tell me—*why* did it seem like us being joined was news to her?"

Bruce felt the sting in Dougie's voice.

"Here I am assuming that you told her so from the beginning. Would make sense, wouldn't it? We're a package deal. There's no getting away from that."

"Do you think she looked…angry?"

"I don't know, Bruce. She looked fine. You two are both so weird, acting like you haven't been writing back and forth for the last five months."

Bruce tried to inhale deeply, his hand still over his heart.

Dougie continued as they marched, addressing the garment bag draped carefully over his arm. "I wonder how she knows Mr. Verhoeven though. It's really funny if you think about it."

The city was a garishly lit ghost town; the wind howled around the twins as they walked north, retracing their steps up the city's sloping incline. Bruce and Dougie, bracing against a sturdy wind, were trekking up an ancient lake bed, the land rising steadily where thousands of years ago there had been nothing but a lake the size of an ocean.

Hurtling home on the train, Bruce read a passage from his book and then abruptly stopped and stuffed it into his duffle bag. He was impatient with his revered M, irritated that he couldn't get to that rapture and clarity in his own life.

> For more than three hundred days, the only solid thing beneath M's feet was the boat heaving through the seas. In his logbook he writes: "On your own you can discover who you really are." It is not known for whom this log was recorded now that M had abandoned the race and sloughed off his former life. A log written for a man bearing witness only to himself. A pod of porpoises had come to sail alongside M's vessel. They made themselves known to the sailor as two or three breached the water, leaping up into the sun before plunging to depths further than one could imagine. What chronometer would accurately measure the lines of their voyage? It would map the globe horizontally and vertically while M simply aspired to keep pace. M felt confident that he had come to understand the point of it all, the reason for these universal particles marbling together in an electric soup. Anyone can know the answer if they let the wind be their engine. The point as he saw it: to become like the light, effortlessly and generously seeking out all corners.

Bruce and Dougie were waiting for Nikki in the vestibule of her apartment building on New Year's Eve. They had buzzed, and over the crackling speaker she'd told them she'd be right down.

"I cannot believe she agreed to be your date to Lana and Gary's wedding."

Bruce had been coasting over a sickly, oily feeling in his stomach all week—worse than before any boxing match he'd ever fought.

"What can I say? Girls love going to weddings. You just have to ask one, you know."

"Doug. Please. Not now. I can't."

Nikki came into the vestibule in a long coat and heels. Her hair was piled high, her eyelashes fake.

"You look amazing, Nikki. Your chariot awaits"—Dougie offered his arm—"but we'll have to hail it first, on the corner."

"You two look great! I've never seen you so dressed up."

"How's your fiancé?"

Dougie glared a gaping hole into Bruce's temple, but Nikki showed no offence.

"He's fine. He's partying with a bunch of his hockey teammates tonight. As usual. Shall we?" A look of annoyance had come and gone across Nikki's face at the mention of hockey teammates.

Dougie jerked the shared middle leg forward, catching Bruce off guard. Bruce pulled up to march slightly faster than Dougie. Nikki held the door open for the twins with one hand while trying to shield her hair from the wind with the other.

At City Hall, Gary greeted the twenty-five guests. "Aloha, everyone. Okay. We're up in three minutes. There are only seats for half of you, but there's plenty of room to stand."

Gary walked over to the twins and opened his arms wide to embrace them both. "We're so blessed you both could be here with us tonight."

A government clerk poked her head into the waiting room. "Yanowski and Ogilvie party? Last ceremony for the day—we're ready for you."

Everyone filed into the chapel room, buzzing and arranging themselves, and then Lana came in and walked herself down the aisle.

Bruce and Dougie and Nikki stood behind the last row of seats. Nikki didn't know this couple, but she was suddenly emotional and carefully dabbed tears away from her lashes with a tissue. She fiddled with her diamond ring, twisting it back and forth on her finger. Bruce was replaying the night in Mr. Verhoeven's living room, trying to get a handle on the look he had seen on Anka's face. She had beautiful eyes. He'd never been that close to her before. A dimpled chin. He'd ruined it. Had he ruined it? He must've ruined it. She didn't give much away. She was solid and steady and lovely and free.

The ceremony was over, everyone clapping and whistling. Documents were being signed. Dougie was talking to Nikki about catching a movie to kill time before the wedding reception started at the restaurant. *Anka Priyanka, Anka Priyanka*, a refrain in the background of all of Bruce's thoughts. He kept reminding himself that he had already decided to give up on pursuing anything with her, that right now he needed to focus on Dougie's recovery and good health. He didn't have time to think about how a relationship could work. *Unghhhhhh*. He didn't actually know if she was interested in him like that. *Fuck. Whatever. It's over. The letters are done now.* But he couldn't deny that every time the galvanized steel mailbox had offered up one of her letters, he had felt something come alive in the air all around him—facets of diamond light dazzling across azure waves in the sun. He told himself he was being very rude by not responding one last time. Especially now that she'd met them in person. In precisely the way he did not want them to meet. He regretted throwing out his confessional letter; he should've delivered it the minute he'd finished writing it. He wanted to tuck himself away somewhere and write to her now. He'd confess to everything all over again. He'd beg her forgiveness for his deception.

"Saddle up, Brucie. I think they're kicking us out of City Hall."

The same government clerk was poking her head through the door, impatient to get on with her New Year's plans. "All done. Excellent. All right, everyone. Congratulations. We're just locking up. Enjoy the rest of your evening. Please make sure you have all of your belongings with you."

Lana and Gary made their way to the door and hugged each person as they left, making sure everyone knew when and where to reconvene. Nikki and Dougie and Bruce walked to a multiplex a few blocks away. Nikki chose a romantic comedy in keeping with the day's wedding theme. They milled around in front of the cinema's door while other patrons filed in, and when they realized there weren't that many people, they went in and found an aisle seat for Nikki near the back. Dougie and Bruce stood out of the way until the trailers started and then sat down on the aisle step when they were sure no one else would come in. By the end of the movie, Bruce was pinching the tears from both his eyes. The morals of the romantic comedy as he saw it: lean into your heart, not away from it; be your own self; don't waste another minute.

"Pull yourself together, Brucie. There was a happy ending. Everything worked out; no one died."

"Yeah, sorry."

"Aww, Bruce. You're a real softie. Here." Nikki fished a fresh tissue out of her purse.

"Well I don't know about you, but I'm starving. Time to celebrate." Dougie was doing a good job of pretending to be himself; the suit helped with that.

From the minute the opening scene had kicked off with the mousy, overworked, single mom in oversized glasses and sweats, Dougie had been focused on something else. He imagined fighting Farroz and Patrice and Cranston and Marlowe. He went through every fighter they had faced that year: Smith and Abrams and Torres and Duchamp. And even further back to Potter, Udoh, Youssef, Patel, Granger, Li, Johnson, Ramsammy. In his daydream the Reuben Beast lost every single bout. Again and again they were beaten to an unrecognizable pulp. By the end of the movie, they were barely breathing, flat out for the count. Had the Reuben Beast fought just one more opponent, then Dougie's daydream would not have ended with them alive. So, sure, happy ending.

On the walk to the restaurant, Dougie had his arm around Bruce's neck as usual, but his other arm was wrapped around Nikki's shoulders. Each of them were mourning something. Nikki had taken off her engagement ring in the darkened theatre. She finally accepted that her fiancé had already broken up with her but just hadn't been bothered to say the words. All around them the city thrummed with the heightened anticipation of saying goodbye to the year. They arrived at the warm glow of the restaurant. It was clear to them that the newlyweds were the only ones who wouldn't wake up hungover and depressed in the new year. And so, for a few hours, Nikki and Dougie and Bruce each allowed themselves to surrender, to abandon the gravity of their separate losses and let themselves be pulled into the orbit of Lana and Gary's happiness.

Jan 1, 2013

Dear Anka,

Happy New Year. I'm so sorry for so many things. I'm sorry that I never told you that my twin brother Dougie is my conjoined twin. I'm sorry for leaving Mr. Verhoeven's in such a rush the night we met. I'm sorry that I wasn't honest from my first letter. I owe you many more apologies, but let these be enough for today.

Please forgive me.

I understand if you are no longer interested in corresponding. I know that I was the one to stop writing, but Dougie recently had a health scare, and I've been wrestling with some things.

Priyanka, I haven't been entirely forthcoming, but I have always been sincere.

May this year be one that you will look back fondly upon,

Bruce Henry Reuben

P.S. Dougie's middle name is Weston. Henry Weston was a boy my parents grew up with who was inadvertently responsible for introducing them. It's a long story.

Bruce spent two days in negotiations with a silent Dougie to go for a run in exchange for delivering his letter. Bruce weighed his options and decided the risks to Dougie's health were worth it.

Anka found herself in Verhoeven's kitchen on one of her days off, knitting him a scarf. Verhoeven poured coffee and arranged cheese on top of crackers.

"Mr. Verhoeven, how did you come to meet your last clients, Bruce and Douglas? Have you known them a long time?"

"Oh! No. Actually it was a matter of being in the right place at the right time and seizing an opportunity."

"Do you happen to know them very well?"

"Hmm. Technically, no. I was only sewing for them for a matter of weeks. But on the other hand, I could say, essentially, yes. I come to know the fibre of anyone I sew for. It's a by-product of this work."

Anka put her needles down, stretched out her fingers, and ate.

"Garments cover the body, but they are revealing in themselves. Not necessarily revealing of a personality but of something else: a temperature, a frequency. I'm not sure how to explain. When I sew for my grandsons, the machine moves fast, I run out of thread, the needles constantly break. There is energy crackling and yet a very slight difference when I approach each boy's garment. I always feel like I want to start on the younger one's project first—he's the leader. With Damian, the older boy, I always have barely enough fabric to sew his project—no matter how much extra I buy, no matter how I lay the pieces out. He will always have just enough to get by."

"What about with Bruce...and Dougie? The same suit for two men?"

"Oh, far from it. Two entirely distinct garments being held together in co-operation and contention."

"Mr. Verhoeven, I know Bruce. A little bit."

"Really? You never mentioned!"

"I'd never met him—them. He started to write to me a few months ago. I wanted to meet, but he never responded. Now I see why; he never properly explained his situation to me."

"Hmmmm. I see." Verhoeven brushed the crumbs off the table in front of him. "They are good men. I didn't have to rip out any stitching. I took my time, but I finished days before my deadline. Mostly because of your help. Their suit would not have been made without you." Verhoeven lay his hand over Anka's on the table.

"I'm having a hard time thinking of your Bruce as the Bruce who wrote all those letters to me. I'm not sure they're the same person."

"Did you enjoy receiving his letters?"

"Yes." Anka unravelled yarn from the ball in order to continue with the scarf. "I did. Very much. But he was lying to me, wasn't he? By not telling me he and Dougie are conjoined."

Anka was avoiding telling Diane that she had met Bruce. She was very aware that she had been the one to warn Diane about getting catfished online. She pressed her fists to her eyes. She was not going to ask her parents' opinions on this. At first when she talked to them she had felt she was just imagining what they'd say, but lately it felt more and more like they were around her, just out of reach. But maybe that was also a figment of her imagination. What she needed was a strong dose of reality. Bruce and his brother came as one. What would it mean to date Bruce? What would it mean to start seeing anybody right now?

"Hmmmmmm. Ummmm." Verhoeven was finishing his mouthful. "That is something, certainly. Is it possible to truly befriend someone who is afraid? Maybe just shift your expectations a bit and see that you have the potential for two new people in your life. You don't have to make it bigger than that. Nothing is forever; you can always change your mind, no matter what you decide."

Ten days after her conversation with Mr. Verhoeven, on a night that was pink rather than dark, Anka walked home from the laundromat and then kept walking past her house, even though she held her keys out.

She had considered responding to Bruce, but none of her efforts hit the right note. One attempt was too casual, one too scolding, one too forced, one too jumbled. She didn't know quite what she needed to say to him. Anka didn't feel as though she had any right to be angry, but now she felt shy in the letters.

She didn't know what she was about to do; it was as if her body was moving of its own acord, without her mind second-guessing things. She walked up to 44 Hudd, past the mailbox marked BSMT, and down the short flight of concrete stairs. She pressed the small button that would sound a bell that would alert the occupants that someone was on the other side of their door, anxious to be welcomed.

She waited.

Her finger reached out to press again but stopped in midair when the door was pulled open. She stood as if pointing at Dougie. She spread her fingers into a slight wave.

Bruce swung back to let her in. "Anka?"

Dougie had very recently become the more sullen twin, and he was here now, shaking his head, unsmiling.

Anka noticed his irritation. "Hi, Dougie." She extended her hand.

Dougie limply offered his left hand to clasp awkwardly; he wasn't going to make it easy for her.

Since Bruce hadn't received a response to his final letter, he had accepted that Anka didn't want anything more to do with him. And yet here he was face to face with her once more.

"Anka, would you like to come in? It's freezing out there." Bruce was being given more than a second chance, and he was concentrating very hard on not being clumsy with it. He hung her jacket on a hook in the hallway.

They sat in the living room; Bruce offered her a clementine, and the smell of sun and freshness filled the room as her thumb sank into the meat of the fruit as she began to peel. The three of them sat silently eating miniature oranges.

Bruce exhaled carefully and started first. "How do you know Mr. Verhoeven?"

"He came into the laundromat where I work, and we got along well from the start. I used to watch his grandsons while he was busy. Sewing for you two, actually."

"He designed a suit for us. A custom suit because we're... you know." Dougie waved his hand down their shared leg.

"Yes."

"Does it bother you?" Dougie was off now, questioning the witness.

"No."

"Were you shocked to meet my brother, Bruce? My twin?"

"Yes."

"Really?"

"Wouldn't you be shocked right now if I took my sweater off and had a third arm tucked like a little flipper under my armpit?"

Dougie was surprised by his laughter, like a sleeping man startled awake by his own snoring. "Do you?"

"No."

"Too bad."

Dougie started to feel himself thaw out a bit. He had been miserable for the last few weeks, and—while still feeling useless and weak and quite sorry for himself—he welcomed this distraction and was happy for this unexpected turn for Bruce.

"I've got these earlobes that are attached to the side of my head." Anka swept her hair up and tilted for inspection.

Bruce didn't see the lobe, just her jaw and her neck and the dip into her clavicle.

"Fair enough. Cover those godawful things back up."

"My turn, Douglas."

"Call me Dougie."

"How long have you guys lived here?"

"Fourteen years."

"Really? I've been at my place about three years, on and off."

Anka looked around and saw that she was sitting in the only chair; besides the couch, there was an assortment of benches scattered around the space, some holding piles of clothes, one under the window with a stack of newspapers next to a wilting plant. A framed portrait of Muhammad

Ali and a t-shirt of a band she'd never heard of were tacked up on the wall. The space was clean and uncluttered. A crocheted granny square blanket was lying over the back of the couch. "Did someone make that blanket for you guys?"

Both twins turned toward each other to peer behind them, and Dougie answered, "Our granddad gave it to us with a bunch of stuff when we moved."

"Bruce, you next. Ask me anything."

"You should stay for dinner."

"Is that even a question?" Dougie asked.

"Yes," Bruce and Anka replied in unison.

Anka was happy to have blindly followed her body here on this pink night instead of letting the weight of her thoughts stop her. There was something easy and natural about being here with the twins. Her heart was steady, her mind calm. She felt comfortable and like her old self for the first time in a long while.

"Bruce told me you're a boxer, Dougie."

Dougie shifted his weight. "Yep. With Bruce." He didn't offer anything else.

"So you're a boxer too, Bruce?"

"We're taking a step back, maybe."

"That's too bad."

"We only have eight months left before we're too old to compete in the amateur league." Dougie sighed. He looked down at his left fist as he opened and shut it tight a few times, the skin dry and peeling around some of his nails. It didn't look like his hand. He stared down at it for a long time, turning the palm up, looking at the lines etched there. The longer he looked, the weirder it seemed.

Anka took them in, sitting before her on their brown second-hand couch. She observed them as a whole and then each on his own terms. It was obvious they were athletes. They were almost identical and yet different. She saw Bruce's forearm, his shoulder, his cheekbones.

"You should write about it."

"About boxing?" Bruce was puzzled.

"About your experience boxing."

"Who has the time?" Dougie said.

"Bruce is a good writer."

"Really? My turn," countered Dougie. "Do you have any siblings?"

"No. Just me."

"Did you grow up in the city?"

"Yes."

"Do your parents still live here?"

"They've passed."

Bruce inhaled sharply. "I'm sorry."

"They were in a car accident. It's been almost a year and a half. A car swerved into their lane and hit them head on." Anka said the words without flinching, but she noticed she was floating slightly out of her body while she spoke.

"I'm sorry. I didn't mean to..." Dougie didn't intend for his line of questioning to cause any harm.

Anka felt herself come back down to the chair she was in. She sank herself down and held onto the arms.

She couldn't feel it, but Stella was giving Anka's earlobe a playful tug to pull her back down to earth. Stella was wearing a leather jacket and felt like a real badass in it, like the first lady of a motorcycle club, and she knew Anka would've loved it. Mukesh was perched on the arm of the couch across from her, next to Bruce. He knew that Dougie had suffered from a blood clot in his cranium that had eventually caused pressure on his optic nerve, that it was a miracle that he was alive and unscathed, that he would soon be on medication that he'd take for the rest of his life, and that in a few years he'd have to watch out for another clot in his spleen. He also knew that the Reuben Beast would've won the Golden Gloves tournament had Dougie's body cooperated. But had that happened, Bruce would also have known, deep down, that Farroz had thrown the match to spite his trainer. Both Stella and Mukesh knew it was better this way, even if no one else in this room ever had any clue about anything. Mukesh was pleased he and his wife had managed to finally push their daughter onward in a new direction when she had left the laundromat that night.

Bruce wasn't saying much, but Dougie could feel that he was considerably at ease. He realized that he couldn't remember the last time his brother had relaxed inside his body. Dougie was finished playing this game of questions now. "Brucie, you should give Anka a tour of our bachelor pad."

All three made to stand.

"This is our living room. It's where we do all our living." Bruce felt as though he'd been in a three-legged race, running as fast as he could while balancing a delicate egg on a spoon. He couldn't believe the fragile thing between them was still intact. Anka broke into a smile that reached her eyes as Bruce led her and Dougie into every nook of their basement apartment.

That night they ordered pizza and drank beer. Dougie realized that he must've seen the Marchesa Casati around, and Anka wanted to introduce them to Diane. And they talked about what it had been like for all of them when they were kids. At the end of the night, when Anka made to leave, Dougie slyly hid himself behind their front door as he swung it open for Anka to step out. She and Bruce stood smiling, agreed to meet up again, and joked about not running into each other at the library since Bruce was lending her his copy of *The Life and Art of Being M*.

Once she had left, Dougie pinched the bridge of his nose in frustration when Bruce confessed that they had not kissed, though Anka had turned back and given him a little wave.

"Well then why the hell was I hiding behind the door like a jerk?"

"Yeah, I thought that was weird."

"I was giving you space."

For the first time since last summer, the rash on Bruce's side wasn't acting up.

When Anka got home, she flipped through Bruce's favourite book, examining the drawings scattered throughout, and read the last page first, as she always did:

> **Editor's Note (2nd edition).** After the first edition of *The Life and Art of Being M* came out, my publisher received a manila envelope from M's eldest—now adult—daughter. She had, sadly, been tasked with going through her late mother's apartment in Paris. When pulling dusty books off their shelves, she thumbed through one and saw the inscription in a volume of poetry: *To my Beloved —M (1965).* But underneath it, in her mother's elegant cursive: *Gifted to me by my selfish piece of shit darling husband. —Claudine (1970)* [translated from the original French]. The manila envelope was stuffed with nineteen or twenty of such Xeroxed addenda:
>
> *Happy Birthday, my love, a lifetime of my adoration —M (1968)*

Gifted to me on the occasion of my fortieth birthday. We had a wonderful party—Lise drank too much and left that night with Pascal, just freshly divorced. I've read this book and didn't much care for it. —Claudine (1970)

Another in a book by the same author:

I read this and immediately thought of you. Were I to be these pages beneath your touch. —M (1960)

Gifted to me at a time when I fell for this claptrap. Ha! What a foolish doll I used to be back then. —Claudine (1970)

For you. —M (1959)

The real gift you gave me was to hold up a mirror to myself. Now lost forever to the sea—and to your young companion on a tropical island a world away—your absence has left a space the size of myself. I can see who I am clearly now, and I can see each of us—who we really are—and our own daughter striding out, sure-footed, the ground solid beneath her. —Claudine (1977)

APRIL 2013

DOUGIE WASN'T SUFFERING from any more headaches, but he hated to acknowledge that every strange sensation always put him on high alert. In the time that he had been holding out hope for a rematch, he had tried to demonstrate to himself and to everyone else that he was invincible. The twins had been discharged with no real answers and no definitive diagnosis. But in the days that followed their release from the hospital, Dougie kept it a secret from Bruce that he felt confused when he was out in large spaces; he was claustrophobic when stuck at home but completely disoriented on a busy city sidewalk. He knew then that he wasn't ready to go back to work out on the lot, though he was stubborn in his certainty that he could still box. However he found that sometimes he couldn't remember random things. For the life of him, he couldn't remember his mother's maiden name or how to spell the word *business*. Bruce would remind him of something he had said that he had no recollection of. He played it all off in the moment, but one morning in early April, in the shower, he finally started to cry when he couldn't remember the name of the girl he had lost his virginity to. "Brucie. Dr. Lars might be right, I think," he admitted. He expected Bruce to give him some rousing speech about M and the wide expanse of a hopeful horizon, but Bruce immediately broke down too. With that Dougie said the thing he couldn't say before: "We're never going to compete again." Bruce and Dougie Reuben let themselves cry, hanging on to one another as best as they could while the water drained itself of its warmth.

Once Bruce and Dougie had calmed themselves, dried off, and made coffee, they called their parents, who were at their door two hours later. And by the end of the month, all four were in a corner of the hospital huddled on one side of Dr. Lars's desk.

"Adults have never been separated. But given the specifics of your case, I think we owe it to you to investigate further." Dr. Lars was relocating towering stacks of patient files from his desk to the floor to address the twins and their parents more directly. Every day put him more woefully behind in digitizing his clinical records. When he was finally done rearranging and none of the new towers were threatening collapse, he sat and continued: "I will assemble a team quickly, but the whole process will be a long one. The major benefit is that you have been so healthy and active your whole lives. The fact that you boxed for so long will be a saving grace here, and I suspect it will make the separation easier for each of your bodies to handle independently."

Dougie had to laugh: his obsession with boxing was the very thing that would make separating easier. Dr. Lars missed the joke, but he wasn't surprised by any patient's reaction anymore. Once he had had a patient throw up on all of his files—this was actually why he cleared his desk during appointments now. He turned to his computer and pecked around the keyboard with two fingers for a few minutes until Dougie was composed again.

"We must be mindful of the possibility of another stroke, and so I'm prescribing blood thinners. You'll be on them until we get closer to the surgery. Once your blood tests return, I'll assess whether you need to be on them as well, Bruce. Once I assemble our team, we'll talk next steps. Any questions?"

Bruce was overwhelmed by the sensation of feeling everything at once. M had written about focusing so intently that he had become one with the object of his attention. Bruce's mind was focused on the fact that one day soon the Reuben Beast would cease to exist. He—as he had known himself for thirty-four years, alongside Dougie—would be annihilated. In light of that, he couldn't think of any one particular question to ask the doctor.

When no one in his family spoke, Walter rose from his chair to shake the doctor's hand. Dr. Lars escorted a solemn Reuben family to the door.

JUNE 2014

"THE DOCTORS ARE READY FOR YOU NOW."

The nurse smiled but didn't linger for any chit-chat, and she was long gone before the orderlies could figure out how to wheel the combined double-stretcher bed out the door. After lots of ungraceful banging about, Dougie suggested they just cuddle up together on one bed and save everyone the headache.

For their long trek down to the operating room, the twins folded themselves toward each another as much as they could, arms encircled.

"Are you scared, Brucie?"

"Yes." Bruce inhaled deeply. "You?"

"Yeah." Dougie exhaled a sigh.

The elevator doors shut slowly. The hospital felt creaky in its old, gothic bones. An orderly named Derek wished them luck. Another orderly named Chris said, "You got this, guys." The elevator doors were comically slow to open at their floor; Derek and Chris waited, very calm and quiet. The twins couldn't see anything around them, only parts of each other; at the angle they were at, they couldn't quite make eye contact.

Bruce put his attention on his heart beating and not on this feeling straining behind his eyes and at the corners of his mouth. The stretcher had one squeaky wheel, marking each rotation down the length of the hallway. Turning right.

Turning right again. Bruce was astounded that so much could change in just two years. How his whole life had been the same for so long until one moment when nothing was recognizable anymore. Abracadabra.

Once the twins had been transferred onto the wide operating table, Dr. Sigrid introduced each of the general surgeons, orthopedic surgeons, anesthetists, nurses, and surgical and anesthesia residents. Twenty-four healthcare professionals in colour-coded scrubs, divided into two teams.

"We will see you both in a few hours, gentlemen. Sweet dreams. The future is now."

Bruce wasn't sure if the doctor really said these words. Dougie was similarly thinking that this doctor was a bit much—*On this side, all the way from Johns Hopkins, Dr. Sigrid heading the green team. And in the purple corner, hometown hero, Dr. Lars*—but he couldn't finish his thought before the anesthesia washed through. Bruce realized that his anxiety was buttressed by an undeniable rush of excitement. It was the same way he had felt as a kid the moment an enormous airplane lifted itself up off the runway. But then he thought about the long hours that his parents and Anka had ahead of them in the waiting room. He began to panic, thinking of himself alone in the bed when they came to see him. What if they put Dougie in a different room? On a different floor? He had to remind himself that pairs of six-month-old babies had preceded him and Dougie on this table and that they had been much braver than he was feeling now. He was forced to sit with these uncomfortable feelings for a good minute as a purple-clad nurse walked around the table, down toward their feet, and up to his side to adjust a problem with his IV drip.

"Okay. There we go, hon."

Bruce stared straight up into the light. "Ungghhhhhh. Hmmmmmmm."

PART TWO

DOUGIE REUBEN
JUNE 2015

DOUGIE WAS TIRED of looking out over the wide expanse of ocean, so he did some squats on the ship's deck. Nikki wouldn't be awake for another few hours. She had been the one to find them these jobs on the cruise ship. He thought back to the day she had suggested it this past winter.

She had come over, and they were lying in bed on his side of the bedroom. He and Bruce still lived at 44 Hudd and still shared a room, but they had decided to switch out their queen for two twin beds, like children bunking at an eternal summer camp. Bruce and Anka had gone out to eat and would be back soon.

"I think it might be good for all of us to get a fresh start." Nikki was curled between the wall and his left side. At the time it made him remember when he and Bruce were folded into the stretcher being wheeled down to the OR last year.

"Hmmmmmmm."

"The money's way better than what we're making now, and as long as your doctor says it's okay for you to travel, I think we should consider it. The contracts are only for a few months, anyway."

Dougie said, "Sure." From the moment he had opened his eyes in the recovery room, separated from Bruce by a yellow curtain between their beds, he had felt an external pressure to be grateful to go at this life solo. He got the impression that he was supposed to be eager to foster his independence and be an adult, that he should be moving forward with his relationship with Nikki. The latter he was on board with, but he didn't mention his feeling that truly forging his independence would've meant doing it without a girlfriend right now. He didn't want to entertain that idea. He knew his therapist would warn against replacing his brother with someone else. He stopped himself from thinking the word *co-dependent*. He remembered waking up in the recovery room and staring over at that insipid yellow curtain, feeling so mad because they had put him on the right side of the room and Bruce on the left—for fuck's sake, it made no sense.

He kissed Nikki and told her he was game and that it was a good idea, that they could talk to Bruce and Anka about it when they got back from dinner. He felt rudderless.

Here on the cruise ship, Dougie had to concentrate on properly redistributing his weight and striking a balance with the liberated right leg. It still felt off-kilter, and to compensate he walked with a left-leaning hobble, which his physiotherapist had tried with everything she had in her to correct. His new body frustrated him more often than not. His large right leg now always felt too cumbersome, and his small right arm was always two steps behind, always in search of a place to hang, it seemed to him. He was certain that together he and Bruce had always moved naturally and gracefully. On his bedside table back in his room was Bruce's copy of *The Life and Art of Being M*, which he hadn't cracked open and knew he never would. He only brought it to have a piece of his brother there with him, on his right side.

He'd done enough squats. He considered some lunges but abandoned the thought when a man came out with some watercolour paints to capture something of the morning's heartbreaking glow. Dougie silently nodded good morning and leaned toward the sea again, allowing himself to feel adrift.

"You're the boxing instructor, right?" came a voice from behind.

A young guy came over to lean next to Dougie and ashed his cigarette over the railing. "I work in the kitchen."

"I'm Dougie."

"Warren. How are you finding the job?"

"It's different. This is the first time for both my girlfriend and me out here. She's a blackjack dealer."

"That's a sweet gig."

Dougie looked down over the railing; the ship was so massive and they were so high up from the water that it made him feel queasy. And small. He had to turn his back to the sea and face the wall of cabin windows rising above him. There were probably more than two thousand people aboard right now. He was an ant in a colony.

Warren flung his smoke out into the great beyond. "I've been on this fuckin' boat for a year."

"You're sick of it?"

"I'm sick of cooking fucking chicken cordon bleu. We're in a floating time warp, I swear." Warren's long hair was being blown about, and he took an elastic off his wrist to gather it up. He turned to face the same way as Dougie. "My first week, a passenger went overboard."

"Jesus."

"They were quick to rule it a suicide and kept it all hush hush. He had been on the cruise by himself." Warren pressed a finger against his lips, securing Dougie's silence.

"He was murdered." Warren mouthed something discreetly that Dougie understood to be *the mob*.

"That's intense, Warren."

"How's your gig?"

"The boxing class? It's not really boxing like I'm used to. I'm starting to understand that it's meant to be a basic cardio class for people to feel better about the buffet later."

"That fuckin' buffet."

Dougie snorted. "Does this place ever stop being weird?"

"Nope. Were you a good boxer on land?"

Dougie shrugged. He remembered socking a left hook to Patrice's jaw. "Just okay." He remembered when Patrice fell out of the ring, and it made him immensely sad. It was still a tender spot, thinking about his last year as an amateur boxer.

"Well here you can tell your students you fought Tyson and won."

"I don't think anyone would believe that."

"The point is that no one will care."

"Fuck, Warren, you're a real chipper one in the morning."

"I haven't slept in two days, brother." Warren mimed some punches, gave a salute, and then sauntered back inside, yanking a hairnet from his pocket.

Dougie looked down the length of the deck, squinting to try to figure out what his next move was. From where he was, he couldn't see it yet.

BRUCE REUBEN
JUNE 2015

BRUCE WAS GOING BACK TO WORK at Ogilvie's for the first time since the operation. He woke up early so he could walk there. He needed to practise moving around on his new prosthesis as much as possible. He pushed the sheets off; his bed was against the wall on the right side of the room, and it was still unnatural to get out of bed on his left side. Dougie's bed was ready and waiting for his return from the sea. It had been a disorienting year since the operation. Everything strange, everything turned around. Bruce decided that when he got home later, he'd push the beds together so he could get out on his right side. So many things had changed that he could afford to hang on to one harmless, lifelong habit.

His phone buzzed with a text from Anka wishing him good luck today.

He texted that he'd come by her place once her shift was done.

He was still on his back in bed, staring at his phone for a few minutes after hitting send.

He texted her a heart emoji, put his phone back on the side table, and then sat up and grabbed his crutches. His leg was leaning against the wall. His parents, Dougie, Nikki, and Anka had all chipped in for his prosthetic leg. It attached at the stump of his left thigh in a way he found to be quite beautiful. The mechanics of sockets and microprocessors replacing the memory of muscles.

He didn't want to walk too fast, but he felt strong, concentrating on keeping a consistent rhythm. On his own he found all his movements still required intense focus. He heard Dom's voice in his ear: *Get into your body, Bruce*. As he walked he had to constantly remind himself to keep swinging his left arm: *left, left, left*. It stubbornly wanted to find somewhere to perch.

He found that he actually enjoyed being out early, in the quiet of a still-resting city. He remembered how much grief he used to give his brother over their five a.m. runs. And now he would have run to work if he could have. He'd need to save up for a specialized prosthetic if he were to start running again. He was wearing a new pair of tearaway track pants that he and Anka had bought at the mall. He knew Dougie would love them. He thought about Dougie the whole time he walked. It was worse than merely having a phantom limb. Bruce wished that he had been able to approach things with more of Dougie's good humour while they were together. He should have let the wind blow through him rather than girding himself so tightly against it and then becoming so helpless and broken by it. While he waited for the light to turn green, he started whistling because that's what Dougie would have done. He couldn't think of any particular song he wanted to whistle. He could feel a weight hanging around his neck. A phantom rub, a soft, soothing pat.

When he had checked the mailbox last night, there was a postcard from Dougie with a picture of two wolves howling. Dougie had penned speech bubbles over their snouts. One wolf was asking why there was so much #*&! snow everywhere. The other wolf replied, "Next time, Nevis!"

He thought about the wolves now as he whistled a tuneless string of notes.

Dougie, we made a big mistake.

The light turned. He stopped whistling and stepped out into the crosswalk, almost at work now. The city had started to come alive all around him.

Lana had taped a bow to Bruce's new ergonomic chair. It had been a long year, and she was happy to be relieved of the constant stream of distracted college interns she had had to train and retrain. She rushed to open the door when she saw him approaching and gasped. She had visited Bruce and Dougie a number of times since their operation, but they were always together when she spent time with them. It was a marvel to see them separated, but very quickly the three of them settled into their familiar way of being with one another. It wasn't until she saw Bruce walking toward her that she truly understood that Dougie wasn't there with him.

"Oh! Bruce! Welcome back, dear! Oh...wow! Look at you. Here, let me help you. Come, can I give you a hug?"

They hugged, and Lana remained close in case Bruce needed to lean on her. He took his time getting reacquainted with his desk. "Thanks, Lana."

He hadn't gotten used to how light he felt, as though he could raise his arms straight up and just float away. He wasn't so warm all the time. Everything was quiet, which he had anticipated, but also a little flat, which came as a surprise. He didn't have Dougie's warm breath or pomade punctuating all of his thoughts.

"Have you heard from Dougie? How is he?"

"He called me last week from a port before they set sail for Alaska. He sounded good. He sometimes gets bored, but his boxing class is always full. He said that Nikki's a real hit, making a killing as a blackjack dealer. They'll be home in a few weeks."

"If you get in touch, give him my best."

"Sure thing."

Lana turned back to her computer, and the sound of typing filled the room. A siren outside wailed for a moment, but then the sediment of silence settled again.

"Thanks for the new chair, Lana. It's really nice."

Lana swivelled back around. "What's that?"

"I didn't know I'd miss him so much."

"Me too, Bruce. But he'll be home soon."

"I don't mean Alaska."

"I know, dear. I know." Lana reached for a tissue.

Bruce turned on his computer and stared at the blinking cursor for a while.

When Bruce got back home that evening, Anka was there waiting by the mailbox. She wasn't crying, but he could tell that she had been. He hugged her. Her hair smelled like coconut.

"Mimi called," Anka said, not letting go of Bruce. "He had a heart attack. Poor Damian found him lying on the kitchen floor and had to call 911."

Bruce didn't let go either. "No."

"He didn't make it. I'm going over to watch the boys while Mimi makes arrangements."

"Do you want me to come with you?"

"No. Stay. I'll come by after."

"Anka, my god, I'm so sorry."

They continued to hold onto each other until Anka pulled away. She leaned in and used the front of Bruce's t-shirt to dry her face.

After Anka left, Bruce didn't go inside. Instead he chose to keep walking, automatically reminding himself: *left, left, left.*

He pictured Verhoeven's grandsons cradling one another behind their mother's sofa, the paramedics navigating the gurney around the furniture in Mimi's home. Verhoeven's straight pins, tape measure, sewing machine. Verhoeven's old hands confidently taking measurements, clapping when he was satisfied, when the case at hand was closed.

Dougie's job on the cruise ship wouldn't be finished in time for the funeral; he wouldn't get the chance to say goodbye to the tailor. Bruce realized these things in a rush all at once. He rounded the block, and then it hit him: he didn't have a suit to wear to the funeral. He'd have to borrow one of his father's. It would be big on him. He kept going, wandering around until he found himself at the Everest lot.

He hadn't been on the lot itself since before their surgery. His first day back working security wasn't until next Friday night. Before the surgery, Bruce would not have predicted that he would want to keep Dougie's job. Now that Dougie had left, Bruce wanted to keep up their old routine in order to feel his brother close. He didn't know the guard on duty now, but he decided to introduce himself, which is what Dougie would have done.

"Hey, I'm Bruce. I'm starting on security next week."

"Mike."

"I'll see ya."

The lot was half empty. It was still light out, and Bruce could see the phantom of the crescent moon in the blue sky. He didn't go inside but wandered around the back toward the alley.

A delivery truck was making its way through the lot; this was strange because usually they came before dawn or during the night. But by some magic, the lot was empty enough for it to successfully wend its way through. Bruce waved the truck into the loading dock as it beeped methodically, slowly reversing. Long after the truck had parked, he kept both his arms raised in the air. He closed his eyes, and his lids glowed. The truck killed its engine, and in that silence a space opened up; the square asphalt lot floated on the surface of the globe as a crisp breeze brought the tide in.

Bruce readied himself to turn and go around a second time.

ACKNOWLEDGEMENTS

This story is set in a reimagined version of Tkaronto, the traditional territories of many First Peoples, including the Mississaugas of the Credit, the Anishinaabe, the Chippewa, the Haudenosaunee, and the Wendat peoples.

The 2006 documentary *Deep Water*, directed by Louise Osmond and Jerry Rothwell, started my / Bruce's obsession with Bernard Moitessier.

When I first met Norm Nehmetallah, he told me that "Making a book is fun," but I would amend this by saying, "Making a book with everyone at Invisible is fun, specifically Norm, Megan Fildes, Kim Griffiths, Siavash Saadlou, and Mallory Burnside-Holmes." It was my long-held wish to one day find a place with Invisible Publishing. The humanity and warmth and good taste and ease and advocacy with which the Invisible team conducts their business is what makes it so dreamy.

Thank you to Professor Matthew Bucemi at York University and his Book Publishing students in the 2022/2023 and 2023/2024 Practicum classes. The former class included my manuscript in the First Novel Contest shortlist, and the latter's editing instincts were exactly right and really appreciated. I particularly hope that you each feel connected to this work and satisfied by the outcome of our collaboration because you guys basically made my numero uno dream come true.

Thanks to Aeman Ansari. Less an editor and more a translator of my chaotic whims into structure and form. I came away from our calls inspired and eager to get to work.

Thanks to everyone in all of the amazing writing groups I was a part of in the decade it took to see this project from beginning to end: Julie McArthur, Rob Shaw, Daniel Perry, Brad Weber, Susan Alexander, Jess Taylor, Sofia Mostaghimi, Menaka Raman-Wilms, Cheryl Runke, Andrew Battershill, Maggie MacDonald, Rose Bianchini, and Katarina Gligorijevic. And also to all the formative teachers I've had. To explore the beauty of literature and the craft of writing under or alongside sensitive, smart, funny people is life-affirming.

Thank you to my parents, Neil and Debra Ragbar, who used to routinely ask after Bruce and Dougie as if they were real people during the long, lean years when I felt stuck and was, in reality, doing zero writing. Thank you, Shawn, Nina, Danika Dawn, and Kai Cerulean. To my whole extended family. To all my friends who are my family. I feel lucky and so grateful for the unconditional support and kindness I receive from all corners.

Thanks, Sam, for all of it.

And all of it for Sloan.

Invisible Publishing produces fine Canadian literature for those who enjoy such things. As an independent, not-for-profit publisher, we work to build communities that sustain and encourage engaging, literary, and current writing.

Invisible Publishing has been in operation for nearly two decades. We released our first fiction titles in the spring of 2007, and our catalogue has come to include works of graphic fiction and nonfiction, pop culture biographies, experimental poetry, and prose.

We are committed to publishing writers with diverse perspectives. In acknowledging historical and systemic barriers, and the limits of our existing catalogue, we emphatically encourage writers from LGBTQ2SIA+ communities, Indigenous writers, and writers of colour to submit their work.

Invisible Publishing is also home to the Bibliophonic series of music books and the Throwback series of CanLit reissues.